LOST HANDS

Oliver Eade

https://www.olivereadebooks.org

Cover design and artwork
Copyright © Fiona Ruiz 2025

ISBN: 978-1-80440-198-9

Silver Quill Publishing

https://www.silverquillpublishing.com

Acknowledgements

I am grateful to my fellow writers in Silver Quill Publishing for encouragement and support and, over the years, help and advice with my writing. Also, thanks to my darling wife, Yvonne Wei-Lun, for her tolerance and for believing in me.

Oliver Eade
May, 2025

Websites

https://www.olivereadebooks.org
https://www.olivereadephotography.org

Contact: via first website above.

For other Silver Quill Publishing books for adults, teenagers and young readers by authors across the world, please visit:
www.silverquillpublishing.com.

Dedicated to the late Phyllis Margaret Eade

'The true character of a society is revealed in how it treats its children.'

Nelson Mandela
1918-2013

Lost Hands

Forward

My beloved late mother, Phyllis, to whose memory I dedicate this novel, stunned me, when I was just fifteen, by saying, out of the blue, "One day you will be a writer. I know it!" Then I got a hug. Admittedly, I had been a bookaholic since an early age, and my mother would feed me from the age of eight onwards with books, rather like a mother hen feeding her chick...

But a writer?

She suffered from bouts of severe depression during most of her adult life, but it was only many years after she died that I discovered, quite possibly, why. I always knew that, from childhood onwards, she had lived in fear of her oppressive bully of a father, a black-gowned headmaster of a boys' private school (he'd been given the push as 'classics master' at Manchester Grammar School... now I know, perhaps, why), and had been forced by him to study classics at college, which she hated, but it was not until I was recently told things by my cousin, who, as a boy, had to live with his grandparents for a while after his own father committed suicide, that I learned just how cruel the man was. He used to beat my cousin with a cane, bent over the bath, held down by our grandmother, just as he would beat his 'unruly' pupils. My cousin assured me that he would have similarly beaten his own children, including my mother. In those days, such treatment of children was not only allowed but encouraged, at least in schools, although nowadays it would probably earn the perpetrator a prison sentence. Physical punishment like that, particularly involving a daughter, amounts to 'sexual abuse' within the

1

family, a much-avoided topic highlighted in an article, by Charlotte Philby, in *The Independent* newspaper in August 2009, entitled 'Female Sexual Abuse: the Untold Story of Society's Last Taboo'. According to the NSPCC about 1 in 20 UK children, mostly girls, have been sexually abused. Figures for the USA quoted by the NIH show that 'at least fifteen to thirty-eight percent of adults were sexually abused in childhood', women more than men. True statistics are difficult to establish because of the 'cover-up' involved. They could be far worse.

In a past life, as a doctor and gastroenterologist, over seventy percent of my out-patient referrals involved patients with symptoms that had nothing to do with illness or disease but were what we termed 'functional' — doctor-speak for 'it's in the mind', though not in a derogatory sense; the irritable bowel syndrome (IBS). The human brain is possibly the most complex creation in the known universe and may respond to the horror of systemic childhood sexual abuse by forming deeply ingrained psychological scars that, decades later, may manifest as symptoms severe enough for the patient to seek medical help. After a published study established that a disproportionate number of patients with IBS, mostly women, had suffered historical sexual abuse, often at the hands of the father, and with the mother's knowledge, I would sensitively check whether this might have been the case with my patients whenever I felt it seemed appropriate. What some of my patients had been subjected to in childhood is far too horrific to relate in print, but what struck me was the cover-up that *always* took place, plus the bravery of those women survivors.

Lost Hands

Apart from books, my parents introduced me to the worlds of visual art and of classical music in a way that helped to determine who I became. On my mother's much-admired Bechstein (Brahms played on a Bechstein) grand piano, I learned to play well enough to team up for duet playing with the sister of a Chinese medical student friend; a teenage girl I fell in love with on our very first musical 'date', and whom I later married. Also, I knew that one of my mother's favourite composers was Johann Sebastian Bach, the absolute master of contrapuntal music in which many separate voices come together, each with its own identity, blending to create a beautiful 'whole'. In this novel there are, I admit, an annoying number of characters, but I hope they come together in a meaningful way, and that the abusers get their comeuppance.

As for art, I was brought up on a diet of Van Gogh, Rodin and other famous artists, by my late father, an artist and teacher of the history of art. He met my mother when she was a student of his at an evening adult art class, and, later, would often practise his illustrated art appreciation lectures with my sister and me seated cross-legged on the living room floor staring up at image after amazing image of the works of the great masters of the past. *Real* art... no pickled dead cows!

So, no apologies for allowing art and music to worm their way into this novel, for they became embedded in my DNA long before I stepped onto the perpetual treadmill of medicine as an NHS hospital physician, re-emerging, years later, after I hung up my stethoscope for the very last time, to fulfill my late mother's prediction.

Oliver Eade, May 2025

Lost Hands
PART 1

Chapter 1

As I sit alone outside the courtroom, staring at my hands — my *lost* hands — I cannot help but wonder whether it might have all been so very different if only those hands had been different. After all, much of the time we can blame our hands for the things we do, or don t do... can t we? Imagine a world of people with re-arranged hands that refuse to do things asked of them...

A pianist, somewhere, might be forced to seek new horizons...

Plus...

"No, dear, I can't iron that shirt for you. My hands refuse to do it!" The husband, wearing a crumpled shirt, might, later, turn up at his office only to discover that his hands have no intention of opening those work files, requiring urgent attention, on his computer. Instead, he might be forced to impotently watch as those same hands feverishly hone their online gaming skills...

And what about the wimp of an unsuccessful lover who, one day, wakes up with new hands? *Romeo* hands! Just think how transformed *his* life might become...

Then imagine the killer with hands that refuse to kill. Might new hands attached to his arms be responsible for a murder? Or could different hands sewn onto the arms of a

Lost Hands

potential murderer save a life?

'No, it's not the hands! Someone, somewhere, must always take the blame,' I think, as I sit by myself, waiting. I will soon be called back to the dock, and I continue to ponder over my hands and about their share in the blame of it.

*****

The six-seater prop-plane about to take us from Queenstown to Milford Sound seemed surprisingly small as we sat squashed together inside the cabin. I was reminded of those ludicrous how-many-people-can-you-squeeze-into-a-mini?' attempts of the nineteen-eighties when a bulging American couple wedged themselves into their allocated spaces in front of us. Sally, seated next to me, grinned and raised her eyebrows as she clicked herself in with her seatbelt.

There is something brutally final about clicking the seatbelt at the beginning of a flight. Up until that moment, the passenger does, at least, have the chance to alter fate with a sudden change of mind, but that click seals their fate, trapping an unknown future.

'Sally, I don t think we should take this flight,' I should have said. *'We re still free agents. Let s just get off the plane. Instruct our hands to unbuckle us. Ask them to disobey the pilot.'*

But a newly married, older-than-his-wife man, like myself, does not do that, does he? Expose his fear, his weakness, for his pretty young bride to see and shun; shame himself in front of her and others. Instead, he allows his hands to do that thing expected of them. Fasten his

5

seatbelt, and, in doing so, his hands show him that *they* are in command. So, if and when things go wrong, perhaps we *should* blame the hands. Shall I tell them this when I'm standing in that dock? Persuade them that the real culprit is not John McEuen but his hands. The ones that, back then, after boarding the plane, told the command centre in his brain to shut up and enjoy the flight'.

That s the other thing, right? Not just the hands' fault.

 Enjoy!' the world out there beyond this courtroom keeps on telling us. Buy an ice-cream or a pizza and... 'Enjoy!' New pair of trousers? 'Enjoy! I m going to the hospital to have this investigation. The one where they shove a bloody great long tube up your... erm... well... yeah, that thing... 'ENJOY!'

'Sit back and enjoy the flight,' the world outside my brain was silently screaming at me. Back then. Perhaps it's the world that controls our hands. Can fates be determined by collective hands? Billions of hands controlling frail destinies. Is that the real cause of those *other* things? The things that should never happen...

Like murder.

Actually, I had only the merest twinge of a why-don t-we-just-get-off-right-now?' feeling before my hands entrapped my body, in that little prop-plane, with the woman who was to be the soulmate of my life, together with a small slice of unwanted (by me) humanity.

'Well perhaps not so small,' I thought, glancing at the American couple.

The Americans were loud. Boy, were they loud!? That

loudness was the last thing I needed during the trip of a lifetime with the only woman of my life.

"Where you folks from?"

A red, rounded face sporting a baseball cap and a generous helping of pimples and warts did an owl-twist and fixed me with two vacuous blood-shot eyes, his voice turned up full volume.

"Scotland, actually. Edinburgh." I dourly replied.

'Appear unfriendly, and the face might go away,' I thought whilst deliberately avoiding to smile.

"Jeeze, honey, these folks come all the way from Scotland." Those warts and pimples were now on offer to the large peroxide head in front of Sally. But not for long.

"Hey, what part of England s that in? It s where all the Scotch whisky comes from, huh?" the pimpled red face asked me.

"It s not," I said, curtly. Sally gave me a sharp elbow nudge and frowned.

"Sure it is. Best whisky comes all the way from Scotland.

"In England," I explained. Scotland s *not* in England."

"Got me there! Could have sworn — "

"Britain. Not England," I interrupted.

"Hey, well how about that, then!? Britain! Like Ireland, huh?"

"Ireland s in Ireland," I said quietly, and got another elbowing from Sally who never truly appreciated my sarcasm.

"Arnie! Arnie Manetti. And this here lovely lady is Joan, my wife."

Lost Hands

Two podgy hands, one large the other small, reached back in unison, and I shook them, hers first.

"John and Sally McEuen," I said. I let Sally do the smiling.

Actually, I *should* have smiled just to hear our names offered up together, in the same breath, for I still had difficulty in believing how lucky I was to have landed Sally.

A nurse, and surely the prettiest girl in the whole of Edinburgh, she had been on the rebound when we met only nine months earlier. She was a lot younger than me. As a shy, overworked, late-middle-aged, general surgeon, I was beginning to think I would be condemned to a life of eternal bachelorhood, with hands that would never feel and fondle true love. Condemned to a lonely, inner death. Then Sally appeared.

She had been seconded to the operating theatre for a year, covering another girl s maternity leave. To this day, I will never know what she saw in me, but she must have seen something, for she allowed me to date her, to kiss her, and... oh, the bliss of it, let me make love to her.

A shot-gun wedding. Registry office, few friends and not much family; myself, without siblings and both my parents 'busy' on the day, according to my father. In truth, I wanted our marriage signed and sealed as quickly as possible. Before Sally could change her mind. Before *her* hands could change *their* shared mind, refuse to put on that wedding dress, refuse to sign the register.

New Zealand for a honeymoon was *her* idea. The dream of a lifetime, she said, but no place for a solitary soul. Now that we were Mr and Mrs McEuen, Milford Sound seemed the only option to both of us after getting married.

Lost Hands

And the flight over the wilderness of Fiordland was to be the highlight of a blissful honeymoon.

"Just married," Sally said to the Americans, smiling. On our honeymoon!"

"Oh my, ain t that just cute!" said the peroxide dyed head, too fixed on its short, wide neck to turn and face us. Two honeymooner lovebirds on our little flight. And all the way from England."

"Scotland, Goddammit!" I whispered to Sally.

I don t think Arnie and Joan Manetti heard me, but Sally did. And she glowered.

Just then, two young men came on board and sank, with confident ease, into the seats behind Sally and me. I heard the clink of their seatbelts as their own hands committed them to the flight, sealing their fates. I felt uncomfortable. Having a woman I could now call my own for the first time, and so late in life, I was fearful of the proximity to my attractive, young wife of two younger men. Something to do with having a surgeon's, not alpha male, hands, perhaps? An animal fear of the dominant male, and surely for a man of my age every unknown male in his prime might be — *must* be — an alpha male. My reaction was to play another card to the one I had shown the Manettis. I hid the dour, British John McEuen and became the affable Scot with my hand safely on Sally s lap, claiming its territory.

"Hi! I m John McEuen," I announced to the two young men. This is my wife, Sally!"

"Righto, mate!"

Mate?

The man seated behind Sally gave a faintly knowing smile. Knew my fear, perhaps? The other only stared. I was getting some of my own medicine from him. Sally appeared strangely embarrassed.

"Wayne. And this, my friend, is Mike," the smiling one finally said in the face of my false, lingering grin. You here for the tramping?"

Tramping? I read about this in the guide book. The New Zealand version of hiking, only you take many days, maybe a week or two, about it, and risk being swallowed up by the wilderness forever.

"Nope. We re on honeymoon."

"Lucky you!" It was Mike, the one who seemed unable to smile.

"Kiwis?" I asked.

"Not bloody likely. Ozzies. From Melbourne."

"Great," I said. Not been there."

"Wouldn t want to, mate. Piss awful place," Mike replied.

"I m sure it isn t!" I said, smiling. He was joking. Of course he was.

"I m sure it bloody is," came the reply. No smile. Not joking.

"Candy?" questioned Wayne. Smiling again.

"Who?" I asked.

"He's offering you a sweet to suck," explained Sally. "Helps the ears for take-off."

"Thanks," I said, taking what appeared to be a large

barley sugar from Wayne's over-sized, dangerously masculine hand.

"Not for me," Sally said, holding up her own hand.

As I sucked on the strangely flavoured, though not unpleasant, sweet, the Kiwi pilot, who had closed the plane door and started up the engine, spoke to us through his microphone.

"Welcome on board for this wonderful Wilderness Paradise Air Tours flight over the paradise of our beautiful Milford Sound, ladies and gentlemen, boys and girls, and believe me, each and every one of you is about to get the experience of his or her lifetime. One that only happens once, ha-ha! Before we take off, though, let me just run over our safety procedures. Just a routine, I assure you, for I stress to you that I have never... and I mean *never*... fallen from the sky. Not yet. Ha-ha! Wouldn t be here talking to you if I had, huh? Now under your seats..."

'Why the 'ha-ha' chuckles?'

I normally switch off at times like that, but my fate was entirely in this weirdo s hands. Rather, *our* fates, all six of us, not just mine. Or should that be five, I wondered? I wanted to get in the way of thinking of Sally and me as a couple... as one .

The engine started up in reluctant bursts, the propellers began to turn, slowly at first, but soon, in a whirring crescendo of engine noise, they became a feint blur, pulling the plane forwards as it bumped along the runway. Sally, grinning fearlessly, mouthed something but I could not hear a word. I had put on ear muffs to minimise the engine roar. I squeezed her hand and smiled and

11

thought about what might be our last moments on Earth... and I wondered what death might have in store for me should we give our pilot his first hard statistic. If his hands were to fail him, and us, I prayed that I might get more of Sally after death, for I reckoned nine months with her was just not long enough. I was not asking for all eternity with my new wife, so I felt it was perfectly reasonable to put that humble request to my Maker. Then...

My head felt weirdly fuzzy. The fear of death, maybe?

'A bit more time with her, please, even if it has to be after the big D" my brain mumbled through that fuzziness.

'Then do what you f------ like with those invisible God hands of yours, Chum.' That was my personal prayer as the plane shot along the runway before lifting itself off the ground only yards before it ended.

Soon, we were high in the sky and still alive. Sally pulled her hand free from mine and shook it, laughing. I had not realised I had been gripping it so hard that I must have squeezed out all the blood from her slim, nurse's fingers. She pointed at an unfolding paradise through the window, but, as the small plane skirted over endless trees, then on and up towards the mountains, I began to feel even more floaty and fuzzy, though somehow more relaxed and able to share the magnificence of the scenery with my new bride. She must have detected a sadness in my expression, with my hand lying impotently on her lap, for she picked it up and kissed it, then held it up to her cheek. God, I suddenly felt so happy at that moment. All fear of death gone, I stroked her cheek, and smiled.

'Really mine? Impossible! Just keep on dreaming this dream, Johnny,' I thought to myself. 'Keep it going

12

forever.'

And, as Sally, grinning, peered out at the magnificent, forest-clad mountains ahead, plus the deep valleys and mirror fiords, I just stared at the perfect contours of her face, at the way the sun caught her shoulder-length, blonde hair, at those lips that had given me so much pleasure with their soft, eager kisses, now parted in their own pleasure at the beauty of the place.

"Well, folks, just feast your eyes upon one of the few remaining paradises on earth," announced the pilot. "Soon, we ll be flying directly over the South Island rainforest, a jewel within a jewel, eh? And you re just so lucky with this picture postcard weather. There s folks who have done this flight a dozen times and not once seen the sun, but just look at that! Hardly a cloud in the sky. Now, ease her up a bit, and we might just miss that mountain straight ahead. Ha-ha!"

'*Shit,*' I thought, '*you don t joke about things like that. Jesus, man, planes crash. People die. I ve only been with Sally for nine months. Not yet, please!*'

Sally turned and looked at me as though she had read my mind.

'I m okay!' she mouthed.

Arnie showed us his pimples and warts again. "You got rainforest like this in Scotland, John?" he asked.

Sally gave my hand a warning slap.

"Not much of it left around Edinburgh," I answered, glibly.

"Jeeze, that sure is one hell of a shame. Jus' look at that

13

view out there! You know, Joan and I, we thought about going to England one day. Seeing the King and Buckingham Palace and those soldiers with their funny hats. We wanted to — "

"Holyrood," I interrupted.

"No, I don t think they call them Hollywood hats. Something like — "

"His palace in Edinburgh," I interrupted. "It s called Holyrood Palace."

"The King of England has a palace in Scotland? Well, fancy that, Joany!"

"He *is* the King of Scotland as well. Buckingham palace is in England, Holyrood in Scotland."

"Did ya hear that, Joany? Their King, he s gotten a palace in Scotland as well."

"That s why it s called the United Kingdom!" I said, abruptly.

'God,' I thought, *I cannot take another hour of this.'*

Another little slap from Sally, and she held a finger to her lips. My foggy mind got the message. Fog? Mist? Scottish mist in an autumn dawn?

"It s a beautiful country, Scotland," I added. You d like it. Very different from the rainforest here, but you d like it."

"Sure we would, John. And you must come visit us in Wisconsin one day, you and Sally. We d like that, wouldn t we, Joany?"

"Why, sure thing, honey!"

14

Lost Hands

No, they weren t that bad, Arnie and Joan. It was *me*. I knew all along that the problem was me, and maybe the altitude was playing games with my increasingly fuzzy mind, but Sally would keep me right from now on. She must have seen something more than just an irritable, solitary surgeon in me, and I had to cling onto this... to this *other* John McEuen whom she had nurtured so carefully over our nine months together.

The plane climbed steeply, forcing us backwards with only an endless, blue firmament to look at out of the window, until we levelled once more above high mountain peaks. The guy was right. It *was* a paradise, though not one that I could feel a part of. It was a like watching a documentary movie, 'The Last Paradise On Earth', unfolding a thousand feet beneath me whilst stretching away to a distant green horizon, filtering through the fog clouding my brain, but I felt no closer to the place than if I had been sitting in front of a television back home in Edinburgh. Perhaps it was because my own paradise, my *tangible* paradise, sat there in the seat adjacent to mine. Plus, my fear was still with me. My fear that *that* particular paradise was so very temporary compared with the world outside the window of the small plane suspended in space.

We all sat in silence, the Americans included, as the plane trawled its black shadow across the lush, green mountains below.

"There she is!" the pilot announced. Milford Sound! What a beauty, huh?"

I peered out at the glass-still Sound, the reflected mountains, the tiny pleasure boats. They looked so very safe, those boats. *'Two parachutes,'* I thought. That s all we need. Two parachutes for Sally and me to drop together from the sky to the stillness of the Sound, to be rescued by one of those boats and to get on with our lives. Together.

"Heading west now, folks. Over true wilderness. Then south over Doubtful Sound. Those boats down there, they re the last you re gonna see of civilisation. The *very* last! Ha-ha!"

I really did *not* like the pilot s laugh. There was something almost maniacal about it. It should have warned me — *all* of us — that laugh, but I guess we just shrugged it off as affable eccentricity. Besides, our hands had sealed us into the plane — his plane — by clicking those seatbelts.

We must have flown for twenty minutes or so with nothing but green, and mountains and more green and more mirror water and more mountains, more green again, when the plane suddenly banked, throwing Sally against me. She gripped my arm, and, for the first time, I saw the same fear in her eyes that I had felt myself on clicking my seatbelt.

"Jeeze, what was that about?!" shouted Arnie.

"He took my job as chief pilot and then my girl, guys," announced the pilot. That was too much, don t you think? I mean, you d all do the same, wouldn t you? Right? Is there anyone here who wouldn t?"

'Do what?' I wondered with mounting anxiety.

The plane curled in the air, throwing us the other way. Sally screamed.

Lost Hands

"What the heck s going on?" Arnie yelled.

We had dropped a few hundred feet in a matter of seconds. The forest below had risen up, dangerously close. We seemed to be heading straight for a sheer mountain face.

"Had to choose the right spot, see. A reasonable number of casualties to hit the headlines so as she ll notice. Wouldn t want to be relegated to a small paragraph somewhere in the middle of the local rag. Small addendum tagged to the bottom of a news bulletin. Need a front-page national press headline. She should feel guilty, right? Couldn t kill *her*, could I, or she d never have known that guilt? Plus, I was a better pilot than him, the bastard. Called himself my friend, the fucker! But you lucky lot, you re going straight to another paradise. No need for a silly brochure about that other place, eh? Get there, for free, from *this* paradise, guys! To the *ultimate* paradise."

I felt Sally tremble as she looked at me with a do something!' expression. Through my fogged mind, I saw the mountain rapidly approach, like some sort of vast and hideous prehistoric monster, and knew that this was where we were going to die. Together.

Arnie shot out of his seat like grotesque Jack-in-the-Box, and pushed his way forwards, a veritable charging bull, towards the pilot.

"Out the way, you jerk!" he shrieked at the crazed, lovesick lunatic. I flew in the Nam. I ll take over."

"Na! Better to go quickly," the pilot said, without

looking up. Wake up in paradise, ha-ha!"

By now, Mike, too, was there, up front. The plane swung round, away from the mountain, after Mike gripped the pilot s arm, trying to yank it free from the joystick. Arnie reached forward over the pilot s shoulder, grabbed the stick and fought to gain some sort of control over the aircraft.

"Do something, John!" Sally, now frantic, urged. Help them, for God s sake! That maniac s gonna kill us!"

Wayne had now joined the other men as the plane juddered, jumped and jerked in the air, uncertain as to what it was supposed to be doing because of grappling hands. Mike dragged the pilot from his seat, and, soon, he and Wayne had the man pinned to the floor. Arnie s great bulk was spread across the back of the pilot s seat as, unbuckled, he desperately wrestled with the controls to gain height.

"Shit, we re almost out of fuel!" he yelled. Someone break the bastard s neck and get the hell back to your seats, guys."

Mike slammed the pilot s grinning face against the floor whilst Wayne pulled the guy's sleeves long and tied them together at the back. The pilot was immobilised and appeared barely conscious. Sally glowered furiously at me, an impotent surgeon, totally out of his depth, as though the whole thing had been my fault. *'For Christ s sake, I m only a surgeon, not an air bloody pilot,'* I wanted to say. I mean, what *could* I have done? But I felt painfully puny in the face of all that macho-male action and the fog clouding my brain thickened like setting porridge.

"He told us to stay in our seats," I said, weakly, by way of an excuse.

"He said go *back* to your seats!" Sally corrected, pointedly. "Like you should've been doing something rather than staying glued to your seat like a dummy!"

How wrong I was about Arnie, and how ashamed of myself I now felt. The large American was a bloody hero. Jammed up front like an out-of-place hippopotamus, he kept his hands on the controls all the time. He must have known the best he could do, being out of fuel, would be to minimise the damage of a crash landing, plus the full impact would be taken by the cockpit, with himself wedged there up front, to reduce the risk of the fuel tank exploding.

We were now flying very low. Something scraped the fuselage, and the plane swung over to one side.

"Brace, everyone!" Arnie shrieked. Now!"

I pushed Sally s head down to her knees and adopted the position myself. No one screamed at the moment of impact. There was a terrific bang, followed by a metallic crunch. Then silence, apart from a hissing like the last sigh of dying dragon.

Still alive, I looked up. No front to the plane, no Arnie. Only a tangled mass of branches, and, with what I took to be bits of Arnie amongst the wreckage. Joan screamed as if it came from some cavernous hollow deep inside her. I checked on Sally. Thank God she was alive, but her face, her expression, these gave nothing away. Now was my chance to show my true, brave self to her. Prove myself.

19

Lost Hands

I was on my side, still strapped in, Sally above me, with what remained of the plane tilted over to one side perched high up in the trees. I unfastened Sally s, then my own seat belt, and reached over to unfasten Joan s. I looked back. Mike and Wayne were both staring at me.

"The door, for God's sake," Wayne shouted.

I was nearest to the door. I fumbled with it, lifting the handle to the emergency position, but nothing happened.

"Open the fucking door!" Wayne yelled through the dying dragon hiss. She might blow any minute!"

He climbed forwards, shoving me aside, and, with the weight of his whole body, repeatedly kicked at the door. Suddenly, it swung open.

"Jump, you stupid bastard," he yelled, pushing me through the opening.

We were stuck in a tree some thirty feet from the ground. I crawled out, gingerly, onto a branch. I have a terrible head for heights. I felt a sudden thump on my back, and slid down from branch to branch towards the ground, the foliage breaking my fall before I landed draped face down, on a large branch, like a dozy leopard.

"I ll take the girl and you help the Yank lady," I heard Wayne shout.

'The girl? My girl? But... whose girl now?'

I turned. I saw Sally above me, her short hiking skirt up around her waist, virgin white underwear on display, her arm around Wayne s strong shoulders, his free arm around her waist. Tarzan and Jayne came to mind. And with that vision ended my honeymoon paradise. I was now entering hell.

Chapter 2

You ll surely be wanting to know more about Sally. After all, it was *she* who was at the centre of this whole affair. *She* who ultimately controlled those hands of mine, indirectly speaking.

Sally s grandfather had been a miner before the Lothian colliery, where his lungs were destroyed, closed down. After that, he earned a little by fruit picking in Fyfe, breathlessly lifting potatoes in the late summer and also working on the roads, if lucky... and able. Sally s mum, his adored daughter, became a nurse, and later, a single mum. With her grandmother working flat out as a domestic, the grandfather never got over his shame of being the secondary earner in the family. He drank to dull the pain of the shame, and most of what he earned passed through him as beer ended up in the bar urinal. Or in the street. Liquid assets! His wife would hide from him whenever he came home pissed, his temper unleashed. He would sometimes beat Sally's grandmother with a belt, just for the hell of it, or so it appeared to Sally when she caught him at it, but he never touched his daughter, Sally's mum. Not once. He was proud of her, as was Sally, because, like the man's granddaughter, her mother was both intelligent and determined.

The grandfather's death was horrible. A Christmas that would haunt the ten-year-old Sally for the rest of her life. The miserable old fellow vomited what looked like a bucketful of blood over the Christmas turkey whilst he stood carving it. He died before the ambulance arrived. A varicose vein in his gullet, the result of years of heavy drinking, had burst, they were informed after the autopsy.

Sally followed in her single mother s footsteps and was the brightest girl in her year at college. Her mother was over the moon when she got her degree in nursing. Somehow a degree seemed to mean so much more than the straightforward SRN qualification that she had sweated to achieve, but, at the end of the day, Sally was just a nurse on a nurse s meagre salary.

For some inexplicable reason, Sally was sad that her grandfather never lived to see her qualify. They had repeatedly warned him about the drink, her mother told her. His excuse: the stress of the mines closing down all those years back during the Thatcher years. Sally remembered praying to God, in her bedroom, as a young child, for her granddad to stop getting drunk most evenings, for she truly loved him despite his alcohol-laden rages. Perhaps, even back then, she knew that he was a good man at heart. After all, *he* was the one who had always made her laugh as a wee child; the man who, in the absence of her own father, who- and wherever he was, had swung her high in the air and had called her his 'wee princess'. She told me that the saddest thing in her life was knowing, after that awful Christmas Day, that she would never see him again.

Sally was almost a closed book when it came to earlier romances, but I was not stupid. For a girl with her looks there must have been many. However, she did tell me about Sean...

Sean happened when Sally was working on an

orthopaedic ward. He had been transferred from Fort William following a mountaineering accident. His leg was a mess, and he was in for months undergoing a series of complicated operations by a leading orthopaedic surgeon to save him from an amputation.

"We just hit it off," was all that Sally would say to me at first, which I took to mean she fell for him hook, line and sinker. Had it not been for her professionalism, she might have climbed into bed with him there and then, in a hospital ward, but she continued to see him, in a non-professional way, as soon as he was discharged. Then, I assumed, she did climb into bed with him. I never asked her what it was like, with Sean, in bed. but, oh God, my imagination played cruel games with me. A mountaineering hunk... even with a damaged leg. How could I possibly compete?

Sean was also described to me as a writer . Funny how I wanted to know all about the man; but not funny how Sally snapped shut like a clam whenever I attempted to probe her on the subject.

"Oh, this and that," was all she said when I asked what Sean wrote about. The faraway look in her eyes revealed a lot more. He wrote about *her*. I knew it. About the sex they had together in that bed of his. Jesus, why did I so desire to give myself the pain of knowing!?

"Famous? Will he become famous?"

"What does it matter, John? It s all in the past."

Which meant that it wasn t. And which meant, to me, that Sean s passion for Sally would be there, written down, for the whole world to see, excluding me from her story.

24

Lost Hands

Something written is something permanent, indestructible; it can permeate anywhere... *every*where.

It lasted for nearly two years, the 'thing' between Sally and Sean. Long enough for me to know they *were* made for each other. Sally moved in with him and, for all intents and purposes, they lived as husband and wife. More, even. They were soulmate lovers, I was sure of it. Unlike with Sally and me, the marriage thing was unimportant for them. Clearly, their 'thing' should have gone on forever, with children thrown in, but it did not. Sally would never talk properly about *that* bit, the bit that pained her so much, and that she could never truly understand.

Once Sean s leg was mended enough for him to head off for the mountains again, which took over a year, he first tested himself in the Cairngorms and, later on, the Cuillins. Then, one Monday, out of the blue, he told Sally he was off to South America. Patagonia. With his climbing companion, Cameron. Sally, apparently, had always sensed it would happen sooner or later, but this did nothing to dispel the shock when he told her. He asked her to give up her job and come with them that very day. Sever her ties and see the world. But she knew this could never work. Also, she would be a liability to them, she said. Hold them back when they wanted to fly free. And they would argue. That, she would have hated more than anything. *Any* arguing.

Plus... she loved her job.

Sally thought she understood why he had to go. They were so close that she reckoned she understood everything about Sean. But it was so very hard for her to take it in when he said he had no idea when he might return. Might!? One year, two years, who could say? He needed that experience to become a real writer, he told her. It made her feel their love was not for real when he said that, and she felt empty when he was gone. Like a shell with nothing in it. She knew that he would *not* write to her. A writer who never wrote letters nor e-mails, but that's how he, the man she loved to distraction, was. But she could never feel angry. Only hollow and empty. Even more so as her own e-mails and text messages remained unanswered. In them, she told him about us. And about her engagement. Never said I was a doctor, not back then.

I knew the *real* reason for her telling me about Sean, but it was too painful for me to think about.

Also, she told me about *another* reason for not joining Sean and his friend, and maybe one that was a more believable excuse. Her mother. Cancer. And despite being a nurse herself, the woman needed Sally like crazy. As a daughter, the girl could not have been more dutiful, and there was a bond between her and her mother which was far stronger than I had known with either of my own parents. Also, of late, her mother s memory had begun to fail, and Sally feared the worst. Brain secondaries? Early Alzheimer's? I told her that I did not mind. Having a demented mother-in-law was a small price to pay for the most beautiful woman in the world.

Looking back from where I am now sitting, in a court room, and wondering where the heck I go from here, I see how much Sally missed the father she had never known when faced with that awful emptiness after Sean took off. A quietly spoken older man, like me, with a calm exterior and the apparent patience of Job when listening to others, at least most of the time, perhaps I was more of a father figure replacement than a fiancé.

The first time I asked Sally out, she swore it was over between her and Sean. She was convinced, well over a year after he had left for South America, that she would never hear from nor see him again.

"Perhaps he s had some sort of an accident?" I suggested when she told me about those unanswered texts and e-mails.

She shook her head.

"I d know," she said through her tears.

"Of course you would," I affirmed, stroking her hand and wishing her memory of Sean would vanish as easily as the man himself. I knew it could *never* be over for her, but I was happy to be her sounding board. Even more so when she allowed me to kiss her.

And the rest? Well, I simply did not know how complicated women are back then. My experience of datable females had been limited to the social stuff and the animal stuff, the sex, whenever and wherever I could get it. I had never been close to the soul of a woman, and with Sally I was totally out of my depth. I loved her with all my heart, and that is the honest truth, but I did not *know* her, had no idea what drove her deeper feelings and, worst of all, I hadn t a clue what she truly needed from, or even saw in me.

"Yes," she said, staring up at the ceiling, when I asked her to marry me after we first made love. I had never known that sort of tenderness in a woman whilst having sex before, and it drove me crazy with desire for more. I wished the lovemaking with Sally would never stop. "Yes, why not!? Yes, yes, yes!" she repeated. Almost casually. If I had been wiser in the ways of women, I would have realised, back then, that by marrying me she was subconsciously getting at Sean, but I was too blinkered. Years of sexual bliss ahead with the loveliest girl in Edinburgh, possibly the whole of Scotland, I just could not believe it. I asked her to say Yes again, a third time, and she did. Several more times. Then she laughed.

Once it s out and everyone knows, the marriage thing has a momentum of its own. As with hands clicking in that seat belt, a point of no return is passed. The wedding *will* take place. And thus, Sally became my bride, and I became the happiest man in the world. And yet... who was she, this Sally? This other man s woman.

Chapter 3

"Help her down, for God s sake," Wayne shouted.

I must have appeared transfixed to the spot as I stared at my young wife s bared legs dangling from branches above me, with her and Wayne locked into what could only be described as an embrace under any other circumstance. I m no climber, but I managed to disentangle my arms from the trapping branches about ten feet from the ground, and reached out for Sally s hand.

"Just grab my bloody legs, can t you?" she screamed.

I had yet to discover just how small a woman can make a grown man feel, but I encircled her legs with my arms and carefully eased her, and myself, down to the ground, Wayne still holding her hand from above.

"Your skirt," I said, quietly, as she brushed the leaves and twigs from her. It was still up around her waist, and she was standing there in her white panties, her shapely legs on full view. I could not bear for any other male to see her like that.

"Oh, for God s sake! Help Wayne and Mike, can t you?" she chided.

"Stand clear!" Wayne yelled as he climbed back up to assist Mike. Joan was jammed in the doorway of the plane and was screaming. My own body, with two conflicting commands to obey — help Wayne or sort out my wife's raised skirt for her — hovered, uncertain. No, I could not — *would* not — be humiliated any longer in front of Sally. She had to see me as a superman, however weak I was. I climbed back up towards the action. Clouds of acrid smoke now billowed from the aircraft, there was a rumbling noise, and, worst of all, a very strong smell of aviation fuel.

"Run, Sally!" I shouted.

I glanced down. Thank God, her panties were no longer on full view. She ran down the slope, through the undergrowth, to a clearing some fifty feet away.

"Take Joan's legs, John, whilst I ease her down to that branch," ordered Wayne. "She s shaking like a jelly in an earthquake."

I put an arm around Joan's legs, and tried to support the large woman on the branch to which Wayne was lowering her, but suddenly her full weight was on me. So different from my sylph-like Sally. There was no way I could support her, and no way she could support herself. Her vast bulk slid from Wayne s strong grasp, past me; her body flipped 180 degrees on striking a branch before she tumbled to the ground. Horrified, I watched as she continued to jerk and twitch, on the ground below, in a weird, rhythmic sort of a way. It slowed down, that jerking, and she became still, her screams silenced. Her head was at a funny angle.

"Oh, for Christ s sake!" yelled Wayne.

Suddenly, with an enormous explosion, the plane burst into a brilliant ball of fire. For a split second, Mike, balanced before the broken door of the plane, was silhouetted like a charred statue before being engulfed in a fury of flames as I fell from the tree.

I must have lain unconscious for several minutes, for

the next thing I knew was the sound of Sally screaming. I opened my eyes. She was bent over the body of Wayne, one arm around the man, and from that moment on I knew that I had lost my wife.

The tree bearing the burning plane was ablaze. As I stood up, the thick smoke tore at my lungs. I choked and staggered towards Sally and Wayne.

"Help him, John," she said, looking up. His leg. It s badly injured. You're a bloody surgeon, for God's sake!"

It was the first time I had been asked to help someone when, as a doctor, I felt out of my medical depth. General surgeon, yes; orthopaedic surgeon, no. Wayne was alive, but clearly in terrible pain. His leg, as Sally had rightly said, had been shattered by the fall. Maybe the bone was fractured. A deep cut, with open flesh, showed through his torn jeans, and he was rapidly losing blood.

Another moment of indecision. Pulled two ways. Again. The man for whom I had reason to feel intense jealousy, just minutes before, now needed my professional help however inadequate that might be. I knelt down, beside Sally, and pulled material away from Wayne's wounded leg as carefully as possible.

He screamed.

"John, *please* don t hurt him!"

"I m doing my best!" I felt angry and I did not know why. Perhaps I *did* want to hurt him. Maybe, seeing Sally with her arm around him, trying to comfort him, reminded me of my own inadequacy.

"Aargh!" Wayne cried out as I removed his boot and sock.

31

Lost Hands

I heard Sally sobbing. Sobbing for him? I stretched the sock, rolled Wayne s jeans up to his knee and tied the sock tightly around the leg just below the knee. The ooze of blood slowed.

"We ve gotta get him away from here. Quickly," I said.

Sally nodded then coughed. We were all choking on the dense, lingering smoke from the wrecked aircraft. Together, we eased the groaning man onto our shoulders and managed to drag him, groaning, to the clearing where we laid him down onto his back.

"The American woman?" I said.

We returned to Joan.

"Dead!" Sally announced, staring at the body of the large American woman. "Just a minute..." She edged towards Joan, fearful of the heat from the blazing tree supporting the wrecked airplane. "John..." She knelt beside Joan, felt the woman's neck then turned to face me. "She's got a pulse. Just."

As I approached Sally, Joan's hand moved as though trying to grab hold of something. Her eyes opened.

Two seriously injured air crash victims in the middle of nowhere; how much worse could it get? That, I would soon discover. Perhaps a rustle in the undergrowth beyond the blazing tree should have raised my suspicions that something else was going on, but by then the doctor in me had taken over. I had two desperately damaged patients with only one trained nurse at my disposal. No surgical instruments, no medicines, no resuscitation equipment.

Joan tried to speak, but no sound emerged from her mouth. I told her to tap my hand once for 'yes', twice for 'no'. I touched her left leg. "Can you feel me touch you?" I asked. One tap. I repeated my question for the right leg. Another tap. Her eyes fixed on mine and seemed to search for the source of my voice before diverting their gaze. I told her to look back at me, raised my hand then asked her whether she could see me waggle a finger to the left of her field of vision. She nodded her affirmation. Likewise for the other side. Then, "Raise your right hand." Joan did so. Left hand, both feet, too. I grinned at Sally.

"Just concussed, it seems," I said, with pride.

"Just?" scoffed Sally. Then, having established as best I could that Joan's neck was intact, perhaps protected by layers of adipose tissue, together we helped the large American away from the fire, and, moments later, all of us coughing and spluttering, were in the clearing watching the flames. By then, Joan was able to sit up unsupported. She looked this way and that before fixing her eyes on mine.

"Where's Arnie?" she asked. "And why are we here? I thought..." she began.

Although I'm only a humble surgeon, I do know something about the effects of head injury. About 'retrograde amnesia', as the loss of recent memory is termed by us medics. I looked at Sally still comforting Wayne, as if asking her permission to tell Joan the truth. Before I could formulate any words, Wayne did the honours...

"Bloody hero, he was, Arnie," he blurted.

Joan's face froze. She stared at Wayne, then at me.

"Was?" she asked in disbelief. Sally left Wayne and came over to hug Joan.

"Like Wayne said," she whispered. "Because of your husband, *we're* still alive."

33

Lost Hands

Leaving Joan in a state of shock, I turned my attention to Wayne. Took off my jacket and rolled it into a pillow to support the man s head whilst Sally, deciding the Ozzie was in greater need of her nursing skills than the head-injured American woman, came back over to kneel beside him and stroke his forehead and cheeks. Too tenderly, for my liking. Meanwhile, I broke off a couple of branches from a nearby tree and snapped them to a couple of feet in length. These became splints to support his injured leg and I used my belt to tie these around the limb. Wayne screamed. Sally winced.

"We ve gotta get help for him, John," she insisted. She glanced at Joan. "Her too," she added, almost as an afterthought.

"Where from? We re in the bleeding wilderness. Remember? Paradise?"

She reached into the back pocket of her hiking skirt and pulled out a mobile phone, offering it meaningfully to me. Mine was lost in the wrecked plane.

"Do something with that!" she instructed.

There was distinct annoyance in her voice. This had been evident ever since the pilot went wacko and I had been painfully unimpressive on the Hollywood hero front. I took the phone from her and switched it on, only to discover there was no reception... surprise, surprise!

"Nothing," I said, showing Sally the blank phone screen.

"Sweetheart," she said, thankfully, something must be done. He can t walk properly. He mustn't suffer like this.

Lost Hands

He just can t. Have a heart, John."

'Like it s all my fault!' I thought. *'Oh, that s it, isn t it? Not enough Tarzan training for us doctors!'*

Maybe I should have shinned up the nearest tree, taken the woman in one hand, Wayne in the other, and leapt to safety from branch to branch with the two of them, like Superman, before returning for the large, weeping, American woman and the Ozzie's mate now spread out in chunks of bloodied flesh, together with bits of Arnie, across the rainforest.

'Okay, then! Blame me for that Kiwi pilot going bonkers if you must, but...'

But I remained silent, standing alone, feeling an idiot, as Sally hugged Wayne close, again stroking his hair. She was a good nurse, I knew that — the very best, my head of department told me when he heard about our engagement — but is it really good nursing, all this stroking and cuddling? Her body language told me otherwise.

Sean, too, had a damaged leg. Same side, right leg, if my memory was correct.

"What is it you want me to do, Sally?" I shouted.

"I don t know. Just get help. Somewhere. I can stay here. With Wayne. And Joan. There must be rangers around. Or people tramping the trails. Just think of something, John. Anything! If you're able."

'Able? Anything? So you can stay here with Wayne, huh?' My bride, my wife, the woman I have waited half a bloody lifetime for, so that she could keep that Ozzie Tarzan nice and warm? With her body? Whilst the gooseberry of a feeble husband of hers got himself lost in the wilderness?

35

Lost Hands

Good time to tell you a little more about my own life before Sally? I mean, you might be thinking, *What a wimp!'* Right? Just like Sally did back there in that wilderness surrounding the beautiful Milford Sound. It is so much easier to dismiss people than to understand them, I ll grant you. But please, just a little of your time to allow me to explain...

I was a single child. Like Sally. With a doting mother. Like Sally. Unlike Sally, I had a strong father, a man who, at the top of his profession, as a doctor, no less, saw all others as inferior, and for whom nothing I ever did came even close to winning his praise other than, 'But you really could have done better, son,' Which meant, *Should* have done better.' Although Sally never knew her father, she told me he must have been a loser and a waster. However, her maternal grandfather did love the girl whilst I received not a single measly ounce of love from my father. Yes, I did have love from my mother and, I hear you say, *'Surely that was enough? You re just a moaner, like all wimps.'* True, perhaps, but I tell you this. When one parent is strong, the other weak, it is the strong one who sets the pace, makes the demands; the alpha male who inflicts mental pain with impossible goals and who makes others believe they are weak, turning any potential Tarzan into a shrimp of a wimp.

I gave up trying to please my father a very long while ago. He is still alive, somewhere on other side of the planet, nice and comfortable in his posh suburban house, doubtless looking forward to saying to my ever-compliant mother, "I told you so!" when I am sentenced for murder. God, how I hate the man. But I could never tell Sally about him. Never expose to her my weakness in the face of a patriarchal bully. Perhaps I feel unable to tell Sally the truth because I have never truly believed in myself. My father saw to that. By not telling my young wife, I was hiding the *real* me from her, and in so doing hoped she would not know that weakling.

I guess this is why I had never before been truly close to a woman. Always a loner. And there is a kind of strength in that — in being a loner — is there not? Just allow me that single positive attribute, please. You see, to face the world alone, you do need a certain courage, even if in a selfish sort of way. "Wimp!" I hear you shout again. But I was doing really well, alone, climbing the ladder of my profession, same as my father's, harming no one, asking no favours. Until Sally appeared. And I fell in love. I didn t ask to. It just happened. I had no belief in myself when I popped the question, and I could not believe she meant it when she said "Yes", her being on the rebound. Later, in New Zealand, as I stood there watching her nurse an injured Tarzan with that comforting body of hers, I knew that I had lost her... of all things, on our honeymoon.

"Okay, okay!" I said. I ve got the message. I ll go and get help. No problem! Just a little jaunt down this steep, densely forested mountain, pick up a wandering lone ranger and all our troubles are over."

"John! No sarcasm. Please! There s a time and place for that, and it s not here and now. We have to try is all I m asking."

"Other way around? I look after Tarzan?"

Lost Hands

"Tarzan? He s just Wayne, John. An Ozzie who's hurt and needs help. We *all* need help. You don t seem to see it. What the hell is wrong with you?"

Her face was red with rage. For several moments, I stood and stared at her... at my *wife*!

"Sorry," I said, at last, squirming with guilt. It s just that..." God, I knew so little about women, and felt overwhelmed by a native fear of that injured alpha male; a fear of being cuckolded so soon into my marriage.

"Sure ! I ll go for help. Keep him warm, huh!?"

I do not know why I said that. I suppose it was the fear — no, the *knowledge* — that she would end up doing more than keeping him warm. A *lot* more.

"Come here!" Sally said.

Like a pet puppy, I went to her.

"Let me kiss you!" she said, quietly.

I stooped and we kissed, but there was no sex in that kiss.

"Another candy, mate?" offered Wayne from down on the ground.

Eagerly, I took another sweet from the Ozzie and popped it into my mouth. The earlier one I took from him had been curiously comforting, but... such a weird flavour.

"Take care!" Sally cautioned before I started to scramble through the undergrowth down the steep side of the mountain away from what I feared was about to happen in that clearing.

I tried hard to focus on what I was doing, where I should put my feet and hands, but all I could think about was Sally. With that man. The one who had been so scornful of me from the outset; whose male ego, even back then, in the plane, had clearly dismissed me as an inconsequential obstacle to his sexual union with the gorgeous Scottish lass sitting in front of him and his equally macho mate. As I pushed my tangled way through the dense scrub, I visualised him sporting a grin as broad as a bloody rugby pitch, tearing at Sally s clothes with those Tarzan hands, feeling her silken skin, her breasts, her thighs. God, he had been so close to those thighs up there in that tree, with his arm around her body. Plus, her underwear on full view, for heaven's sake! He saw, and knows, that she s wearing pure white panties.

I began to talk to myself as I grabbed onto, and fought with, moss-covered branches and bushes on my steep descent towards the fiord way below...

"Sally, don t do this to me! It s Sean, isn t it? Has been all along. Sean, Wayne, Shayne, Tarzan, Warzan, Sharzan... what the heck?" I muttered.

My head felt even more feeble and fuzzy as I sucked desperately on Wayne's strangely flavoured sweet.

'Flavour? Flavours of heaven? No, favours of heaven from a nursing goddess for a bastard with a broken leg? Or nurse goddess? Or goddess nurse? Oh what the...?'

I stopped mumbling when I heard a rustling sound behind me. Heavy breathing too? I turned and searched the dense forest with misting vision. Just trees, trees and more trees. No... only my imagination. Feeling even more floaty, I continued on down.

"God, don't do it, Sally. All those years, I ve waited. For you. You know that, don't you?"

39

Lost Hands

Could not stop talking to myself. Strangely, I now seemed to be climbing uphill, not down. Weird! Back towards the clearing?

"Funny, but is that where the rangers are?" I asked myself. "Rangers in the sky, ha-ha! Suspended up there, watching a porn movie starring Tarzan and Mrs Sally McEuen. Tarzan with one leg. No two legs, only the second one is inside Mrs McEuen right now. Deep, deep inside. Sally, no! Don t do it! My hands, they won t obey me if you let him do that thing he wants from you. I promise, on their behalf!"

Having traced a large circle through the steeply sloping forest, I was again level with the smoke and the flames reaching up into the sky high above the clearing. The wind must have been blowing away from the unfolding scene there. The porn movie. At least, inside my head where the smoke was being replaced, molecule by molecule, by something dark yet colourful.

I felt the hint of a breeze on my face.

"Nice wind! *Kind* wind! You should be on *my* side, wind. The side of righteousness, for I am her true and rightful husband, for heaven's sake."

My mumbling stopped when I saw something on the ground at the edge of the clearing down there. Blue. Trees and shrubs in the way. Could not see clearly enough from where I stood holding onto a branch. *'Easy does it,'* I thought as, deathly quiet, I lowered myself to another tree a few yards down. Better view of that flimsy, blue garment...

Sally s little hiking skirt! All by itself. On the ground.

How sad! Or... was it just in my confused head? My mind could not be certain about the reality of what appeared
40

inside compared with what actually happened outside my brain. Whatever, that little blue skirt was no longer on Sally. Obviously. And hands would be needed to remove a skirt...

Strong Tarzan hands?

'God, how many skirts have those hands of his peeled off beautiful women? Why does the bastard have to add Sally to his list? And with her accepting only because Sean s still there, refusing to be displaced, somewhere deep inside her.'

There is something fundamentally animal about the sound of unhindered sex between two consenting humans. *'Not a bad thing,'* I hear you say. *'Evolution in the making. The sweet music of evolution, huh?'* Whatever, I saw 'it', the 'thing' that goes on between two human animals of opposite sexes...

"Oh... oh... oh!" gasped Sally.

"Uuurgh ... uuurgh!" grunted Tarzan... Warzan... Sharzan?

My young wife's shapely legs were splayed out like open scissors across the injured man, his hands gripping the yielding flesh of her bouncing buttocks as she jerked up and down, rhythmically, in time with his thrusts and with the two lovers' mingled gasps and grunts. And, oh my God, those too. Sally's breasts were free, kissing and bouncing on his bared chest.

"Slut!" I screamed, scrambling towards them. That's when I must have fallen. Some thirty feet, at least. Banged my head on a tree trunk, then it bounced off a rock, then... then... then... nothing...

Chapter 4

"For God's sake, what happened?"

I opened my eyes, blinking. Sally was peering down at me, a look of concern in her lovely eyes. But my brain refused to believe those eyes. It still screened that porn movie somewhere at the back of my cerebral cortex. Painfully, I staggered to my feet, ignoring my wife who was now fully dressed. I picked up a broken-off branch and retraced my steps towards the clearing.

"John, it's... not... what... you... think!" Sally panted as she hurried after me back to where Wayne and Joan still lay stretched out on the ground in the clearing.

"Stop it!" she yelled, just before I raised the branch and swung it down at Wayne s head. Wayne reflexly turned his head at the same time, and I only grazed the top of his scalp, although enough to momentarily stun him.

That s when the hands took over. I can honestly say I had no clear idea what I was doing. Sally, seemingly still bursting with sex, sprang forwards, her own hands clawing at the back of me as my hands encircled Wayne s neck. I was stronger than her, though, and... now just think of this... I was even stronger than a stunned Tarzan. My hands thought that his neck fitted in very neatly there, between them, as I squeezed.

"Don t John! Don t, don t! I had to do something. No painkillers. Only endorphins. You know that. You re a doctor. Sex releases endorphins in the brain. Helps to kill pain. He was in agony. Please stop it, John. There s no need. I love you."

The clawing stopped. Wayne went still. I let go.

'Endorphins?' I thought as Wayne's face turned from purple to red, and the Ozzie grunted. *'I could do with a few endorphins. Can I have some, too, Sally? After my hands are finished here.'*

A terrific crack on the side of my head sent reeling me sideways. Momentarily stunned, I came too for a second time a short while later. Sally stood above me with the same branch that I had used on Wayne now in *her* hands.

"Slut!" I said, rubbing my head. I got up onto my feet and swayed towards her. I had no inkling of what my hands had just done. I m a doctor, for goodness sake. I don t hurt people. But I really do need a wife. "Oh my dear, sweet wife," I said out loud to the Sally I knew inside my head. "I love you so much. All that tenderness. Those times we ve had. We re going to have such a life together, you and me. In paradise."

Sally screamed again, dropped the branch and ran into the undergrowth, me lurching after her, talking all the time to the Sally in my head, not the beautiful slut running away from me. I was gaining on her. No, I would not harm her. Not even the slut. Only make her say it was over between her and Wayne... or Shayne... or Sean? That s all I wanted. My own Sally back. Then we could live on in this wilderness paradise. Make babies here...

'With all that tenderness in you, Sal, what wonderful babies they ll be. But why that look on your face? You were

Lost Hands

a naughty girl, after all, so I ve every right to be angry,

and I don t always know what my hands are gonna do,

but say it! Say Sean is dead for you. Not that guy back

there. Sean! Say he s dead!'

"Slut!" I shouted, again, at the other Sally. The one who couldn t, or wouldn't, hear me.

Sally turned, her eyes wide with fear. She was perched on the edge of a rocky cliff.

"No need to be afraid," I told the inner Sally in my head. "I can get it up just as well as Tarzan. Or Shayne... I mean Wayne... ha-ha!"

She lost her footing. That s what happened. Can t blame my hands for that, can I? Her arms flew wide open, she gave a piercing shriek and was gone. *That* Sally, anyway. The slutty one, not my dear young wife, my paradise princess. No! It wasn t *all* bad. My *true* wife and I could go off into paradise now and find that little bit of peace we d been searching for. No more planes, fat Americans or Tarzans. Just me and Sally. Together.

I could not be bothered to return to see what my surgeon's hands had done to that testosterone-driven, alpha male back there in the clearing. I took a detour. Rather, *we,* my hands and me, took a detour, encircling the clearing, to reach the cliff edge again. I peered down to see whether the other Sally was there. Her body maybe? But there was nothing, and perhaps, I told myself, that *other* Sally had never really existed. Just the projected imaginings of that bastard who had ogled my wife in the

44

plane triggering a porn movie inside my head.

"Hold on tight, Sally," I warned my other wife, the one inside me, reaching back, offering my hand to her in the emptiness behind as I began the slow, steady scramble down the steep mountain towards the valley below. A short way down, I heard the whir of a helicopter somewhere high above the forest.

"No need for any of those, Sal," I said out loud. "Planes, helicopters, they only lead to death. Us, we re going to paradise. Together. What we ve talked about since we first met, Sal. Remember? Our love. *That s* paradise. 'Of course it is,' I hear you say. Agreed! Of course it is!"

Chapter 5

I felt annoyed with that helicopter hovering high in sky above our heavenly paradise. It was an intrusion, like Wayne-come-Shayne-come-Tarzan had been. Plus the large Americans and that loony pilot.

"Thank God for the forest, Sally," I muttered as I slid over rocks, clung to roots and branches in my slow fall-and-tumble down the steep mountainside. "Thank God for paradise, eh? And thank God we got away from that lot up there. I saw how he looked at you, Sal. Him *and* the other guy. On the plane. The one that got blown to bits. *He* would've raped you, I m sure of it, given half the chance.

Narrow escape there. And the other one with the leg? It was my hands that saved you, Sal. Hollywood hero hands, eh? Got yourself a *real* Hollywood hero now. In paradise. H... H..." I couldn't say the word again. It became all scrambled up in my mouth. "Wow, Sal! Think of that. Here... give me your hand."

Her invisible hand felt so warm and yielding in my firm, surgeon's grasp.

"Wait for it!" I said.

I leapt, yowling with joy, some six feet from a rocky platform to a carpet of dark green moss and ferns.

"How s that for Tarzan stuff?" I called back aloud. Go on! Jump! I ll catch you!"

Sally hesitated, then jumped. I caught her, invisible in my arms. Light as a feather. Or was she really just a feather? Or perhaps a wingless bird?

Lost Hands

"Why that look of surprise?" I asked, brushing her imagined hair away from her eyes. You didn t know I could do that? Is that it? Listen... hear that sound?"

I held up my hand.

"No, not the helicopter," I said. The other sound. The music of paradise. From over there."

I pointed in the direction of a distant rumble.

"Water, Sal! First priority in any paradise. Water!"

The sound reminded me of my damnable thirst. I took her hand, and we continued our slow scramble through the forest, descending all the time. I felt curiously happy. The thundering sound of cascading water became louder by the minute until, through a gap in the trees, I saw a shimmering cloud of white spray below. For some unknown reason, it reminded me of my childhood when, during those blissful weekends I spent with my granny in the country, away from my bully of a father, I would walk alone through the nearby woods thinking about... well, nothing. Just feeling the wonder of everything around me. Closer, and I could feel the fine spray cool my face.

The roar of the waterfall became deafening.

"We ll have to climb down," I shouted to Sally. Can t reach the water from here, but just take a look at that! Paradise, huh? We have our crazy pilot to thank for this, you know. Had no idea, up there in the sky, what it was *really* like down here."

I much preferred talking aloud to Sally now that she was actually there, sort of, with me. Or, better still, *within* me. After all, what is the point of inner speech when you can hold a person s hand, speak out aloud and leave the

47

Lost Hands

words hanging in the air? Oh boy, those strange-tasting sweets Wayne gave me were awesome! I just wished I could have another one... two... three... a whole bloody bagful!

Once beside the waterfall we slid downwards, over the moss, the damp rocks, the rotting, dead tree-fern trunks soaked with fine spray. The spray of almost-forgotten memories. I could hear Sally s laughter above the roar of the water, and I smiled to myself that we were now free of the others. What a close one it had been with that bastard, Wayne, and I praised my hands for what they had done as they clutched onto roots and holds in the rocks on our way down.

"You had to do what you did together, hands. Team work, like in the operating theatre, huh? His hands were gonna take my Sally for himself, you know. God, what a shite!"

The ground began to drop less steeply. The waterfall became a fast-flowing, gurgling stream.

"Drink, Sal? I could do with one. Those funny sweets have left me with a strange taste in my mouth!"

On wobbly legs, I crouched beside the tumbling stream and scooped handfuls of water into my mouth. I had not realised, until then, just how parched I was. I blamed the sweets for this and waited for Sally to drink, then, sitting down next to her, took out some 'food' from my purse belt. Two packets of fruit gums and a bar of chocolate.

"These'll have to do for now, I m afraid. No Tesco s near here, huh? Don't have any of that bugger's sweets with you, do you, Sal? No? Guess we ll have to make this lot last. Like our love. And our marriage. That s gonna last, isn t it?

48

Lost Hands

No more Tarzans or Warzans to threaten it now. My hands saw to that. You ll vouch for them, won t you, when the time comes? Tell 'em he was gonna rape you. They ll believe you, Sal. Piece of chocolate? No? Not hungry? I can have your piece, you say? Wow, that s true love, Sal. Sharing!"

I quickly downed Sally s piece of chocolate as well. Had not realised how hungry I was. Blamed those sweets. Again.

It was getting darker. Clouds had gathered and I felt cold. Shivery. A little away from the stream was a rocky alcove, and I was sure that Sally and I could turn this into a makeshift shelter with a few branches and a bit of ingenuity.

I could tell that Sally, too, was tired. She always went silent when tired. So, when the shelter was ready, I helped her into it, then crawled in after her. She curled up beside me, and, with her body up against mine, in no time I had drifted off to sleep.

Chapter 6

Something kept slapping my cheeks. My eyes opened. Sally's face, so close that I could feel her breath. She smiled. I blinked, then frowned. She was fully clothed, thankfully. Nothing like in that porn movie I had been forced to watch from behind the trees near the clearing.

"Thank God you're okay," she said. To my horror, Wayne stood beside her holding a branch for a crutch, his right leg splinted. By me. And I thought I had strangled the bugger.

"Gave us a hell of a fright, mate," Wayne said.

Mate?

Another figure entered my field of vision. The large American woman, Joan.

"You okay?" I asked her.

"Better than you, by the look of that bruise on your head," she replied.

"What...?" I began.

"He's alive. Out there somewhere," Joan said.

"Who are you on about?" I asked, rubbing my head. I sat up. "Who's alive?"

"The pilot."

"What?"

"Wayne spotted something moving through the trees after you left," Sally said. "Same coloured top as the pilot. He was following you."

"Thank God I found my feet again," Joan said. "He was gonna kill you, I know it. You just didn't seem to be aware of him. Like you were on another planet. Even talking to yourself. I screamed at him after he hit you, and he simply vanished like a puff of smoke. Here…" She offered me her hand before pulling me up onto my knees.

"God, you're strong," I observed.

"Gonna have to be with Arnie gone," she replied.

"But for your husband, we'd all be dead," I said. "So that bastard clobbered me, then? Funny, I thought…" I glanced at Sally, then Wayne.

"What?" questioned Sally.

I said nothing.

"You thought *what*, John?"

"My mind playing tricks," I lied, for I knew what I had seen.

"That was a heck of whack you got, mate," Wayne told me. "Sure you're okay?"

I nodded. "Your leg?" I questioned.

"I'm good," he replied, looking down at his splinted limb. "Thanks to you and Sally here."

Sally? Not 'your wife'?

Sally smiled. The same smile she used when reminiscing about Sean.

"Can you stand, John?" my wife asked.

"Think so," I replied. With Sally's help, I struggled onto my feet, swaying like a Saturday night Sauchiehall Street drunkard in Glasgow.

"We'll stick together from now on," suggested Wayne. "Down to the shoreline. Sure to catch the attention of a pleasure boat."

"Heard a helicopter," I offered. "Surely they'll see us here in the clearing."

"Fire's getting too close," observed Wayne. "That tree

51

there's alight already. We must get going, unless you and your young wife want to be kebabbed." He glanced back at Sally. A *lingering* glance.

"What if that crazy pilot jumps out at us again?" I asked.

"All the more reason to get the hell outa here!" remarked Wayne. "You guys follow me."

A sorry foursome, we headed down the unmarked trail that I thought I had taken earlier, with Sally, but now wondered whether it had all been imagined in my comatose state. Perhaps not, I reckoned, after hearing the same distant sound of a waterfall again. Like before, it grew louder and louder until, once more, I became aware of a fine spray stroking my cheeks.

"Sally, please tell me we *were* here together. Before you found me again. This is exactly as I remember it."

"John, you were badly concussed. We've never been here before. I promise you. It's all in your imagination."

'Including that porn movie?'

I remained silent as we approached the waterfall and descended to the rushing stream below.

I halted and crouched down to drink from the fall where Sally and I had, earlier (in my head?) refreshed ourselves. Wayne, who had caught up with us together with Joan, fumbled in his pouch and took out another sweet before offering this to me. I snatched it from him and popped it into my mouth, quickly grinding it between my teeth and swallowing the slightly bitter, sugary fragments.

Wayne laughed.

"Another?" he suggested.

No way would I refuse. Those little sweets had a

curious hold over me, creating a hell of a thirst which I slaked whilst (again?) crouching beside the stream.

"Could be a little tricky for Joan and me getting down there," said Wayne scanning the terrain, below, from a rocky promontory. "You and Sally take the lead."

'Sally? Not Mrs McEuen? Was the porn movie truly imagined?'

With Sally in front of me, the two of us inched our way down a scree slope till the ground, covered with dense scrub, levelled off.

"Stop, Sal!" I screamed. A man-shaped shadow flitted between two nearby trees. "Over there. That pilot guy!" I gesticulated at the forest beyond.

Sally looked and saw nothing.

"John, you're still suffering from concussion. Nobody's there."

Cautiously, I caught up with her. I picked up a rock and slowly approached the tree behind which the shadow had vanished. Nothing! I pricked my ears for sounds of someone moving around in the forest scrub, but the noise of the waterfall was too deafening. I looked back, and saw Joan helping Wayne down the scree towards me.

"Everything okay, John?" he called out.

I shrugged my shoulders and followed Sally on down the mountainside towards the fiord below. There was now a well-worn trail that zig-zagged beside the fall.

'Perhaps,' I thought, *'Sally's right. I really do feel odd. Like my feet are sponges and... oh my God, the patterns of broken sunlight filtering through the trees. Awesome! Why can't I just turn into a tree and enjoy this for all eternity? Can trees be eternal?'* I asked myself.

Chapter 7

I sit on my hands in the dock whilst the judge waits for members of the jury to respond to his request for a verdict. They all look to one woman who nods her head, then stands. I am ordered to also stand, which I do, wishing I could leave those guilty hands behind on the hard, wooden seat.

"Does the jury find the accused, John McEuen, guilty or not guilty of the murder of Anthony James Wood?"

"Guilty, your honour!" pronounces the woman of the jury.

"John McEuen, you have been found guilty of the wilful murder of...."

I switch off. Wish those hands could cover my ears and blot out all sounds. Better still, encircle my own throat and do to myself what that jury have just accused me of doing to that crazy pilot. But no. I am sentenced to life imprisonment in a country I had dreamt of as being 'Paradise on Earth'. Instead, I would end my days in Hell on the other side of the planet. Never again will I guide my hands as they attempt to save lives in the operating theatre. Clearly, having saved, perhaps, hundreds of lives with those hands counts for nothing in a court of law. As I am led back down to my cell, my mind returns to that fateful day when I found myself scrambling down beside a waterfall, in the wake of my wife, towards the fiord below. To say my mind was on another planet would be a gross understatement. Not even another universe. I was in a totally different dimension. Whilst my legs and arms did their job, their 'animal' stuff, my brain, soul, whatever you want to call it, disconnected from my surroundings, danced about with the colours and patterns of the forest. It glorified the feminine shapes of the woman ahead... the woman whom I had married yet who now seemed to strangely personify all that is good about the female of our species.

'Is she a goddess?' my left brain asked my right brain... the thoughtful half, a neurosurgical colleague once jokingly informed me. *'Indeed, she is. The one and only Aphrodite!'* was the response the left half got, moments before 'it' happened...

That shadow, no longer a shadow, sprang out from the undergrowth between Sally and me.

"Watch out, Sal!" I screamed. As Sally halted, holding onto a branch, turning to look at me, the figure, a carbon copy of the pilot, shot forwards and pulled her down onto the ground.

The word 'rape' bounced about in my mind. Whatever dimension I had found myself in, I knew it was my duty to rescue a goddess. Slipping and stumbling towards the rapidly unfolding scene below me, I thought of only one thing. To stop that ghost of a pilot from harming Sally. I grabbed him from behind... or, to be more precise, I encircled his neck with my hands... my surgeon's hands... with all the strength I could muster in my confused state.

"Stop, John, stop!" screamed Sally, now thankfully free of the maniacal brute.

"Can't!" I said, truthfully, for those hands were disconnected from my brain. In that other dimension, they were doing their own thing. For a goddess.

Lost Hands

I heard sounds behind me. Breaking branches. Then... nothing! Again.

*****

I woke up on board a pleasure boat, lying across the length of a bench designed for paradise-hungry tourists. Sally, Wayne and Joan were seated on the bench in front of me.

"Sal?" I mumbled. "You okay?"

Sally turned to look at... no, to *scowl* at me.

"What have you done, John?" she asked.

I wanted to say, 'Rescued a goddess!' but the woman eyeing me was most definitely not a goddess. Was she even still my wife?

"Did they get him? The guy who tried to rape you. The mad pilot."

"Are you completely insane?" Sally's eyes burned with anger. *The Goddess of Fire, perhaps?* my still fragile mind questioned. "He was helping me when I stumbled. And you bloody killed him!"

"Shh!" warned Wayne. "There may be hidden ears on this boat."

Wayne came and sat on the bench behind my bruised head. He leaned down to whisper in my ear.

"We, Joan and me, we were too late. He was dead. The pilot. So whilst you were out for the count — thanks to Joany — we filled him with rocks and tipped him into the fiord. Just hope it's deep enough to swallow the guy forever and that they believe our story. That he died in the crash. It's up to you, John. The police will be waiting for us at the quay. Better have your story worked out before we dock, huh?"

"But he was going to rape you!" I plead-shouted at

Sally.

My wife shook her head and raised a finger to her sweet lips.

I so wished for another of Wayne's very special candies. "Have you got...?" I began. Then paused. I had a damn-awful thirst. "A glass of water?" I asked.

Wayne helped me to sit up whilst Sally disappeared off to fetch a glass of water. Joan stared at me with disgust, shaking her head.

"It's not true... is it?" I asked.

Slowly, the large American woman nodded.

"But he killed your husband," I insisted. "*And* he attacked Sally!"

"Not from where I was standing. And what do you mean, 'He killed my husband'? That was a dreadful accident. But to blame the poor pilot you strangled, how low can you get?"

Some physicists talk about the existence of a multiverse with an infinite number of possibilities whenever anything happens, the only reality being that there can never be any connection between such separate universes. But does the word 'never' have any meaning at all if the possibilities are infinite? Whatever, what I had witnessed and experienced was so different from what Sally, Wayne and Joan were now telling me that either I was... *am*... either completely insane, or we were, or had been, temporarily, in different universes.

Lost Hands

Chapter 8

I could barely stand unsupported when the vessel docked at the landward end of the fiord. Two police officers escorted me off the boat, accused of murder, to a parked police car. Why and how they knew about the dead, crazed pilot, I had no idea. Had our conversation been overheard? Or, my worst fear, had Sally decided to turn me in?

Turning to look pleadingly at my wife, I already had an inkling that this might be the last I would see of her. Stripped of my mobile phone, I had no means of communicating with Sally and, later, confined to a remand cell in Queenstown, the lawyer appointed to act in my defence told me, in no uncertain terms, that my wife did *not* wish to communicate with me.

"But that bastard tried to rape her. I just don't understand. I know my head felt a bit fuzzy (an understatement if ever there was one), but I'm sure of what I saw."

"Not according to her statement to the police. She told them she desperately tried to stop you filling his pockets with stones and tipping him into the water... and he might even have still been alive, she said."

"But it's what they all agreed," I insisted. "Poor Joan. Her husband died because that crazy pilot deliberately crashed the plane. To kill all on board."

"Three against one on that, John. You really are making my job very difficult. Look, you said your head felt fuzzy. What, exactly, did you mean?"

"Fuzzy. Like not all there." Should I have said, 'Like in

a different universe, let alone another planet!'

"Does this happen often?" Anita, my lawyer, asked.

I knew what she was getting at. Temporal lobe epilepsy, in which abnormal electrical activity in a particular part of the brain changes reality for an apparently conscious sufferer. I am a doctor, after all, albeit a surgeon. But... Dr Jekyll and Mr Hyde? Is there a Mr Hyde lurking somewhere inside my temporal lobes, only for him to emerge on that one occasion?

"No," I replied, truthfully. "It was *not* some sort of a fit, I can assure you."

"Had you eaten anything strange?" she questioned.

"Just a few sugary sweets. From an Ozzie on the plane. The one who survived." Wayne? Shayne? Whatever! I said nothing about seeing him copulating with Sally after (or before?) that bump on the head. "I did get bashed on the head by the mad guy. They said at first. Out for the count. Not sure how long for, but — "

"That's another thing your wife and the other two survivors of the plane crash told the police. They claim you just fell and bashed your head on a rock. You're a medical man. You'll know only too well how a head injury can affect judgement."

I could see what Anita was getting at. Hoping for leniency for me on the basis that I was suffering from the effects of concussion totally screwing up my interpretation of the events of that period of time following the crash which, she suggested, may have also distorted my sense of reality. Plead guilty, and I could get off with only ten years, if lucky. My exemplary record as a hard-working NHS surgeon, could, she reassured me, also help to slash prison time off my sentence.

I was allowed one phone call a day. Unable to get through to Sally, who declined to answer, I managed to speak with my mother... my *tearful* mother!

"It's not possible, John. What Sally told me. You, a murderer? How could you? Your father— "

"Mother," I interrupted, for my oppressive father was last person in the world I wished to hear about, "I know what I saw. A crazed pilot who had crashed his plane to kill us all, later attempting to rape Sally. My bride. I swear I'm telling the truth, and I have no idea why Sally is now denying my version of events. I was protecting her, for God's sake!"

"I want to believe you, John. Don't know why, when everyone else says something different, but I never once knew you to deliberately tell a lie."

"My only defence is the bash I got on the head. My lawyer is hoping the judge will take that into account."

"And let you off? So you can come back home?"

I could almost see my mother's warming smile hover on the wall behind the prison phone. No way could I wipe it away with the brutal truth.

"We'll see, Mother. Could you call Sally for me?"

"I will, Johnny. But she comes off the phone every time I try to get in touch with her."

'Why?' I wondered, over and over. 'Where did I go wrong?'

Days became weeks became months. No Sally, no change in my recall of those fateful events in 'paradise', no hope of any return to my former life. The only two dim lights in my life in that awful prison were my lawyer, Anita

Mulholland, a wonderful person whose legal skills had been stretched to the limit by my stubborn truthfulness, and my mother. She wanted to come out to New Zealand to see me in person, but that dastardly father of mine said, 'No way!' In truth, I felt she should wait till after the trial, scheduled for some nine months after the event.

'Nine months, huh? The gestation period for humans... and for pigs!'

Lost Hands
PART 2

Chapter 9

"No!" yelled an eleven-year-old Sean Taylor when they told him. Covering his ears as though this might erase what he had just heard. That his beloved elder sister had died in hospital during the night after a lengthy operation. Too young to truly understand, yet too old not to, he slammed his bedroom door and threw himself, face down, on top of his bed, perhaps hoping the bedspread might swallow him up and take him to the place where his sister now was, wherever that might be. Of one thing he felt sure... The crying would never stop.

A gentle knock on the door. It opened a crack.

"May I come in?" his mother asked.

Sean rolled over to face the door.

"Yes," he replied, weakly.

His mother, also tearful, entered and sat beside Sean on his bed.

"Why?" the boy asked. "You said last night they would make her better. With that operation. Dead's not better, is it!?"

His mother felt she could almost reach out and touch the anger in her son's eyes. A necessary emotion in coming to terms with what happened, she realised, knowing how fond the boy was of his big, tender-hearted sister, Verity, but she also knew how dependent Sean was on the girl. *She* was the one who had always helped him to control that temper of his, make him see sense. It seemed as though she could connect directly with the 'better' Sean hidden inside the boy and ensure that he got let out when the angry version of her little brother had imprisoned the good one behind bars of fury.

"Her appendix burst. There was nothing they could do to save Verity," Sean's mother told him, hugging him close to her chest.

Like Sean, the girl's father had a temper. He regularly took this out on Sean's annoying younger sister, Felicity, and spanked her teasing little bottom at every opportunity, which Sean loved to watch. Like his son, the man almost worshipped the elder sister. Verity had wanted to go on to study medicine, of which her father was immensely proud; how ironic, Sean pondered, later, when she 'got killed by a rubbish doctor' as his father put it.

Mr Taylor senior refused to accept the hospital's version of the events that led to Verity's tragic death. The surgeon involved in the case *must* have bungled the operation and caused the appendix to burst. Or he did not open her up soon enough? Either way, it was clearly *his* fault that Verity was taken from them. No one, not even Sean's mother, could persuade him otherwise, and he made a formal complaint which, after the surgeon in question had been exonerated, was followed by a civil action being taken out against him by the deceased girl's father. The lawyer for the prosecution insisted that the three-hour delay in getting Verity to the operating theatre, whatever the surgeon's excuse (trying to save the life of some old fellow bleeding into his stomach who, anyway, also died), was instrumental in allowing her appendix to rupture and cause a fatal peritonitis.

For young Sean, the months leading up to the court case seemed to go on for ever. Somehow, this helped to cement the father-and-son relationship. Whilst before his beloved elder daughter's death, the man as good as ignored his son, afterwards they would spend hours together fuelling each other's anger. Felicity, Sean's little sister, seemed almost pleased that Verity was no longer around, but her attitude encouraged more beatings, now with a stick that the man called a 'cane', from her sadistic father and which Sean was encouraged to watch. The boy tried to imagine the girl was the surgeon responsible for Verity's death, and he felt strangely roused by seeing his naughty younger sister thus punished.

Sean's mother sank inexorably into a deep depression and seemed almost unaware of what was going on in her broken family. Not even the antidepressant pills prescribed by her GP, and dispensed by her husband — Mr Taylor, the local pharmacist with a small photographic studio at the back where he took portrait and passport photos — fogged the suicidal thoughts which eventually took her life after a fourteen-year-old Felicity ran away and turned up at her maternal aunt's down in London where she remained, much to her father's displeasure.

For several months before this, the beatings by her father in his 'photographic studio' at the back of the pharmacy, had been filmed and recorded by the girl's brother at their father's request. The man's excuse... that if and when she finally learned to respect his authority, she could be reminded of the consequences, should she again fail to behave, by watching those movies. Not even Sean, then sixteen, and the same age as his beloved elder sister when she died, knew the real reason for those filmings, but he did enjoy being the eye behind the camera lens.

Before her death, Verity would help out in the family pharmacy whenever she could, at weekends or during holidays. It was why she decided to become a doctor, she said to her mother. Sean, back then, was already interested in the photographic side of his father's business, and soon became knowledgeable about cameras and all aspects of photography. However, his real love, other than what he felt for his elder sister, was sport. He began to spend more and more time in the gym, growing muscles to impress the girls, and was a key player in the school rugby team. Apart from filming Felicity being beaten with a cane, his interest in the art of photography began to wane, and he took to writing stories on his laptop.

It all changed for father and son, one Saturday lunch time, when Sean forgot to switch the pharmacy door sign from 'OPEN' to 'CLOSED'. Mr Taylor senior was administering what he deemed well-deserved punishment across fourteen-year-old Felicity's bottom with his cane, eagerly filmed by Sean, when the door to the dingy backroom studio opened, and an attractive, well-dressed blonde woman entered, interrupting the proceedings by announcing, in a foreign accent, that she had wanted to know what the screams were about. Mr Taylor told the woman to leave immediately, and berated Sean for leaving the pharmacy 'OPEN', but the woman intervened…

"I see you are making a movie," she said with a

distinctly Russian accent. "Your movie could make you big money. Come... we must talk."

Leaving his sobbing daughter still bent over a table, ogled by brother Sean, the pharmacist, holding the cane, followed the young foreign woman back into the empty shop. He swivelled the shop sign to 'CLOSED', turned to face the woman, then demanded,

"Explain!"

"I know people— " began Sonia.

"So do I!" interrupted Mr Taylor. "Lots. But that has nothing to do with you interrupting me disciplining my daughter for her bad behaviour."

"These people, they can make you big money with that movie the young man was shooting in that little room."

The pharmacist studied the strangely attractive woman for a while before responding. Her bright, piercing blue eyes seemed to bore into his brain like a pair of electronic drills, seeking out his lust for the perverted pleasure of administering corporal punishment on his daughter's backside to merge it with a lust for money. The pharmacy business just about brought in enough money for them to survive, what with Sean bringing in nothing and his wife, Elsie, unable to work because of depression caused by Verity's death... and Felicity's bad behaviour. Any opportunity to increase his income needed to be carefully considered.

"What do you mean, 'big money'?" he asked. The five figure sum offered by the woman silenced him for several seconds before he asked her to repeat what she had just told him.

"Twenty-thousand pounds for a dozen movies. Good

quality, of course, but I see you have a good camera. The boy... he knows what he's doing with that expensive-looking equipment?"

"I have him well trained," Mr Taylor replied. "And I have way more than a dozen movies dating back — "

Sonia held up her hand.

"Not too young. Your daughter?" she questioned.

"Eighteen," the pharmacist lied as teams of mental pound signs did somersaults inside his head. The woman fumbled in her handbag and took out a card with her name and contact details. She handed this to the pharmacist.

"Thank your daughter," she said. "Young for eighteen, huh? She can make us both rich. And the boy? Is he your...?" she began.

"Yes," interrupted Mr Taylor. "My son. Sean."

"A handsome lad. Let me know if— "

"Keep him out of it," responded the pharmacist. "He must know nothing about our little conversation! I'll be in touch. Now, if you'll excuse me, I have a naughty girl back there who still needs to be taught a lesson. Or two."

Sonia winked at the man.

"Or three or four?" she suggested before turning to leave the shop. Mr Taylor ran to the door and called out after her.

"What is it you wanted from the pharmacy?" he asked.

"To see *you*," Sonia replied, flourishing a wave of her hand in air.

Back in the studio, Mr Taylor, after giving his tearful daughter a few more whacks, told the poor girl to pull her skirt back down and get on with helping her mother with housework back home before he asked Sean to find *all* the movies taken of his sister being beaten and put them on a memory-stick.

"Why?" his son asked.

"Never you mind! Just do it!" barked the father.

Soon, considerable sums of money, albeit nothing approaching the promised amount, appeared in a special bank account opened by the pharmacist; sums that still far exceeded the amounts earned through sales of medicines and sundries in the pharmacy shop. Sean's movies, of which his mother knew nothing, were, unbeknown to him, soon enjoyed by sick old bastards across the planet thanks to Sonia and her Russian overseers. The pharmacist upgraded the 'authenticity' of future movies by purchasing, on-line, a black, academic headteacher's gown and mortar board and telling Felicity that this was only because he was doing what the headteacher at her private girls' school should have done to ensure she grew up to be a respectable young lady. Using the same excuse, he demanded she wear her school uniform when being 'punished'. Felicity never dared say anything to anyone, least of all her mother, in case it led to yet more beatings, but one weekend, a surprise, albeit brief, visit from her Aunt Maggie who lived down in London, implanted a thought in her troubled young brain. A thought that seemed, to the girl, like a seed from which a new life might emerge.

The following weekend, Sean was almost disappointed that his little sister, already a 'young woman' body-wise, had disappeared, never to return, after stealing money from the pharmacy till, following a beating, whilst her father and her brother were still busily editing their latest 'movie'. But Sean's services in that 'studio' at the back of the pharmacy continued, thanks to Sonia.

"No problem!" explained the Russian woman when told that the pharmacist's disobedient daughter had gone down South to stay with his sister-in-law in London. "I can find girls. All ages."

"Where?" asked Mr Taylor.

"Very naughty girls. From other countries. All ages."

Soon, other girls replaced Felicity for the 'filmings'. Some about Felicity's age, then nearly fifteen, a few younger, and also grown women were told to squeeze into Felicity's school uniform to be filmed taking their punishments. Sean was sworn to 'tell no-one else', and if anyone asked him, he was to say the girls were all over the age of eighteen and had asked to be filmed to help them get work in the film industry.

Sean, now a maturing adolescent, knew that some of the girls were a lot younger, and that, judging by their accents, many were of East European, or even Middle Eastern, extraction. He eagerly helped his father in what was called 'the studio' at weekends, whenever the shop was closed, or in the evenings. He wished he could do more with the girls than film them being beaten, but never got any further than escorting them, afterwards, in tears and rubbing their bottoms, out of the shop when a woman called Sonia came to 'collect' them. Both before and after the 'filmings', as father and son called those sordid 'photographic sessions', Mr Taylor would rehearse in front of the mirror in the toilet, cane in hand, practising his lines with the gruffest, severest voice he could conjure up, and distorting his otherwise featureless face into one of stern authority. He envied his son's ability to mimic different accents. Sean's Cockney, he thought, was superb whenever the boy's mother mentioned his Aunt Maggie. He never understood why Elsie got so upset, or why she went on about her sister, also a Scot, was now a little more 'RP[1]' but definitely *not* Cockney.

Making any sort of meaningful relationship with a girl was a problem for Sean. Highly sexed, and tainted by his father's sadism, most girls instinctively backed away from him. A control freak, he wished nothing to do with 'easy-to-get' girls or with prostitutes. Meanwhile, despite being sports-wise, he remained a loner. Sean's love of rugby waned when his teammates realised they could never rely on him, and he took to mountain climbing, sponging off his father whose sideline making sadistic porn movies considerably fattened his income, although the son did find work in Fife during the fruit picking season, plus other odd jobs. He also attempted to set up his own window cleaning business, but that soon fell flat, particularly after his father warned him not to use this as an excuse to become a peeping Tom. Mr Taylor senior, a pillar of the community, being the local chemist, was extremely sensitive about being found out as porn-monger of the very worst kind.

It was an old friend from school, Cameron, who suggested mountaineering to Sean. After their first long weekend together, climbing in the Cairngorms, Sean was hooked like a fish on a line. Within a week his savings had been spent on serious mountaineering equipment, and three months later, when Cameron, an experienced Alpine climber, and who was out of work, could take a fortnight off, the two men headed for the Italian Alps. Whilst roped

---

[1] Received Pronunciation, or unaccented spoken English

up against a precipitous mountain face, perched above a thousand foot drop, seeking wedges, grips and footholds, he could forget all about his girl-less life, although every evening, in the hostel canteen, his eyes would forever be seeking out feminine beauty and charm in need of his male dominion. Never could his mind totally erase film-clip images of his little sister being beaten with a cane.

Meanwhile, Felicity truly blossomed with Aunt Maggie. The truth about what happened at the back of that pharmacy in Edinburgh never emerged. Felicity feared it might mean having to face the man again. So Maggie became a much-needed, loving mother substitute who knew nothing of the horrors the girl had been subjected to by her father, and she quickly realised that the teenager who landed, one evening, on her doorstep, was a real gem. Into sport, like her hated brother, Felicity also wanted to help other people, unlike Sean. She was bright, and because of this, and her love of physical activity which helped her to forget the cruelty of her childhood, she became a physiotherapist specialising in sports injuries. She knew of her brother's interest in mountaineering and tried to avoid, not always successfully, having anything to do with climbing related trauma. Every time she heard mention of her brother's name, she attempted to shut herself off from the conversation, and would get up and leave the room if her father was the subject of discussion.

Aunt Maggie always knew something more than 'he doesn't care about me' was afoot, but it wasn't until years later, thanks to a brave young Lithuanian girl, after it all came out, that Felicity, in her late twenties and engaged to a young doctor, a rheumatologist at the same hospital in

London where she worked, finally spilled the beans to her aunt. That she had been subjected to what amounted to sexual torture at the hands of her father, and that her big brother, rather than protecting her, was involved in the abuse by recording on camera what went on. Not even Felicity knew the worst of it; that filmed recordings of her being beaten with a cane became a source of income for the very man who should have protected her. Aunt Maggie hugged her niece close and vowed revenge on her brother-in-law, if only for her beloved deceased sister's sake...

But what to do about her nephew, Sean, with whom she'd had no more than fleeting contact, troubled her?

Chapter 10

Sally Guthrie loved her work as a staff nurse on an orthopaedic ward at the Edinburgh Royal Infirmary. Her mother, a district nurse, had always been such an inspiration for the young Sally that thoughts of any other career never even entered the girl's head. Also, she had promised her grandfather, before he drowned in his own blood that fateful Christmas Day, that she would follow in her mother's footsteps. She still lived at home, so the two women had plenty of time to talk about their nursing lives on the ward, and in the community, over meals at night. Like the day Sally just had to share her feelings about a certain patient helicoptered down from Perthshire with a major injury to his leg following a mountaineering accident... one for which only the senior surgeon on Sally's ward had the necessary expertise to fix.

"He's gorgeous, Mum!" Sally remarked before biting into a slice of a pizza delivery. Neither of the two women was fond of cooking.

"No, Sally, *you're* gorgeous and he, whoever he is, is your patient. Never forget that invisible barrier that protects us from our patients and vice versa!" She gave Sally a wink, then offered a little chuckle.

"What about you and my dad?" asked Sally.

"Ah, yes. Your dad. Not *exactly* a patient," replied the older woman. "Relative of. But, yes, that wasn't my finest hour. Left you without a proper father. But please be careful, Sally. Who is this guy, anyway?"

"Serious injury to his right leg. Climbing in Perthshire.

Don't exactly know what happened, but— " Sally paused and peered, starry eyed, at nothing in particular.

"Mr Reynolds, Scotland's best orthopaedic surgeon, fixed him, right?" interrupted the older woman.

"Hope so. He's not married, you know. No girlfriend that I've seen."

"You spying on the poor man?"

Sally laughed.

"Would if I could, Mum."

Miss Guthrie senior reached forward and took her daughter's hand.

"Do be careful, Sally. I know how traumatised you were when that bastard from Dundee dumped you, but you're still young and— "

"Twenty-bloody-eight, Mum! Couple of old friends from school are already mums!"

"Like I was saying, you're still young and beautiful. Plenty more fish in the sea."

Sally groaned. How many times had her mother said that, for goodness sake?

"He said he has to get better *because* of me," she said sheepishly.

"Like he'd curl up and die if you weren't nursing him? Pff! Sounds a right chancer to me!"

Sally put down her fork and looked across the table at her mother.

"It's not like that. We understand each other. Surely you know what I mean."

"What you mean is you're falling in love with your patient. What's his name?"

"Sean."

"Scottish?"

"Uh-huh!"

"That's something, I suppose. Guess he'll be going nowhere soon with that sort of injury. Long rehab, physio, O.T. Just don't climb into bed with him!"

Sally laughed again.

"If only!"

Over the following month, whilst the young mountaineer made remarkably rapid progress, thanks, he told Sally, to her presence on the ward, she truly did find it difficult *not* to get into bed with the hunk, but their brief but frequent talks revealed a lot about his past. His beloved elder sister had died from a burst appendix because a botch-up by the surgeon on call.

"My dad, a pharmacist, even took out a civil action against the bastard, but got nowhere. A stitch up! Professionals cosying up together is what happened."

"*I'm* a professional!" objected Sally.

"*You* are different, Nurse Guthrie."

Sally glanced over her shoulder, came up close to her patient and whispered,

"You can call me 'Sally'."

And he did.

"Do you have any siblings, Sally?"

"Nope! Just me and Mum."

"Still at home, then?" The way Sean asked suggested that this might be a problem for him.

"Still at home," Sally affirmed. "Mum's a nurse, too. On the district."

"Just me and my dad, now," the mountaineer patient said. "My mother died. Depression after my other sister ran

75

away. Killed herself. And all because of that surgeon..." Tears welled in Sean's eyes. "I really loved my big sister, Verity. You know, she wanted to be a doctor."

"I'm sure she'd have made a wonderful doctor, Sean. Do you keep in touch with your other sister?"

"Felicity? Not really. She went to live with our Aunt Maggie. In London. She's a physio now. Right little tearaway as a child. Drove my poor parents mad."

"A medical family, then. Your father a pharmacist, sister a physio, and poor Verity who would have been a doctor."

"Hmm! They say I'll be getting out soon. Can we still talk?" Sean asked. "Like this? When I'm back home?"

Sally smiled, and quickly slipped the piece of paper he handed her, with his phone number on it, into her pocket.

"A pleasure, Sean," she said, quietly.

She called the number the day after Sean's discharge from hospital. They had sex the following day, and within a week, much to her mother's concern, Sally had moved in with the jobless climber.

Chapter 11

Miss Guthrie senior assumed, and hoped, that her daughter's questionable fling with an ex-patient would fizzle out within weeks, but this was not to be. It seemed Sean Taylor, to whom she took an immediate dislike, had a curious hold over her daughter. And when she hinted that Sally's ex-patient, who had sponged off his dad, and now her daughter, was a 'layabout', Sally, uncharacteristically, blew her top.

"How can you, Mum!? He's had such a terrible childhood, his own mum committing suicide because of his sister's death at the hands of some rogue surgeon, his disobedient little sister being looked after by his aunt down in London and his poor, poor father doing his very best. Sean helps him with his photography business, anyway. That's what he gets paid for. Mum, he absolutely is *not* a layabout!"

"Sorry, Sally, but I just don't want to see you getting hurt. That's all."

"Hmm!" A grin slowly emerged on the daughter's face. "He's a fabulous cook. Can I tempt you to come round to our place for a meal?"

Sally's mum chuckled.

"Anything to make a change from yet another pizza delivery. When?"

"Saturday? You and I are both off, right?"

"You'll really like him, Mum. I know you will."

Saturday came and went. Anne Guthrie agreed that her daughter's lover was an excellent cook... some sort of a chicken dish, which was truly yummy, washed down with red wine and followed by homemade trifle. But 'like him'? She was unsure. 'Shy', Sally explained when her mother asked why Sean hardly uttered one word the whole evening, but the way those keen eyes not only looked at her but seemed to bore into her brain troubled the older woman.

"He's a photographer, Mum," Sally said when asked why Sean just stared at Anne in silence. "Working out how to take really great shots of my beautiful mother! *And* he writes."

"Has he any photography qualifications?" Anne asked.

"Taught by his dad. Cooking too. The old guy's into that as well,"

"I'd like to meet this Superman pharmacist father of his."

"Mum, don't joke. Sean and I really do love each other. I've never known a man like him."

After seeing him, Anne Guthrie felt the same way. She had never met anyone quite like Sean, although not necessarily in a positive way. But gradually, over the course of the following weeks, months then almost two years, she grew to accept the man she assumed would, one day, become her son-in-law. But she never did see Mr Taylor senior, the pharmacist. For some unspoken reason, he was 'off limits'.

*****

Living with Sean was not easy for Sally. She quickly learned new boundaries set by her lover; things she could not ask; places, including his father's pharmacy, she must never visit. Although not violent towards her, the young man's tempers did frighten the nurse who thought, mistakenly, that her profession had taught her everything there was to know about human behaviour, good and bad. The 'good' she experienced with Sean was better than anything she imagined possible; the quiet times together on the sofa, watching (and not watching) the television, the walks in the Pentland Hills and in Perthshire... and the sex. The sex made her feel even more than alive. It seemed to illuminate her like a sort of inner *sons et lumières* display. And afterwards, he was always so loving, as if needing some kind of forgiveness from Sally. Curiously, the sex was most amazing whenever he came home after helping his dad with his photography at the back of the pharmacy. Why, she asked herself, could he barely wait to take her to bed after a photographic session?

Not only did Sean keep Sally away from his father, he also kept her apart from his mountaineering life and mates. It annoyed her how, come a Saturday, he would sometimes simply announce that he was off climbing in Cairngorms for a few days. No warning.

"I'm sure I told you," he would say if she found him, early in the morning, already dressed and loading his mountaineer's rucksack in the hallway. But she soon learned *never* to show the frustration, even anger, that she felt at times like this. Nevertheless, she was delighted that he could get back to what he loved the most. Loved even more, perhaps, than being with her? Scaling the rock faces, facing death with limitless courage, achieving the impossible. The hospital physiotherapist had told him he would never climb again. How wrong she was! But when, one Monday morning, she found Sean rummaging in a drawer for his passport only to be told, blankly, that he was off to Patagonia with Cameron, she remained rooted to the spot, still in her nightdress, speechless, as she watched him slip the passport into a rucksack pocket before heaving the huge load onto his broad back.

"Let you know when I'll be back," he said casually, without conviction, and without even kissing her farewell. He was out of the door, and into a taxi already pulled up and waiting in the street, before Sally could think what to say... what to do.

Chapter 12

Justina Banis, just sixteen, lived on the outskirts of Vilnius with her mother, a seamstress. Since her father, a refuse collector, died from a massive heart attack aged only forty-one, leaving the mother and her twelve-year-old daughter struggling to make ends meet, the girl, a loner despite being by far the prettiest girl in her class at school, buried herself in what she loved more than anything...

Art.

Her art teacher, a kind, grey-haired woman, took the gifted child under her wing, inspiring her with the idea of following in the footsteps of the great Lithuanian environmental artist, Aleksandra Kasuba. She felt transported to other worlds, other dimensions even, by the works of Kasuba who, she learned from her teacher, left Lithuania for the United States after the horrors of World War II, but sadly died pre-Covid. Having shunned the unwanted attentions of her pimpled teenage male classmates, which resulted in her having to suffer teasing and bullying by other girls, Justina's adolescent dream was start a new life, abroad, like Kasuba, for herself and for her mother, but her determination to secure a future in America also made her prey to dark forces out to ensnare eager, innocent young girls.

Ponia Ivanova, the art teacher, warned Justina *not* to enter the competition when the girl showed her a slip of paper that appeared in the Banis's letter box that morning.

"How can they possibly know about your love of art?" she asked.

Lost Hands

Justina shrugged her shoulders.

"Someone from church, maybe," she replied. "Surely no harm can come from trying. A scholarship for Edinburgh College of Art would be such an opportunity for me. All expenses paid. Maybe they could pay for my mother to join me. Who knows? Please say 'Yes'. The idea I had for an installation about 'Spring' that I showed you... do you think I should submit it?"

Grudgingly, Ponia Ivanova helped her gifted student with her submission design which would be picked up from her mother's workshop the following week.

"Why no forwarding address?" the teacher asked.

Justina shrugged her shoulders again, a habit that annoyed Ponia Ivanova although she would never make the girl aware of her irritation. She knew only too well about the bullying, and had taken her concerns to the principal who didn't even look up from his desk when she went to talk to him about the matter.

"She's not the only child who has problems fitting in," he said staring at his computer screen whilst still typing. "It's up to her to make the effort. I'm sorry, but I am awfully busy!"

Within a week of entering her submission, of which Justina felt certain even the great Aleksandra Kasuba would have been proud, the schoolgirl from Vilnius received notification that she had been awarded the prize for her 'extraordinary entry'. She felt so excited she could barely wait to tell her art teacher but simply could not understand why the woman still seemed to have reservations about the whole business.

"Who *are* these people?" she asked.

Lost Hands

"They're from Scotland," the girl answered. "They'll know all about Kasuba and her work and about our traditions here in Lithuania. Just think, Miss Ivanova. From Scotland I could get to America. With mother. Start a whole new life."

"Hmm!" frowned the art teacher.

Things moved fast. All her free time, when not helping her mother about the apartment, was spent brushing up on her English... a subject in which she always excelled in class and learned mostly from watching American teenage romance movies online. It was all planned for her by the sponsors of the competition. She would fly to Edinburgh, during the holidays, with an 'escort', a well-dressed woman who listened attentively to Justina's life story to date and felt for the girl after hearing about her torment at the hands of fellow pupils at school.

"Put it all behind you from now on, Justina," the woman with a Russian accent said kindly to the girl, beaming a smile, on the plane. "Just think about your heroine Aleksandra Kasuba looking proudly down at you from heaven as you make your way up the ladder in the world of art, starting in the great city of Edinburgh. Have you heard of Rennie Mackintosh?"

Justina, grinning, shook her head.

"You've a lot to learn then, child... a *lot* to learn!"

At Edinburgh, the woman held on to Justina's passport and documents.

"Can't have you losing these, can we?"

"But Ponia Ivanova said— " began the girl in the taxi on the way to the 'hostel' where she would stay whilst being introduced to the teachers at Edinburgh College of Art.

Lost Hands

"Ponia Ivanova knows nothing about this great city or their Scottish laws," interrupted the woman who simply gave her name as 'Sonia'.

Rather than taking Justina to a fine hotel like the ones she had seen in the movies, the monosyllabic driver of the car that picked her and her escort up from the airport took her to a dingy, grey block of flats in a drab area, on the outskirts of Edinburgh, called Muirhouse. Here, Justina saw a very different Sonia. The woman, who spoke in Russian to the driver, grabbed the girl roughly by the arm, took her rucksack from her and pushed her forwards up the staircase that smelt of urine and vomit. Protesting in Lithuanian that, "This is all wrong... where are we?" Justina was taken up several flights of stairs before being shoved into a dingy flat that also stank of urine and vomit. Sonia handed the rucksack to another, even older Russian woman, together with Justina's passport and mobile phone, before disappearing.

"Don't leave me here!" the girl screamed in Lithuanian after her 'escort' who left with a mere backward wave of her hand, without turning round, before slamming the front door shut behind her. The older woman pulled a reluctant Justina along a dark corridor, opened a door and pushed the girl into a blinded room with four bunk beds, clothes strewn about all over the floor and several other young women lying like fish on fishmonger's slabs, stretched out on shared bunk beds. She pointed to an empty bunk at the far end of the room.

"Yours! Rest. You eat later." the woman said in heavily accented English.

When Justina, beyond tears, attempted to leave the

room and escape what was effectively a prison, the stone-faced woman slapped her across the face, pushed her backwards then closed and locked the door.

"Lithuanian?" a soft voice called from one of the top bunks.

Justina looked up at the dark-haired face of young woman in her late twenties peering down at her.

"Yes," the girl replied.

"You're *very* young. How old are you?"

"Just sixteen."

"Oh my God. You're only a child. This just gets worse and worse. What's your name?"

"Justina. Where are we?"

"I'm Lina. And where are we? Welcome to Hell, Justina!"

Lina, dressed only in her underclothes, climbed down to sit on Justina's bunk and patted the flimsy cover for Justina to sit beside her. Justina, still in a state of shock, did so. The woman held her close and stroked her hair as the Lithuanian girl sobbed her young heart out.

"I'm here for you, Justina. Together we will fight these devils. And we will win. I can see you're a strong girl. And a virgin. This, I see in your eyes."

*****

Justina and Lina stuck together as though superglued to each other, speaking in Lithuanian. English was the common language for all the other imprisoned women, some from other East European countries, others from Africa and one from Thailand. Justina was the only child, earning her respect from the others. At meal time, later that first day, she was offered extra food, and she was allowed to be first in the bathroom the following morning. Most of the women were high on drugs, but Lina warned Justina not to be tempted.

"They think it dulls the pain," Lina told her at breakfast, "but, in truth, it turns them into mindless zombies."

"What's going to happen to me?"

"A child? I don't know. For the others here, it's men. But you? A virgin for sure. So... too valuable for street work as we call it. Of one thing, you can be sure. Sonia will come up with something for you. Maybe porn pictures or movies. Who knows?"

"But I won a competition to study art here at Edinburgh College of Art," protested Justina. "I just don't understand!"

"Oh, you poor child," said Lina, hugging the girl up close.

Later that morning, having spent most of the night imagining her escape — even, in her mind, creating an art installation of this with the route mapped out in gold glitter — Justina found out what was in store for her. She was taken, by Sonia, from the apartment to the same car, same driver, and driven to another part of the city. Justina thought the city looked so beautiful. In the centre was a small 'mountain' on which perched a castle. How she wished she could just get out of the moving car and climb to the top of that castle then scream and scream and scream.

Being a Sunday, there were few people about. The car pulled up beside a pharmacy shop in another part of the city. Why? Was this to buy drugs for her and the other women? If she were let out of the car, would she be able to draw to the shop assistant's attention her desperate plight. *'Surely in a city of this size there must be at least one kind person?'* she thought to herself.

Sonia got out of the car and opened the rear passenger door for Justina to do likewise. As the girl was forcibly led to the pharmacy shop, she could see the place was closed up. Sonia knocked on the door and it was soon opened by a young man with the physique of a body builder. Staring at Justina, he asked Sonia how old 'the girl' was.

"Eighteen of course," came the reply.

Justina felt a fuse burst inside her head.

"I'm just sixteen," she shouted, "and I'm here to see the Edinburgh College of Art. I'm going to be like the great Aleksandra Kasuba."

"Who?" asked the young man, grinning as though he had just heard the joke of the century. Sonia shrugged her shoulders.

"Some other silly little Lithuanian tart, I imagine" the Russian woman replied. "I'll be back for the girl in an hour. Your father must teach her a lesson. She's been *very* naughty. But nothing more. She's valuable. A pleasantly *young* eighteen, huh?" The Russian woman gave Sean a crocodile smile and wink. "By the way, her name's 'Jenny'."

Justina stared in horror as the woman left the shop and the young man locked the door behind her. She took note of the fact that he left the key in the lock.

"So, Jenny, your teacher tells me you've been a very naughty little girl and must be punished."

Justina turned to see who had spoken. A man wearing a long black cloak, like Dracula, with a weird, square, flat black thing on top of his head, holding a long stick, stood in the open doorway of a room at the back of the shop.

"Who are you?" she asked. "This isn't the Art College. I know it!"

"Cheeky young Madam!" responded the man. "Sean, give her the school uniform. Knickers too. Looks to be the same size as Felicity. She can change in the toilet. And make it snappy."

Intimidated by the cruelty in the eyes of the Dracula figure, and by the sheer size of the younger man, Justina followed the latter, past Dracula and into a room with a large camera perched on a tripod pointing at a desk on which were the clothes Dracula had talked about. These were handed to her before she was shown to a toilet.

"Put these on," the young man said. He wasn't bad looking. Handsome even. He smiled at her. This made her do as he said inside a pokey little space that passed as a toilet, and she soon emerged dressed in the uniform of a local girl's private school, but without the tie on. She held this in her hand and showed it to the young man, wearing an expression that informed him she had no idea how to put it on. She felt the touch of his strong hands on her neck as he adjusted the tie for her.

"I'll ask him to be gentle with the cane," the man whispered just before the Dracula figure appeared in the doorway. "Not too hard on her, please," he said more loudly to Dracula. "A first timer, for sure."

"Lighting," ordered the older man, ignoring the other's request. "Get started. And I want this very naughty little girl across that desk, please."

In a flash, Justina realised what was happening. The

evil Dracula figure was going to beat her bottom using a stick with a curvy handle that he held whilst the younger man photographed or filmed her ordeal. What neither of these men knew about was her determination, nor the karate classes she attended in Vilnius when one of the teasing bullies in her class at school became physical. She soon became as good at karate as she was with English and art. Timing, she knew, was essential, and with the key still in the lock she could make her escape. Plus she was a fast runner.

Justina waited until Dracula *('No! Just an old pervert wearing a silly cloak...'* thinking of the man as such made him seem less dangerous and the younger man's eyes were *'almost friendly'*) was standing beside her in front of the wooden desk holding up his stick with a curvy handle. The younger man had switched on a bright light which he turned on herself and on the old pervert before peering at them both through the camera eyepiece. The older guy started to talk to her as the camera began to whir. She caught a few words, including "...Across the desk, Felicity *('Felicity', not 'Jenny'?)*, you naughty girl!" But she wasn't taking it in. Instead, she stood still, planning her moves. Correct timing to the nearest split second would be vital. When Dracula tapped and looked at the desk of which he spoke, with two quick movements, arm and leg, she had the beast tumbling about trying to regain his balance. She snatched up the fallen stick and whacked him full force across the face with it. He screamed, fell to the floor and rolled himself over, clutching at his face, only for the girl to stamp on the small of his back. How he howled!

The younger man, frozen in disbelief, merely stared,

speechless, at Justina when she paused, her foot still firmly on his father's back immobilizing the older guy. She looked at Sean, eyes narrowed, daring him, almost twice her size and age, to take one step closer. He watched as she elicited another grunt from his father by stamping on the felled man's back yet again, and he edged away from the camera as she came towards him. He did nothing when she grabbed the camera tripod by the legs, raised it up and smashed it on the ground, damaging it beyond repair, then calmly handed it to Sean before running for the door to the street.

"Jūs turite būti kalėjime, velniai[2]!" she sneered without turning. Suddenly, realising what she had just done, after turning the key on the outside of the pharmacy front door, and throwing it blindly into the air, she ran, in tears, along the empty street, hoping to find someone, a friendly face at least, who might listen to her. On turning a corner, she saw a woman carrying a bunch of flowers. She approached her and, sobbing, asked the woman,

"Church! Where is church? Must find church."

The woman, clearly puzzled at being asked such a strange question by a local schoolgirl, on a Sunday, with a strong and unfamiliar accent, pointed up the street and indicated to the right. Justina got the message, thanked the woman and ran on. At the next crossroads she saw the spire of a church a few hundred metres away and ran to it, praying that it might save her life. Repeatedly, she looked back to ensure she wasn't being followed, although she knew that the Dracula monster would not be able to keep up with her and, perhaps, the younger man, whose eyes were less cruel, wished for her to escape.

---

[2] You should be in jail, you devils!

Lost Hands

She heard the sound of an organ. Music from heaven! The church door was open. Passing on into the body of the church, she realised what she took to be mass was being conducted by, of all things, a woman.

'Thank God, a woman priest. Never knew that was possible. Is that why Aleksandra Kasuba left Lithuania for America,' she thought as she wondered what to do. Several heads turned and scowled at her whilst the female minister up front, a Black woman, addressed the congregation. One head did not scowl. Instead, its owner, an elderly man, got up and came over to Justina. He took her gently by the arm, and ushered her back out into the vestibule.

"What is it?" he asked. ""Ye seem fair gubbed, young lass."

Justina wiped her eyes, and looked at him, puzzled.

"What?" she asked.

"Upset," the man explained. "You." He pointed to her. "We're in the middle o' a kirk service here. Ah ken it's got tae be serious."

Justina, confused by the man's dialect, understood the word 'serious'. She nodded.

Gently, again, he led her, by the arm, through the door and on into another room lined by chairs. He suggested she sit on one of the chairs, then said, kindly,

"Bide here in the church hall, lass. Dinnae gae anywhere. Someone'll come an' see ye, nae matter whit the problem is."

Justina got the gist. She did not have to wait long. Soon the door opened again, and, to a background of communal hymn singing, a youngish woman appeared and came to sit beside Justina. The girl could hold back no longer. In a burst of tears, she buried her face on the woman's shoulder and allowed herself to be hugged close as she sobbed and sobbed. The woman held her close and patted her back.

"There, there," she said softly. "Take your time. You've come to the right place and our minister will be out soon. I'll take you into her office at the close of service. Don't want a whole bunch of inquisitive old biddies listening in whilst they slurp their coffee, do we!?"

When the hymn and the blessing were over in the body of the church, Justina, still crying, was led along a short passage to an office and the woman waited with the Lithuanian girl dressed as a posh private Edinburgh schoolgirl until the minister appeared. Like some of the women in the 'hostel', she was clearly of African descent. The other woman stood, and the minister took her seat beside the tearful girl.

"Oh my, you go to the same school as my daughter! Do you know her? Melanie Osondu. About same age as you. Fifteen."

The girl looked up and wiped the tears from her eyes.

"I be Justina. From Vilnius."

"Lithuania? But... the uniform you're wearing?"

"Two men make me wear. At pharmacy shop. Then..." the girl paused and looked at the warm, concerned face of the African minister seated beside her.

"What?" the Revd. Osondu asked. "What did these men do? And what were you doing at the pharmacy? Is that the one just nearby? Around the corner? Mr Taylor? One of my parishioners, but not at church today. Nor most Sundays."

"He look like Dracula," the girl explained.

"Mr Taylor? He's no Harrison Ford, but I never

thought of him as Dracula. In fact, he even seemed short of a tooth or two last time he smiled at me. And that's going back a long way. Oh, I'm sorry, Justina. Getting carried away. What happened? Tell me everything. Nice and slow. Take your time."

"I win competition. To study Art at Edinburgh College of Art."

"ECA? But that's wonderful. Melanie would love to go there. She, too, loves her art."

"They send for me to visit college in holiday. Escort called Sonia, Russian lady, take me by plane then drive in taxi to hostel here. Bad place. Smell of..." Justina couldn't think of the English word for urine. "Toilet," she added. "Take my passport, my rucksack, everything, then today... I must be photographed, she say. Movie. Wear this... (she indicated the old school clothes of Mr Taylor's younger daughter) and... under skirt too. How you say?"

Frowning, the minister offered,

"Knickers?"

"Think so."

"This Sonia, she was there?"

"She go. Come back, she say, in one hour."

Revd. Osondu glanced at her watch.

"When did this happen?"

"Just now. I come straight here. Ask for church."

"Clever girl. You did the right thing."

"I worry I kill Dracula man. After he try to beat me with a stick. Across... across desk, he say. Another man, younger, he make movie of everything. But Dracula man fall to floor. My karate teacher tell me self-defence. I hit older man's face with that curvy stick. He cry like baby. Then I smash

93

camera on ground. Young man do nothing, so I escape and come here. Do I go to jail? Please help me."

The minister hugged Justina, then told her to hurry, with herself, to her car parked outside. In the car, she used her mobile phone to contact her personal friend, DCI Calum Scott, who, being off duty, was thankfully at home..

"Calum, this is really serious," she said. "Meet me at Taylor's Pharmacy ASAP. It involves the serious sexual abuse of a minor."

Chapter 13

Sean helped his father up off the floor after hearing the front door slam shut.

"The wee bitch!" the older man cursed, rubbing the bleeding red streak striping his cheek rather than those other cheeks of the young foreign girl who had so easily outsmarted him.

"You had it coming, Dad. Reckon you got off lightly, unless..." Sean paused, recalling the anger and the determination of the first of Sonia's girls not to comply with the 'punishment' due to her according to his father. Punishment he used to inflict on his irritating younger sister. But why did the man call the girl 'Felicity' when she was supposed to be called 'Jenny'? She looked so very like Verity the year his elder sister died at the hands of that rogue surgeon that Sean had felt uneasy about filming her being caned by his dad. Because of her resemblance to Verity, had Sean been unable to pretend this spirited foreign girl was truly Felicity, allowing the girl to escape?

Felicity's behaviour was the reason her elder sister 'caught' appendicitis, Dad always claimed 'on expert advice'... and, after all, Dad *was* a qualified pharmacist, so he knew about such things. Sean hated Felicity for her apparent role in causing the beloved Verity's death, and easily accepted his father's 'punishments' for those other girls that Sonia brought to the pharmacy by imagining each and every one of them was his little sister. But, somehow, this girl, even when dressed in Felicity's old school uniform, which fitted her perfectly, was different. Perhaps the old man also recognised Verity in her and could only proceed by calling her 'Felicity'. Sean even wished to protect the girl from his father, though, despite living with Sally, he was still financially dependent on the man and knew that defying him was not an option. Living in Edinburgh, Sally's nursing salary would certainly not support the two of them.

As with Verity, there was a curious strength in the girl's determination. What, he wondered, might Verity have done in her shoes? Never would Sean's dad have dared to raise his hand against his elder daughter, let alone beat her with a stick. Nothing could have prevented Verity from contacting the police should that have happened.

'Oh my God!' thought Sean. *'The police! I must get out of here. My finger prints will be all over the camera.'*

He grabbed the broken camera and tripod.

"I'm off, Dad. Had nothing to do with what's gone on here in your grubby little studio since Verity died. Those movies of yours were all shot by yourself. Remember!? You're on your own."

After hurriedly stuffing the damaged camera and tripod into its canvas bag, Sean left his father still wearing his 'headmaster's' gown, with the squashed mortar board on the floor, and fled from the pharmacy carrying his equipment. Thankfully, Sally was working that Sunday. Back home, Sean stuffed the camera and tripod into a refuse bin in the alley, then spent the remainder of the day making arrangements. Cameron was delighted. As easy going as any five-year-old might be if tempted with a bagful of his favourite sweets, Cameron said 'Yes' before Sean had finished his sentence about flying off to South America the following day. Cameron laughed. Sean, his usual morose self, did not. Besides, he was thinking about Sally. About quite possibly never seeing her again after the following morning.

Cameron's dad, a wealthy businessman with more money than sense, never said, 'No!' to his son who was now approaching thirty and, like Sean, had never had any meaningful employment for more than a few months. He jokingly described himself as a 'professional scrounger'.

In truth, he and Sean had often talked about climbing in Patagonia. There was something dangerously appealing about the Andes. So remote, so unspoilt compared with the Alps and the Himalayas... and so mysterious. Since developing an interest in writing, Sean also had a curious fixation about the ancient civilisations of the Americas, particularly that of the Inca people. For a while, he had had a time-travel novel, working its way around his brain, involving a climber, like himself, and a beautiful long-dead Inca 'princess'... or whatever they called their young noblewomen. He had even tried to explain it one evening, in bed, to Sally, but she quickly fell asleep having been on duty, all day, in the hospital.

Sally!? How to tell her about Patagonia? What to say? Perhaps he had taken to the long-winded process of novel writing (three, self-published, with sales of each book in low, single figures) because of his difficulty with the spoken word. This was another reason he had to hate Felicity and those 'movie star' girls his father punished for old perverts with money to throw away and to pleasure themselves over.

A coward at heart, Sean decided to leave the telling till the following morning. Anyway, the woman was exhausted after a difficult day on the orthopaedic ward.

Lost Hands

'Just pack my bag, mountaineering gear and all, then leave! Can't risk giving Sally any information other than, "Off to Patagonia, mountaineering. Arranged at the last minute by Cameron,"' he lied to himself. *'Maybe I can, at least, protect Sally from the truth, even if Dad spills the beans and they catch up with me in Argentina. Great place to simply disappear, though, I reckon. I do love Sally. Always will, even if and when I find that Inca princess.'*

Chapter 14

Revd. Osondu's car arrived, before the police, outside the pharmacy, with Justina in the front passenger seat.

"Are you okay coming in with me?" the minister asked the girl.

"Coming in?" queried the Lithuanian teenager.

"The pharmacy. To challenge Mr Taylor about what he was up to dressed as Dracula and threatening you with a cane. More to the point, get him to help the police track down that Sonia woman."

"Ach!" exclaimed Justina. "A devil woman!"

"Well... certainly *not* a Christian. But Mr Taylor?" The minister shook her head. "And a parishioner of my church! But he'll not harm you now. Not with me present. Seems he has more to fear from you, from what you told me. And I'm sure you haven't killed him with that stupid stick of his that he wanted to beat you with. Come. We'll give him a chance to explain himself before my good friend, DI Calum Scott, arrives."

"I stay here. In car. Please," begged Justina.

The minister smiled, patted the girl's hand and said,

"I understand, dear. Wait here. I'll lock the car door to keep you safe. If anyone tries to get to you, just press the horn."

Justina grinned and nodded her understanding when the reverend gave a long, loud blast on the car horn. The noise prompted the face of the paedophile pharmacist to appear in the pharmacy window, a sticking plaster covering the cut on his left cheek caused by his own cane.

Lost Hands

"Not dead, I see," Revd. Osondu announced. "So, no prison," she joked. "Not for *you*, anyway," she added, meaningfully.

She left Justina alone, but safe, in the car and strode into the pharmacy, a veritable Queen of Sheba, after Mr Taylor opened the door for her, politely stepping aside, out of her way. He glanced at the girl seated like a frightened rabbit in the minister's parked car, her head down. No longer wearing the headmaster's black 'Dracula' gown, nor the funny hat, as the Lithuanian girl had called the mortar board, he looked pathetic.

"Not at church this morning, Mr Taylor?" the minister asked.

"It's not what it seems," the man said.

"She thought she had killed you," the imposing woman said. "Worried she'd end up in prison." The man visibly cringed at the word 'prison'. "I don't think paedophiles have a particularly enjoyable time in prison. Something about a basic human instinct to protect young children."

"They said she was eighteen. And willing. Wanting correction."

"They!?" roared the minister fixing the man with her large, piercing brown eyes. The man visibly shook, like a statue about to topple over. "Who... are... they?" she barked, and with each slowly uttered word, the woman took another step towards the trembling pharmacist.

"I have to sit down," came the almost whispered reply. "My face hurts."

"Better your face than that young girl's bottom," the reverend responded. "Who brought the girl? The police will be here very soon, so you might as well tell me first. My good friend DI Scott has two young daughters himself. I think you'll find he'll want some answers. He could be here any minute now."

"A woman called Sonia. Russian."

"And what enquiries did you make as to where the girl — just sixteen it seems — came from?"

The man looked at his feet.

"I *must* sit down," he said, weakly, before taking himself behind the counter where he sank onto a chair.

'Perhaps,' the minister thought, *'the man thinks this restores for him a smidgeon of professional respectability.'*

Leaning over the counter, fixing him with eyes like those of an entomologist might do with an insect whilst using a pin on a cork board, she repeated her question.

"I... I..." stuttered the man before the door opened. DI Scott, a small man with a large, almost fearsome face, entered followed by a young female DC.

"Is that the girl in your car parked outside?" the detective asked.

"Yes," responded the minister. She handed her police officer friend her car keys. He handed these to the young woman.

"Go and sit with the girl, Elaine," he prompted. "Find out what you can. Mary, my dear minister friend here, and I, will find out what Mr Taylor has to say for himself," DI Scott said. And whilst the young DC sat with Justina in the car, comforting the child and learning how a schoolgirl from over one thousand and seven hundred miles away ended up dressed as a schoolgirl from a local private girl's school in a pharmacy in Edinburgh, the senior police detective and his Church of Scotland minister friend extracted something close to the truth from the pathetic, ageing pharmacist with a sticking plaster decorating his cheek. Encouraged by the possibility of a lighter sentence, he hoped, by showing the detective where his stash of videos and photographs of 'schoolgirls' (some genuine, others 'adult') was permanently hidden from prying eyes and from the law, two vital pieces of the jigsaw puzzle remained missing after the pharmacist was driven away, in handcuffs, to the local police station to be formally charged.

Where was the camera that was supposed to record Mr Taylor punishing the girl for the sick pleasure of others who paid handsomely for the experience? And who was the 'handsome' young man behind camera, spoken of by Justina?

Mr Taylor swore that he always worked alone, and that the girl only imagined someone else was involved. He had lost two daughters. Whatever the cost, he had to save his son.

Sean did not even look back at Sally standing in the doorway staring at him in a state of stupefaction. He couldn't. He feared she might see, in his eyes, the real reason for his rapid departure. Being a nurse, she would surely have some sort of a sixth sense where people are concerned. Also, if he were to look into the eyes of the only woman he had truly loved, he might be tempted to stay and face the music. The music of hell. In prison.

He met up with Cameron at Edinburgh Airport, his good friend, eager as always, and unsuspecting even when Sean repeatedly looked at his watch as though he could hardly wait to get on the plane.

"The Andes will still be around for a few million years, Sean," joked Sean's climbing buddy. "They won't erode away in a day or two."

"Hmm!" humphed Sean; then he grinned. "But someone might snatch that Inca princess away before we arrive."

"Weren't they in Peru rather than Argentina? The Incas."

"You need a geography lesson, mate. The Andes are like the backbone of the whole of South America. Top to bottom. Almost. That's a lot of peaks to climb."

"Could take us a few million years, then. Can't wait to get started! And why do they call it Patagonia, the place we're going to, Mr Know All?"

Sean shrugged his shoulders.

At the check-in desk, Sean asked Cameron to go first, hoping his friend's daft monkey act might distract the young woman scanning boarding passes and passports.

"Me and my mate here are off to Patagonia," Cameron said. "Climbing. He's a novelist, you know."

The woman smiled at Sean.

"Have I read any of your books?" she asked. Sean looked down at his boots as though they might tell him what to say... how to remain undiscovered. He looked up and merely shrugged his shoulders.

"Well, I hope I hope you both have a great time in Patagonia. Take care."

Take care? How bloody careless he had been to allow himself to be used by his father. He repeatedly thought about asking Sally whether there could be any truth in his dad's claim that Verity's appendicitis had been brought on by Felicity's attention-seeking behaviour, but was always put off the idea in case the veracity about what happened in that 'studio' at the back of the pharmacy should come out. Now it most certainly would. After all, no way could that wee Lithaunian girl, brought to them by Sonia, have been eighteen.

*****

After connecting flights that ultimately took the mountaineering pair to Córdoba in Argentina, Cameron somewhat regretted having asked his friend about his unwritten novel. Sean had already spent weeks researching the history of the native peoples of South America and it all came out in a tedious soliloquy that grumbled on even when Sean's buddy had fallen fast asleep. It was the only way Sean, normally as silent as a sea-shell, could keep Sally out of his thoughts. But, after overnighting in a doss house on the outskirts of Córdoba, the love of his life being still inside his head helped him to survive the long, uncomfortable ride on multiple coaches to a rough mountaineers' hostel close to the village of El Chaltén, the nearest habitation to the peaks of Fitz Roy, a mountain images of which had so excited Sean since even before he first met Sally on that orthopaedic ward.

*****

"She's coming home with me," the minister told her detective friend, Calum. "You can get your forensics boys and girls to come to my house for DNA off those school clothes they've dressed her in, if necessary, but please don't take them away."

"Why not?" the detective queried, puzzled as to why the minister would wish to keep these. "Surely your daughter has her own uniform even if the two girls are a similar size."

"You'll see!" the woman said with a flick of her hand. "I know there is one woman at the hostel Justina told you about who she's particularly concerned about. Her name's Lina. Not a child like her, it seems. Could your guys bring her back to the manse after you've questioned her. She's also Lithuanian. Apparently, she speaks very good English. Might help Justina better communicate with us."

"Revd. Osondu, for you I would do *anything*!" the detective replied.

"Except come to church every Sunday morning," observed the minister with a mischievous wink.

"Can never seem to find my posh shoes, Mary," DI Scott offered by way of an excuse for his lapse in church attendance that morning.

"Bet you were still in bed!"

"No alibi, I'm afraid! My wife, being a Catholic, wasn't

back from her over-coffee blether in the church hall after mass."

"How is Isabel? Must ask you both round sometime. Melanie's an awful good cook, you know. Gets it from her Dad. Big time into Nigerian cuisine, both father and daughter."

"We'd love that, Mary. I'll give you a call, then, after we've processed the pharmacist."

"You make him sound like a sausage!" chuckled the minister.

"He'll be wishing he *was* a sausage after *I've* finished with him."

Mary Osondu frowned.

"Remember, you are still a Christian even if you weren't at church today. Mr Taylor is a good pharmacist if nothing else. Be sure you get *his* side of the story. *His* reason for looking like 'Dracula' as Justina called him."

DI Scott laughed.

"I've arrested some pretty unsavoury characters in my professional life, but Dracula takes the biscuit. See you soon, Mary!"

Back in her car, Mary Osondu, after the young woman police officer looking after Justina had joined DI Scott, gave the still tearful Lithuanian girl a long, heartfelt hug, then started up the engine."

"You, my child, are coming home with me. You must meet my daughter, Melanie. I just know you'll both get on together. We can have lunch, then it'll be off to Costco to get you kitted up with clothes and toiletries and anything else you need."

"Clothes? Me?" Justina queried.

Lost Hands

The minister patted her precious passenger on the knee.

"Clothes *just* for you, my dear."

*****

Sally was off work all that Monday. Thoughts of walking the Pentlands with Sean on her day off had filled her mind during a long, sleepless period the night before. Thinking about the countryside around Edinburgh sometimes helped her to get back to sleep; displace worries and anxieties about her patients. Now, it seemed as though she had been cast ashore somewhere near Leith, down the road from her, like a piece of seaweed, by a freak un-forecasted storm. *She* knew that *he* knew he hadn't told her about South America. The Cairngorms would have been bad enough, but South Bloody America? What worried her was the thought that he might be in serious trouble... so serious that he was unable to tell her.

For a while Sally had come to realise that part of the love she felt for the irritating man was due to his childishness. Childless and nearly thirty, had her infantile partner become a child substitute? Was this why she now felt so miserable about him disappearing to the other side of the world without any warning whatsoever? Childless, she also desperately needed a stronger, reliable, father-substitute figure. If, as she feared, Sean were to never return, might there be a single, male doctor in the Infirmary who could fancy her if she happened to send out the appropriate signals?

*****

The pharmacist admitted to everything apart from there being another, younger man as the girl brought to him by the Russian woman, called Sonia, had insisted. No way was he going to lose his son, but he quickly realised, under questioning, that just went on and on and on, that his police interrogators weren't daft.

"Where's the camera equipment," he was repeatedly asked.

"Disposed of. She broke it."

"How? Where?"

"I want my lawyer," was all Mr Taylor senior could come up with, hoping desperately that Sean would put some distance between himself and the crime scene before the truth came out. Which it did. About the younger man that Justina spoke of earlier that Sunday morning. Almost. "All right, all right," the pharmacist finally came out with after talking to his lawyer, a certain Donald Ainslie and a good customer of his. "An unemployed guy off the streets. Came asking for drugs. Just happened to be an out-of-work photographer. Wouldn't give me his proper name, so I called him— " A brief pause was noted by the detective inspector. "—Jason. Because he looked like a Jason."

"Looked like a Jason? Jason What?"

The pharmacist shrugged his shoulders.

"DI Scott is leaving the room," recorded the young woman officer, who had comforted Justina whilst Mr Taylor was being arrested, as a her superior, tiring, and supposedly 'off duty', left the room.,

Minutes later the detective inspector was replaced by a steely-faced detective sergeant who, by the look in his eyes, would tease the truth out of a mummified corpse given half a chance.

Chapter 16

Mary Osondu talked to Justina non-stop in the car all the way back to the manse. She spoke about Edinburgh, the 'greatest city in the Northern hemisphere' according to the minister, she spoke about her daughter, Melanie, who was the joy of the lives of her and her accountant husband, and she spoke about her daughter's love of art. Justina understood much of the one-sided conversation and could hardly wait to meet up with Melanie.

On their arrival, Melanie, having been texted about Justina by her mother, immediately opened the manse door on hearing the sound of their car drawing up outside, and she rushed out to greet her new friend for she had already decided this Lithuanian girl, whom she only knew as 'a girl I met in the pharmacy wearing your school uniform' would become a bosom buddy.

After Justina had been taken upstairs to the spare bedroom which was to be her 'safe place' whilst she remained in Edinburgh, Mary took Melanie to the kitchen, closed the door and explained the whole horrid story to her daughter.

"So there's another guy involved?" Melanie asked with a look of disgust.

"Sure of it. Justina wouldn't lie. Likely they'll get an identikit image of him to all airports in case he does a runner, but... I don't know, I cannot believe Mr Taylor got himself mixed up in something like this. Or perhaps I just don't *want* to believe it."

Lost Hands

"Never liked the man. The way he looked at me. Gave me the creeps."

"Pretty young girl like you? Ugh, it's only too obvious now. But to think one of my parishioners spends the sabbath filming young girls being abused. It's just too..." The woman paused as though trying to find the right word to describe both the horror of what happened to those girls and young women — possibly far worse for the older ones — and the shock that the only offender caught, so far, was 'one of her own flock'.

"You're always saying 'God works in mysterious ways', Mum. Perhaps it's a blessing that Justina and I have met up like this. To share thoughts about what we both love. Art. She says she'll teach me karate, too!"

"Oh, I'd better watch out, then!" the mother joked.

After having Justina change into new clothes that the minister had bought for her, and after washing away the tears still smudging her face, the two girls hugged each other and Mary Osondu stood back and almost wept for joy to see how, like two peas in the same pod, they were going to get on. There were no Black kids in Justina's school back in Vilnius, and Justina thought her new-found friend had the prettiest face and the brightest big brown eyes that she had ever seen. But what immediately cemented their friendship was their shared love of art. Melanie had never heard of Alexandra Kasuba, but after the girls pored over images of the environmental artist's work in Melanie's bedroom, on her i-Pad, she could see why Justina was so taken with the Lithuanian woman.

"I'm more into drawing, myself," Melanie said. "More of a two-dimensional girl."

Lost Hands

"Two-dimensional?" queried Justina.

"Flat! Me!" the other girl replied, using a hand gesture to demonstrate flatness. Both girls laughed. Downstairs, in the living room, Mary Osondu smiled to herself, delighted to hear her daughter's happy voice chatting away to this brave little Lithuanian artist. What she did not yet know was that Justina, too, had been bullied at school, like Melanie... Melanie because of her colour, her family connections with Nigeria, and Justina because she simply did not fit into the system back in Vilnius.

*****

The pharmacist, with his lawyer, Donald Ainslie, seated beside him, responded to DS Roberts' needle-like questioning like a recalcitrant schoolboy. The main sticking point, still, was the identity of the young man spoken of by Justina.

Later, the AI-produced image created from the Lithuanian girl's description was circulated to airports and broadcast on the news bulletins long after Sean had departed, with Cameron, for Patagonia. Not even the girl at the Heathrow check-in desk recognised the sketchy image of the silent, solemn figure that had stood beside a clown of a mountaineer who rabbited on about his friend being a novelist off to seek out an Inca princess. Mr Ainslie, however, knew at once that it was Sean, a man he had known since the pharmacist's son was a timid little boy tagging along behind his delightful, elder sister, Verity, both in the pharmacy and at church, with their dad, long before the new minister took over the parish. Later, the co-operation of his client, released on bail, with the police, was clearly helpful in freeing those captive women and girls in that dingy Muirhouse apartment, saving them from the torture of a life in hell, and in tracking down and arresting the Russian 'escort', Sonia Sokolova. Fortunately for the pharmacist, Sonia said that she had no idea who Sean was. For her, he was 'just the guy who took the movies and snapped the shots that helped to bring in more money,' she lied.

Sonia, of course, was merely a small cog in an international, Bratva[3]-led, Russian human trafficking network, but, with her help, DS Roberts was determined to worm his way into that stinking, foul empire of inhuman abuse. Sonia, too, had been forced into prostitution as a young teenager on the streets of St. Petersburg. Being bright, she taught herself English to better communicate with Americans and other English-speaking clients, an attribute that got her fed into the Russian criminal network spread across Continental Europe and the UK where she showed no compassion whatsoever for her 'captives'.

*****

Cameron seemed unable to stop talking. Sean barely opened his mouth to speak as his friend verbally regurgitated whatever appeared in his head. Quite possibly, this explained why they got on so well together. The pharmacist's son could, perhaps, 'hide' behind the other man's constant patter of words, sometimes pouring out in excited bursts, other times dribbling like a leaky tap from the lips of his ridiculously wealthy friend. Whilst 'hiding', he would escape the reality of what happened in that little studio at the back of the pharmacy in Edinburgh, and of his financial reliance upon his perverted father, and the

---

[3] Russian Mafia

awfulness of having to wrench himself away from Sally, the only woman he could ever truly love, whilst trying to re-invent her, inside his head, as an Inca princess whom he rescues from a high Andean time-warp cave that a mountaineering hero — himself — stumbles upon. In his unwritten novel, the princess from the past has been condemned to a cruel death, alone, sealed up in the cave as a human sacrifice to the mountain deity after a landslide destroys a temple in the valley below.

*****

"There she is," Cameron whispered over breakfast in the hostel the morning they planned their ascent, with a paid-for guide, of Monte Fitz-Roy.

"Who?" asked Sean.

"Your Inca princess."

Sean glanced at the attractive, native-looking girl sitting beside another girl, both speaking excitedly in Spanish, and both repeatedly looking meaningfully in their direction. Sean, a born linguist, understood every word.

"It's you she fancies," Cameron said, forlornly, at which Sean immediately transferred himself to the girls' table, delighted to hear they spoke English, now wondering how his fictional mountaineer would be able to communicate with his new-found fantasy love entombed in that ritualistic Inca cave.

"Let me introduce you to an Inca princess," the non-native girl said, at which Sean merely stared in shocked horror at her small, smiley friend. Had she read his mind? Was the girl a goddess rather than a tribal princess?

Lost Hands

Chapter 17

After lunch, Mary Osondu contacted Justina's mother, over WhatsApp, with the Lithuanian girl seated beside her. Not one word of what happened in the pharmacy was spoken. DI Scott had wished for total silence on the matter until there were more leads to help break up the Russian network which he suspected had far-reaching tentacles infiltrating multiple categories of crime.

Mother and daughter listened, both grinning, as Justina gabbled away in Lithuanian about how wonderful Edinburgh was, how it had an old castle perched on a little mountain in the centre of the city, how she was being put up by the lady priest seated beside her and about the woman's daughter also being a budding artist who loved the work of Aleksandra Kasuba... and so on and so on.

"A woman priest? With a daughter?" questioned the mother in Vilnius, incredulous. A devout Catholic, for her there was no such beast as a 'woman priest'.

"Yes, Mum. It's all so different here," the girl said in Lithuanian. "But they have the same God. The same Jesus." A statement that truly came from the heart of the Lithuanian girl after the help she'd received from the Osondu family since her escape from the pharmacy.

"And what about the College of Art?" Justina's mother asked the Revd. Osondu, in English.

Some quick thinking on Mary's part. Fortunately, her accountant husband had a good friend who worked there. A flamboyant character called Daniel, married to a New Zealand guy, David, who was a lawyer. Ade had acted as an accountant for the gay couple often humorously referred to by Mary as the 'two 'Ds', and friendship was formed after they insisted he teach them about Nigerian cuisine. Daniel, a foodaholic, was planning a collaborative piece about global cuisine, to be produced by his final year students, for the Edinburgh Festival, and Ade Osondu, a fellow fanatical foodie, was delighted to help an any way that he could.

"Tomorrow we'll introduce your daughter to Daniel," Mary responded, with confidence, knowing that her husband would agree to anything she asked of him and that the two men would come up with something together. Ade had already promised to show his friend some of Melanie's paintings, so it could be a 'two-for-one' job with it being a school holiday that week.

The following day, DI Calum Scott showed up at the manse with Justina's rucksack, together with her passport... and with Lina.

The manse was certainly spacious enough to accommodate yet another Lithuanian guest. Lina had Justina's room as the girls preferred to share Melanie's room, anyway, and chatter away together till the early hours of the following morning when, after a fitful sleep for Justina, and with Lina's help translating, Melanie, whose artistic talent excelled in draughtsmanship, produced a perfect pencil-drawn image of the pharmacist's son.

"That's him!" the Lithuanian girl said of the head and shoulders picture of the young man, behind the camera, who was to film Justina's ordeal planned by the pharmacist. "Not a bad man, I think," Justina asserted. "Didn't stop me escape. But didn't stop Dracula wanting to beat me with stick."

115

Lost Hands

The image appeared on the national television news that evening. Sally never watched the news but Sean's sister, Felicity, down in London, did...

*****

"What's wrong, dear?" Aunt Maggie asked of her niece as the younger woman froze whilst staring at the hand-drawn sketch, on the television screen, of a young man from Edinburgh wanted by the police for producing pornographic images and movies involving underage girls.

In truth, she did not need to be told. Ever since a fourteen-year-old Felicity suddenly turned up on her doorstep in London after her sister in Edinburgh committed suicide in a state of deep depression following Verity's tragic death from appendicitis, Maggie had suspected there was more to the girl's tearful excuse of, "They just don't want me. I can't stay there any longer." She always knew that 'they', her brother-in-law and her nephew, Sean, had been guilty of more than neglect, but Felicity merely snapped shut like clam shell whenever questioned about the 'real reason' for leaving Edinburgh. Wrongly attributed to the girl's 'bad behaviour', because of her sister's tearful complaints about her younger daughter since primary school, Maggie never probed more deeply into what went on in the family north of the border. Early on, at times, she did wonder how truthful the girl's deceased mother had been because, as far as she could tell, Felicity's behaviour was exemplary.

"Just keep her if that's what she wants," the woman's bother-in-law said over the phone back then. Maggie, an unmarried accountant, thinking this was what both Felicity and her father wished for, even agreed, unaware that the pharmacist's teenage daughter had already been replaced as the victim of 'online schoolgirl-inspired punishment movies' in the pokey studio at the back of his shop, with the girl's hated big brother always the 'eye behind the lens'.

Felicity was much-liked at her new school, particularly by the boys, and excelled in all subjects academically. Her love of many forms of sport awarded her with faithful friends, and, after seeing the problems encountered by injured sports friends, she was determined to help those with injuries by becoming a sports physiotherapist. The week before an image appeared, on the television screen, like a ghost from her horrific childhood past, and unmistakably that of her detested brother despite the passage of time, Felicity had announced her engagement to a doctor at the hospital where she worked. Ranjit. A young rheumatologist who also specialised in sports injuries.

"Just something I have to tell Ranjit," said Felicity when her aunt asked why she suddenly got up to leave the room whilst they were watching the BBC evening news together. "About my brother."

"Sean? That wanted man's picture they just showed? You think it's Sean?"

"Not 'think'. Know!"

*****

"I don't know what you're talking about. Never watch the news, anyway."

The pharmacist turned off his phone before his sister-in-law could explain, and immediately texted Sean...

'Don't contact Sally.'

He reckoned this was enough to get the message across. On bail, still working in his shop, his focus now was to protect his son from both the police and from the international network of Russian mafia gangs. When asked where Sean was, by customers or friends, of which he had precious few, he merely said,

"Looking for another job."

But when, a week after his arrest, Sean disappeared from his 'Find my Friends' app on his i-Phone, the one with which he had previously liaised with Sonia and kept hidden in a never-to-be-dispensed box of Gaviscon tablets on a pharmacy shelf, thankfully undiscovered by the police search, he feared for his wayward son. He knew the wealthy guy with whom he went climbing was a clown, but were they in trouble? Sean had last showed on his i-Phone app somewhere at the foot of a mountain in Patagonia, still moving about. No longer. Had there been an accident? But if so, why would his name also vanish from the app?

*****

"That *was* Sean. I know it," Felicity said after her aunt came off the phone to her father, tears brimming. Maggie had insisted on first contacting her brother-in-law. "They don't say why he's wanted apart from 'in connection with a Russian criminal underage pornography network'. God, that bastard brother of mine. To come back into my life, now of all times. Just when Ranjit and I have got engaged!"

"You don't *have* to tell the police, Felicity. Just forget what you saw on the news. Leave it to them."

"And regret it for the rest of my life? I've got to see what Ranjit thinks. He knows everything. About what Dad put me through as a child. About that horrible lie about me causing Verity's appendicitis because of my behaviour. He said he'd never heard anything so stupid in all his life. Or evil."

"Do as you must, dear. Probably better the police know the whole truth."

Later the same day, Dr Ranjit Prakash was put through to DI Calum Scott of Police Scotland in Edinburgh. The detective inspector listened, absorbing every horrific detail, as the truth about the childhood beatings of his fiancée, Felicity Taylor, by her father, came out, and how the girl's brother eagerly filmed what went on at the back of that pharmacy in Edinburgh.

"Thank you so much, Dr Prakash. May I speak with Felicity, please?"

Ranjit handed the phone to Felicity cuddled up beside him on the sofa at her aunt's house. Aunt Maggie, pretending to be busy in the adjacent kitchen, stood listening behind the half-open door. She had never been happy with the verdict of suicide to explain her sister's untimely death. Just before her niece was about to hang up, she burst into the living room.

"Tell him I'm coming up to Edinburgh. To see him. Not about this, but about your mother's death."

Felicity had never before seen her normally passive aunt in such a state. She handed the phone to the woman, and both she and Ranjit sat open-mouthed as Aunt Maggie asked whether the case of the apparent suicide of Elsie Taylor, over fourteen years before, could be re-opened.

"Has this any bearing on our investigation into your brother-in-law's apparent connection with a Russian crime syndicate?" he queried.

"Maybe!" she replied.

After a pause, the police detective asked whether

Maggie could make it to Edinburgh the following day.

"Yes," she replied before taking down details of the police station where DI Scott was based.

Chapter 18

"**What** do you mean, an Inca princess?" asked Sean, frowning, after he had absorbed the shock of the other girl's introduction.

"Just joking. Don't take it to heart. She whispered to me that she fancies you, so I thought you might be interested in a 'princess'. Anyway, she's from Ecuador and her name's Bibanca. And I'm Catalina."

Still frowning, Sean replied,

"I'm Sean. And my pal's Cameron. Both from Edinburgh."

Cameron joined them and soon took over the conversation, but Sean kept glancing at Bibanca, small but well-proportioned, he reckoned, and with a pleasing little face. He desperately needed another woman with whom to make love and forget Sally, if possible. After a not too-gruelling day testing the lower slopes of Monte Fitz-Roy with their guide, the two men returned tired, but not too tired to cuddle up with Bibanca and Catalina in the girls' dorm whilst the other climbers drank themselves silly in the communal area of the hostel. Sean found Bibanca more than willing... even more passionate than Sally of late. He felt more than happy to use her as the Inca princess in his novel, but kept harping back to Catalina's introduction.

'Can it be just a coincidence? I've only told Cameron about my new novel. And no one has access to the novel plan on my i-Pad. No, I mustn't read too much into it. Has to be coincidence. Anyway, I've read all about the Ñustas... daughters of Inca nobility, and about that sixteenth *century Peruvian native woman called 'La Coya', daughter of Emperor Huayna Capac and often referred to as 'The Inca Princess'. Just part of their culture, I guess.'*

Why the two young women, who never climbed, were ensconced in a hostel for mountaineers, the two men never questioned for the feminine attention they both got from them was wonderfully relaxing after attempting increasingly challenging climbs each day until...

It was week after their arrival in that Patagonian paradise. Sean came to breakfast before Cameron, who was always a slow riser, expecting to enjoy sharing a table and food with their respective lovers, only to be greeted, instead, by an older woman with a strong Russian accent.

"How do you know my name?" asked Sean. "Did Bibanca tell you?"

"Oh, that naughty little native girl. How your father would wish to punish her, eh? Spank her bottom, right?"

"Who are you?" Sean asked after a long period of silence during which he stared at the woman as if hoping this might make her disappear.

"More to the point, who are *you*, Sean Taylor?"

"What do you want? Money? My friend's got loads of money. His dad's — "

"I'm not interested in your friend or his father. Only in you. And in your father."

Cameron appeared, and the woman disappeared after a meaningful backwards glance at Sean.

"Who was that woman?" Sean's friend asked.

"Dunno. But we're leaving. Right now!"

Cameron thought it was all a great joke as Sean hurriedly packed his rucksack, but, like a pet doggie, he followed suit. They paid up and left the hostel, heading for the RN-40 highway.

"Where are we going now?" Cameron asked his friend who kept peering over his shoulder.

"Córdoba. Then…"

Sean paused as a thought suddenly occurred to him. He halted, took off his rucksack, removed his i-Phone then deleted his father's name from his contacts' list and the 'Find my Friends' app.

"We'll work things out in Córdoba," he said, knowing that he would soon be asking Cameron to return to Scotland, and that *he* would have to simply 'disappear'.

*****

For over fourteen years, in a bedside drawer, Maggie had kept the hand-written letter sent by her younger sister, Elsie, the week before she allegedly killed herself in a state of deep depression. According to the pharmacist, at the inquest, his wife helped herself to a handful of sleeping pills from the pharmacy where she sometimes assisted behind the counter whilst her husband carried out genuine photography sessions in the studio at the back. Before packing her case for the train journey to Edinburgh, she took out the letter, sat on the edge of her bed and re-read it. Several times…

Dearest Maggie,

I don't know how much more I can take of this. With James, it's like it's got to be all Felicity's fault that Verity died now that he's got nowhere by blaming that surgeon. I knew there's something very wrong about him and Sean taking her to the pharmacy to be punished. Particularly after I asked him where those unaccounted-for sums of money appearing in our bank account are coming from. He became quite threatening and said I must never say anything to anyone 'or else'! That's why I didn't dare e-mail you. It's really, really doing my head in, Maggie. I wanted to go back to the doctor I see about my depression, but I'm scared it'll all come out about James' behaviour, and she might ask to talk to him. Could you take time off to come up to Edinburgh? Soon? Before the 'or else' happens to me!

Your loving baby sister,

Elsie XXX

With anger, and determination such as she had never before experienced, Maggie secreted the letter in her bag, then left for Kings Cross Station, and, on the train, she repeatedly took it out, again and again, re-reading it each time, before arriving at Edinburgh Waverley Station. After checking in at a Premier Inn hotel, she headed straight for the police station, clutching the letter, to share her long-held concern about her sister's so-called 'suicide' with DI Calum Scott.

*****

Melanie was so excited about getting her dad's gay, foodie friend at Edinburgh Art College, Daniel, to finally see a portfolio of her paintings and drawings thanks to the girl from Lithuania.

Daniel, bald on top, with a dark stubbly growth

covering his chin, hugged both girls after being introduced by his culinary accountant buddy, Ade Osondu. Mary, having been instructed by DI Scott not to let the Lithuanian girl out of her sight, came, together with Lina, as translator, and, with her husband, she watched intently as Daniel took his time shifting through her daughter's art work laid out on a table. He paused, looked sternly at Melanie who appeared ready to burst into tears at what she felt sure was going to be a rejection of her talent, then suddenly broke into a broad smile and uttered only one word...

"Brilliant!"

It was Mary, not Melanie, who shed tears as she hugged her daughter.

"Same word her art teacher at school used," she told Daniel.

Daniel turned his attention to Justina.

"And you, young lady. Ade told me about what happened. You were brought here by some Russian woman thinking we were offering you a place to study art in Edinburgh only to end up in a pharmacy threatened by Dracula. Seems Bram Stoker's anti-hero met his match, huh? And you had been duped by the Devil. 'Him' or 'it' in charge of the Russian Mafia."

"Duped?" questioned Justina.

"Because you're so passionate about art, you never saw the danger."

"She told me all about Aleksandra Kasuba," Melanie said, attempting to change the direction of the conversation.

"Yes, yes... Kasuba and her amazing installations. Well, girls, it just so happens that next term I have a little project

125

for my senior students here. One I'm sure you can both help me with."

Daniel winked at Ade who had already guessed what was coming.

Lost Hands

Chapter 19

All that first week, after Sean left for Patagonia with his mountaineering friend whom Sally could never make out, for surely 'daft' was not an advisable attribute for someone dangling on a rope against a thousand-foot rock face, she texted him during almost every free moment and without a single response. Whenever she tried to phone him, she was immediately cut off. She knew from her 'Find my Friends' i-Phone app that he was somewhere in Argentina, and moving about, therefore still alive, thank God, but why did he want to remain incommunicado, and with her increasingly agitated e-mails unanswered? Unfortunately, she had no contact details for his funny-in-the head companion. Her mother, who had never taken to Sean, might even have been pleased, and she denied knowing anything about the 'other' man. Yet another cross for Sally to bear, for her mother, who had been off work for several months because of cancer treatment, was now showing clear signs of early dementia.

Reluctantly, for Sally always hoped, almost imagined, Sean might suddenly open the front door and reappear in her life, she moved back in with her mother when it became clear that the woman's memory loss was putting her at risk. Sally was relieved that the scan showed no signs of secondaries in the brain, but what it did show, early Alzheimer's, seemed almost worse as it signalled a long, slow slide into mental oblivion. Sally, her only carer, would no longer be able to escape the torment should Sean fail to return now that he was off the radar.

Lost Hands

Days, weeks then months slipped by. After a year, she took Sean's clothes and shoes to be recycled and threw away anything else of his still lying about. The man was gone and she needed to erase him from her mind. Her girlfriends tried to find a Sean-replacement for her, but without success. The guys were always too much 'in her face' for her liking, too wrapped up in themselves or too assuming that all she wanted to do was to climb into bed with them. She focussed most of her attention, when not at the hospital, in caring for her mother. She would take her for walks in The Meadows, treat her to tea and cake at M&S and even watch the occasional movie at the cinema, until she realised this was pointless as the woman invariably fell asleep within the first ten minutes.

Sally was pleased to be asked to stand in for an operating theatre staff nurse who was going on maternity leave. It would be a welcome break from the pressures of ward work. Even if a hunky, fallen mountaineer *were* to suddenly turn up in one of the orthopaedic beds, he could never replace Sean. She found assisting in the operating theatre a welcome challenge for the focus it demanded took her mind off her vanished lover...

As did the eyes of a certain senior general surgeon, Mr John McEuen.

There was something about those eyes that made her want to know more about the man behind them. Mostly, she only made out his eyes and eyebrows on the man's masked face, but during coffee breaks, and before scrubbing up, she could see more of him, and what she saw she liked.

John McEaun was so unlike most of the brash, self-congratulating, male surgical staff, particularly the younger ones whose eyes merely peeled of her surgical scrubs. 'Shy' and 'respectful' were the two words that came to mind when she tried to describe him to her mother one evening.

"Is he going to take you away?" her mother asked.

Wishing that he would, Sally laughed and said,

"No, Mum, that could never happen! He's a consultant surgeon and I'm just a poor wee staff nurse."

But she wondered, from the looks those blue eyes gave her over the top of his mask, and when he stood beside her, scrubbing his hands in the long, operating theatre sink after a particularly difficult emergency abdominal operation that had undoubtedly saved the patient's life, and had told her she was 'the best scrub nurse' he'd ever had to assist him, Sally's heart leapt. Even more so when she found him waiting for her in the corridor outside the operating theatre.

"I really would like to ask you out," he said shyly. "That is, if—? "

"Yes," she replied, before he could finish his sentence, kissing him hurriedly on the lips. "I'm free tonight. See you outside the A&E entrance. Five-thirty. Don't be late!"

Far from being late, the surgeon waited from five onwards, coming up with a variety of excuses when asked by staff and colleagues why he stood alone outside A&E. Sally was ten minutes late, though never divulged the true reason why. Never let on about those tearful ten minutes she spent in the toilet struggling with her conscience. How many times she had told Sean, in bed, that there could never, ever, be any other man in her life? Perhaps, she told herself, it was anger over Sean's disappearance, that she

129

finally decided to break that vow with the surgeon, for she had lost count of the number of times he had gone on and on about some rogue surgeon, years back, who had killed his beloved elder sister. Finally she gave in to her animal attraction to John McEuen. Every time their eyes met, she knew they both wanted the same thing...

Sex.

Sally was pleasantly surprised to learn that the senior surgeon seated across the table from her, in a restaurant in George Street, was unmarried. Although the thought of climbing into bed with another man's husband had rather excited her, this made things a whole lot easier. And when she did climb into bed with him, a week later, his shyness gave way to a passion every bit as intense as that of Sean. He drove her home, she asked him in, and with her mother already fast asleep in her bedroom, they made love all over again on the sofa.

"Will you marry me?" he asked, his shyness back again in the anxious look on his face.

"Yes!" she replied after peering at the ceiling as though the answer to his question might be written across it by some mysterious, divine hand. She looked at the older man who had just proposed to her for the first time in her life, grinned, then added...

"Yes, why not!? Yes, yes, yes!"

Aware that by marrying the surgeon she was both getting at Sean from her past and escaping from a tedious, sexless Seanless present, she was quite happy with the speed with which things happened after John's proposal. She quite understood. Being a surgeon, he just wanted to get things done. An appendix is inflamed, it has to be removed. ASAP. John McEuen gets engaged, he has to be married. ASAP.

"New Zealand!" Sally decided after hearing John's list of suggestions for a honeymoon destination. She had first looked away when John mentioned the country, for the shock hit her like a bullet fired from a gun discharged on the other side of the planet.

Whilst John, grinning happily, went on about the paradise of Milford Sound, and about seeing that paradise from high up during one of those small plane flights he had read about online, Sally, in her head, was back in bed with Sean. The previous week she heard that her vanished lover was alive and well and living in New Zealand. He had contacted his Aunt Maggie in London, telling her to ask Felicity to forgive him for the part he played in those awful punishments meted out by their father, now accused of murdering their mother. Somehow, the news of his whereabouts had filtered through to Sally.

Chapter 20

"James Taylor, I am arresting you for the murder of your late wife, Elsie Taylor. You do not have to say anything, but it may harm your defence if you do not mention, when questioned, something which you later rely on in court. Anything you do say may be given in evidence..."

The pharmacist, who had been busily dispensing pills and potions for a customer, looked up at DI Calum Scott and DC Elaine Matheson, both of whom stood, grim-faced, in front of the pharmacy counter.

He glanced at the puzzled, elderly customer standing beside the detectives before asking the arresting senior police officer whether he could finish making up a prescription. He appeared surprisingly calm as he checked each medication against the list on the counter, and even smiled after handing the bag of health-enhancing goodies to the man who could barely leave the pharmacy quickly enough. The door closed, Mr Taylor came out from behind the counter then held up his wrists for the young woman police officer to do the honours. It came almost as a relief for him. After all, they, the Russians, were unlikely to get to him whilst languishing in prison. And to be imprisoned for murder was surely a better option than to be sent down for child pornography... a charge the detective inspector was holding back from whilst he and colleagues in other crime units across the country were homing in on the massive, evil Russian human octopus that had its multiple tentacles into almost every dirty aspect of crime. So far, the pharmacist had been useful in providing information; even more so after, thanks to his sister-in-law from London, they discovered a mobile phone, dating back many years, hidden in a long-expired box of Gaviscon tablets at the back of one of the pharmacy shelves.

*****

Earlier that week, Margaret Gillespie had held nothing back when, seated at the interview desk opposite DI Calum Scott and DS Michael Roberts, she told the detectives what she thought of, and everything she knew about her pharmacist brother-in-law.

"Just didn't like him from the very start," she said. "Shifty. Controlling. And I knew something was wrong when Elsie said how he used to punish poor Felicity. In front of Sean. And when my sister told him enough was enough, that's when he began to take the poor girl to the pharmacy to be punished. With Sean."

She went on to say how she found out that Felicity had been warned by James not to tell her mother about her punishments or 'or else', but Elsie sensed something was seriously wrong when the girl always ran straight to her room afterwards, locked the door and sobbed her little heart out. James became quite unpleasant when Elsie asked him what really went on during those so-called punishments. Instead of getting a proper answer she was made to swear on the bible that she would *not* go 'gossiping', as he put it. Also, she would be reminded how Verity's appendicitis was brought on by the girl's behaviour, and that 'God would wish for the child to be punished for that alone'. He had recently taken to joining Elsie at church, and would sometimes come out with inappropriate Bible quotations to justify his methods of disciplining their daughter.

Elsie knew not to touch the shelf with Gaviscon tablets, his excuse being that there were 'problems' with some of the batches, and that he always had to personally check the boxes before they were dispensed. Not pharmaceutically trained, and only occasionally being deployed to help out in the shop at the till, Elsie thought nothing of this until a few days before scribbling that letter to her sister in London. It was a brief telephone call from Elsie since James, in the next room, would watch his wife's every move; something that had significantly contributed to the woman's worsening depression.

"There's something not right about that Gaviscon thing," Elsie said over the phone, almost in a whisper. "I asked the nurse at the GP surgery, and she said James was talking rubbish. I'm scared, Maggie. Scared for Sean 'cos I'm sure he's in on whatever's going on. And scared for myself. Could you come up to Scotland? Help find out what he's up to?"

Maggie said she'd see if she could take a few days off. The day before she planned to travel up to Edinburgh, she got a call from her brother-in-law to tell her that Elsie had taken an overdose the previous evening and died in hospital earlier that morning. Even over the phone she could tell that James' tears were fake.

*****

DS Roberts left the interview room to obtain a search warrant with which he and DC Elaine Matheson, later, entered the pharmacy and soon found the relevant, long-expired packet of Gaviscon tablets, hidden behind other packets on a shelf, and containing a mobile phone. The pharmacist told them he had used this to contact Sonia Sokolova, which, the forensic team found out to be true, together with information that explained unaccounted-for money credited to his other bank account, but they also uncovered a message that lead to his arrest...

'The wife found out. Taken care of.'

Lost Hands

Chapter 21

Sean Taylor realised that the only way to forget Sally was to become someone else and start a new life. He had always been good with accents. Sally's i-Phone Siri spoke with an Ozzie accent. Why, he had no idea, but he could do a good Crocodile Dundee, a movie, from his childhood, that he loved, so he chose to be Australian and found various odd jobs as he travelled up to Peru with a pouch full of US dollar notes thanks to his comical climbing companion now back in the UK. In a bar in Ecuador, he met a guy who, for a handful of those dollar notes, could get him a new British passport, perfect in every detail, under the name of...

First he thought of anagrams of 'Sean'. 'Enas'? Like 'Elon' for 'Noel'? No way! 'Anes'? Too much like 'Anus'. And he wondered about 'Ansel'... *almost* an acronym, and with shades of that great American landscape photographer, Ansel Adams. Finally, he dropped the 'S' and added 'Y' and 'W'... Wayne. Which he expanded to 'Wayne Minto'. Short for 'Mine too', referring, of course, to Sally.

As an 'Ozzie writer-come-whatever', Wayne travelled from Ecuador to Peru then on to Colombia where, briefly, he rubbed shoulders with a member of a drug cartel. A lucrative, albeit temporary, partnership, which taught him all he needed to know about mind-bending drugs, significantly fattened his purse, but after a drug runner contact of Native origin 'disappeared', possibly thanks to a rival cartel, he felt encouraged to take flight. For Australia.

He was eager to test out his fake Ozzie accent for real, and ended up in Melbourne where he set himself up as a photographer, working from home, specialising in capturing images of 'people and pets'. When questioned about his peculiar accent, he claimed to hail from Perth, tainted with Kiwi genes 'from a New Zealand born grandfather'. He had left his literary Inca princess behind in Peru where, being the spitting image of Sally, he decided to have her embalmed forever. Instead, he began working on a new crime novel set in New Zealand, involving a mountaineer in the Southern Alps who comes across the body of Māori girl and assists in tracking down the culprit... a rogue Scots surgeon obsessed with the story of Frankenstein.

Mike, who drank in the same backstreet bar as Wayne, enjoyed bouldering but had never climbed a mountain. Friendship formed. Mike was over the moon when Wayne, out of the blue, suggested sharing a trip to the New Zealand Alps. His expense! Neither could boast of any current serious girlfriend, so both were eager to rectify this in the realm of the kiwi.

After arriving in Christchurch with newly purchased climbing tackle, Wayne spotted a BBC News item on his i-Pad. He often trawled through UK News coverage, perhaps, unwittingly, to ensure nothing drastic had happened to the love of his life for, surely if she were to be 'murdered', the fate of his beloved elder sister according to his father, thanks to that horror movie surgeon, this would appear somewhere online. But it wasn't an item concerning Sally that caught his attention. Instead, it was about his father, 'Edinburgh pharmacist, James Taylor'. Accused of the historical murder of the man's wife, Wayne's mother in another life.

Lost Hands

Sudden guilt that he'd got it wrong about the younger sister inspired him to contact Sally. He still remembered her e-mail address. Praying that she had not changed this since his sudden departure for Patagonia with Cameron, he sent her an e-mail stating how he was surprised to hear, on the news, that a climbing mate of his, back in Argentina, called Sean Taylor, had told him that his mother committed suicide after being driven insane by the behaviour of the man's younger sister, and that no way was the guy responsible for his wife's death.

Within fifteen minutes, Wayne received a reply. In bed with her fiancé, soon to be her husband, Sally, who had just been pinged awake by her i-Phone beside her bed, lay in a state of shock, staring at the e-mail message, before taking her phone to the living room to e-mail a reply...

Hi Sean,
I don't know what your father did to your mother, but I could murder you for lying to me and disappearing out of my life like that.
Where are you? As for me, I'm in bed with my fiancé. He's a surgeon at the Royal Infirmary. We're getting married next week, then honeymooning in New Zealand.
Love,
Sal XXX...
P.S. Why Wayne?

Over the following hour, messages flitted to-and-fro, across the planet, between Edinburgh and Melbourne. Sally learned that the man she was to marry, John McEuen, had the same name as the surgeon who, years back, with

138

Felicity's help in causing the girl's appendicitis through poor behaviour, a piece of nonsense no-one had been able to erase from the brain of the pharmacist's son, had killed Sean's elder sister. Plus, Sean added...

'No way did Dad kill Mum.'

Chapter 22

For the first time since arriving at that filthy 'hostel' in Muirhouse, Edinburgh, Justina felt happy. With Lina by her side, translating whenever necessary, she continued to give that 'funny man' called Daniel her views on how she might contribute to the art installation about global cuisine. She simply could not stop smiling. Melanie too. And for Justina it was as if those awful moments in the dark little room at the back of that pharmacy had never happened.

"Give me two Lithuanian dishes that will blow my mind and make me want to book flights to Vilnius for me and David tomorrow," Daniel said with such a serious expression, when Ade took the two girls to the art college, that they both burst into fits of the giggles. Justina whispered in Lina's ear, Lina nodded her agreement, and Justina came out with...

"Cepelinai and Šaltibarščiai!"

"Then 'sep and shush' will feature in our installation. What are they?"

Justina let Lina, in fluent English, explain how Cepelinai, potato dumplings, are not only delicious but are also airships.

"Airships?"

Justina and Melanie giggled again when Daniel pulled a funny face.

"Zeppelins. Airships," explained Lina. "Cepelinai is Lithuanian for Zeppelins. Because of their shape."

"And size?" queried Daniel, his eyebrows travelling up towards his receding hairline. The two girls giggled.

"Big enough," answered Lina. "And a bit like German Kartoffel-Knödel only a thousand times tastier."

"Hmm! I like tastier." He licked his lips. Justina laughed again. "So..." Daniel turned to face her. "Your sepairship thing must be up there touching the marshmallow clouds, watching over our culinary world." He looked at Ade. "Write down the recipe, Ade. We must try it out some time. You know how mad David is about potatoes." He turned towards Justina again. "David is my husband and the love of my life. He's a Kiwi."

Lina translated for Justina who appeared puzzled.

"He's married to a bird?" she queried in Lithuanian.

"What's she saying?" asked Daniel.

"She thinks David is a bird," Lina said. Daniel's turn to laugh at the thought of his husband being a kiwi bird pecking his way around their Morningside apartment whilst Lina explained to Justina how New Zealanders are often referred to as 'Kiwis' in the UK.

"And the other dish from Vilnius?" Daniel asked. "The 'shush' thing?"

"Šaltibarščiai. A cold beetroot soup."

"Mmm! Like borsht, eh?"

"Yes. Borscht is the Ukrainian word. But we think ours is better."

"Dark red. I like it. Red always catches the eye. Red with a dash of white, ay? The sour cream. Ade, it'll be borscht and Zeppelins for Mary, you, me and my bird of a husband next time you come round. And you, Melanie? Your favourite Nigerian dish?"

"Erm... Jollof rice?"

"Love it," said Daniel. "David's always telling me to

make sure your dad does his Jollof rice when he comes round to ours for a foodie get-together. Never asked where the Jollof bit comes from."

Melanie shrugged her shoulders and looked at her father.

"A region in West Africa," Ade explained. "Like a part of the great Mali Empire till it got split up. Their kings were called 'Mansa'."

"Kings, eh?" Daniel, eyebrows raised again, stared seriously at Melanie who had difficulty keeping a straight face whenever she looked at Daniel. Even more so when he spoke to her. "Could you add a crown to your Jollof rice for the installation, Melanie?"

Grinning, Melanie nodded.

"So, Jollof rice and...?"

"Dodo!" responded Melanie.

"Another bird? But aren't they all extinct?"

"Not in Alice in Wonderland," the girl answered. She looked at Justina. "Do you have Alice in Wonderland in Lithuania?" she asked.

A brief exchange between Lina and Justina in Lithuanian resulted in a grinning Justina responding with something which translated as 'rabbit hole'.

"Excellent!" exclaimed Daniel. "A rabbit hole in the installation. But what about that dodo dish? Not extinct, I trust."

"Fried plantain," explained Ade. "Not easy to get hold of in Edinburgh.

"But delicious all the same. We'll have your dodo in there, Melanie. Pecking on a plantain beside a rabbit hole, right?"

Lost Hands

Ade, happy to leave the girls in the hands of his friend, said he'd be back later with Mary. She had a couple of sick parishioners to visit in the hospital and Ade had a client he needed to see.

"You'll be safe with me, girls," said Daniel. "I'm as a queer as three-pound-note. Besides, apart from David, my only love is for art. Guess art makes us three guys soulmates, eh?"

Lina translated for Justina, and the two girls nodded eagerly.

"Seriously now, I'll have you girls work together on a huge sheet of paper almost the size of my brain to come up with a plan for your installation. Oh, and I nearly forgot. David's sister back in New Zealand. Lovely lady. Anita Mulholland. A lawyer, like David. Heavily into Māori art. We can get some Māori food ideas from her. Ever tried huhu grubs?"

Lina shrugged her shoulders, and the two girls followed suit.

"Kind of caterpillar. Best eaten raw and before it pupates. Tastes a bit like chicken."

"Please, I make giant caterpillar that lights up," suggested Justina.

They all looked at Justina for several seconds, then everyone erupted into laughter.

Ade left the college to join Mary, planning not to return, till late afternoon. After visiting the hospital, Mary called by at the police station to speak with her friend, DI Calum Scott.

"Got any further with breaking up that Russian criminal gang?" she asked.

Lost Hands

"Not that easy," was the detective's answer, "But I'll tell you one thing. Both the pharmacist and that Sonia woman are *gey* [4] pleased to be locked up out of harm's way. Don't think they can be got at in the nick by their Russian friends, but outside they're dead meat for what they've given us already."

"That poor girl, Justina!" Mary said. "So brave! Are your police contacts in Lithuania being helpful?"

"Very. But where Putin's devils are concerned, you're never entirely safe. They have to be cautious, for Justina's mother's sake."

Mary returned to the church to say prayers for Justina, for the girl's mother, for her art teacher back in Vilnius, as well as for all those poor women and girls who had been imprisoned in that enclave of hell in Muirhouse, Edinburgh; for the pharmacist now rotting in jail, and for all humanity at risk of being extinguished by, at best, a paranoid schizophrenic who had worked his way up from the gutters of St Petersburg to the Kremlin via the KGB, and a man on the other side of the world who believed God had saved him from being shot dead only to create mayhem in His world.

---

[4] Scots for 'very'

Lost Hands
PART 3

Chapter 23

A week after the trial, Anita Mulholland visits me in jail. Seated across a table, she speaks softly so as not to be overheard by the sharp-eared, eagle-eyed warden.

"Something's come up," she whispers.

I stare at her, wondering what on earth she's talking about.

"What?" I ask.

She leans forward. There's a curious sparkle in her eyes. What a woman, I'm thinking! She just never gives up.

"He's alive."

"Who? Who's alive?"

"The man you're convicted of murdering. Anthony James Wood." Stunned, I watch as a smile slowly begins to form on my lawyer's face; a face that filled me with impossible hope the very first time I saw her. "I always knew you wouldn't — *couldn't* — commit murder."

I know that Anita — I like to call her by her Christian name for she's one of the few people I know whom I could call a *true* Christian — would never, ever lie to me, and I truly wish to believe her whispered words, 'He's still alive', but it just makes no sense. They, including Sally, saw me kill him before throwing his weighted body into the Sound, although they told the police they had watched *me* do that. Drugged to the eyeballs, I honestly had no idea which version was true.

"I wish I could believe you," I say, "but I fear it's not possible. Those three witnesses. And he got tipped into the fiord, for heaven's sake."

"*They* said. But did he? Did *any* of it actually happen?"

"You mean...?"

"Not mean. Know. Just have to prove it. Look..." She turned to glance at the warden whose eyes had been boring into the back of her head as though the whispered words emerging from her brilliant brain might be visible to him. "Just believe me," she continued softly. "I have contacts. I *will* get to the truth, and you *will* get back to using those surgeon's hands of yours for what they were trained to do."

She gets up, smiles and nods, meaningfully, leaving me in a strange state of confusion, joy and anger. I always knew it wasn't in me to kill. I'm a doctor, for God's sake, and proper doctors *never* purposefully take lives, but it was three against one when I claimed to have been trying to save Sally from being raped. That the pilot was a sick psychopath had never been the issue, legally, nor the fact that he had survived the plane crash despite seemingly still being unconscious on the floor of the plane when it blew up. After all, it happened so quickly, and we were all so stunned, he could easily have slipped away before the fire engulfed what remained of the aircraft, but to emerge live and well after being disposed of in the fiord?

I doubt whether Anita has *ever* told a lie. Plus there are those other things that just do not add up. Like my certainty that Sally and I had already been along the track leading to the waterfall despite the others saying this was all in my imagination as a result of a head injury. People do not dream whilst unconscious because of head injury. Any doctor will tell you that, so I know this to be untrue. And what about those 'candies' Wayne kept feeding me with. I felt so peculiar that I'm now more than certain I had been drugged by whatever was in the weird-tasting and strangely addictive sweets. This could well have accounted for my seemingly odd behaviour, but not the reality of going to, and seeing, the waterfall for a second time.

If what Anita says is true, which I know it must be, then the whole thing — my engagement, my marriage, our honeymoon and the plane flight over paradise — was all staged.

Chapter 24

Anita Mulholland left the prison with only one thought in her mind. To seek justice for her client whom she knew had been wrongly imprisoned for committing a crime of which he was incapable. Even before trial, during which she felt sure the good doctor's feeling of guilt had overridden his commonsense, she kept going back to the question of whether or not that pilot really had been killed since the body was never found.

Anita's husband, Jimmy, who sadly passed from a massive heart attack the year before she was asked to defend the Scottish surgeon accused of murdering the Wilderness Paradise Air Tours pilot after his plane crashed on a mountain overlooking Milford Sound, had shared, with his wife, a love of Māori history and culture and cuisine. A private detective, he had teamed up with a guy of Māori descent, Andy Rongo, who, Jimmy always said, had a 'nose for the job'. After Jimmy died, Anita and Andy often met up to reminisce and share their love of good food. Andy now ran the private detective agency built up by Jimmy, employing two assistants, both Māori. Although they focused predominantly on discriminatory issues concerning people of Māori origin, his reputation was such that his 'nose' was sought the length and breadth of Aotearoa[5], the land of the 'long white cloud'. Andy often jokingly said the 'white cloud' was now the white man covering truth with deception, and Anita knew what he

---

[5] Maori term for New Zealand

meant. Particularly after a certain US President, who seemed unable to distinguish between fact and fiction, had been re-elected on the other side of Te Ao [6].

"He's alive. I know it," Andy told his ex-boss's lawyer widow over a Māori 'boil-up' of pork, dumplings and root vegetables. Jimmy always said that Andy's boil-up came straight from heaven, and on the anniversary of her husband's sudden death, Andy and his wife had invited Anita round for a meal of 'boil-up' and Pārāoa Rēwena Pudding... softened sourdough potato bread and honey. Anita brought along a bottle of Scotch whisky left behind, after Jimmy's funeral, by her gay little brother married to a crazy Edinburgh College of Art teacher, who, she told the Rongos, was surely the funniest man on God's Earth.

"Who's alive?" Anita asked, feeling a little swimmy in the head after two tots of whisky.

"That pilot killed by your client in prison. The surgeon."

"Wait a minute. What are you trying to tell me?"

"Not trying. *Am* telling. No way is the fella dead."

"Anthony James Wood? Still alive?"

"A set-up. I've been looking into it ever since you told me about the so-called murder and the surgeon being a real nice kinda guy. He's there. Your dead pilot. Hiding out in the wops[7]. I know it!"

"If Andy knows it, it's true," said Amy, Andy's Ozzie wife. "Not like the crazed utterings of 'He who cannot be named'," she added, for earlier they had been discussing the imminent danger the whole world was now in following

---

[6] Natural world
[7] The wilderness

the US presidential election. The whisky helped Anita to laugh with her friends instead of scream at Amy's reference to the newly re-elected President.

"How d'you know it?" Anita asked when the laughter had subsided.

"Remember how, after the trial, you said something was very wrong. And that Sally McEuen seemed only too happy to refute her husband's version of events in court. Well..."

He paused. Anita grinned.

"You had her followed?" she suggested. Andy nodded.

"More than that," he replied.

Anita's jaw dropped. "Surely you didn't?!"

Another nod.

"I told John to keep quiet about it. He's too bloody honest. I got help from a buddy in the police who agreed there was something shifty about the Scottish nurse and that weirdo who pretends to be Ozzie."

"Wayne Minto?"

"What sort of a name is Minto?"

Anita frowned.

"Minto? I looked it up. A small town in Scotland near the English border. But..." She paused. "There's another thing. John went on and on about those candies Wayne fed him with, both on the plane and after the crash. He'd put the funny feelings he had down to a bash on the head, the crash and the fumes from the burning plane fuel, but what if...?"

Anita paused. Eyebrows raised, she looked at Andy.

"Drugged?" he suggested. "My thought too, which is why I went to visit John in prison."

"He never said."

"I told him not to, Anita. No way. But I'll tell you what. He gave me his wife's contact details. And she bloody fell for it."

"Fell for what?"

Andy looked at Amy.

"You really should tell her, Andy," the man's wife urged. "You know she'll keep quiet."

"Yeah, I should've told you straightaway, Anita. But it's why we asked you round for a boil-up."

"I'm all ears," Anita said, leaning forward and cupping both ears towards Andy.

"Like I said, got help from my mates in the force. But you never knew that, did you?"

Anita gestured zipping up her mouth.

"Amazing, their hardware. Anyway, she fell for it when I said I was at her service to help in any way I could to scupper his appeal 'cos I knew what a bastard he was, that husband of hers, and no way should he go free. Also said I'd been a good mate of that pilot fella, Anthony James Wood."

"Naturally!" grinned Anita.

"Long and short, Anita, is I went round to their place. She's staying with that Wayne bugger now. Planted three bugs there. Got me a goldmine of info."

"I like goldmines," remarked Anita. "Tell me more."

"Well, you'll really like this one, too. Quick rummage in Wayne's bathroom whilst pretending to have a piss revealed a hand-scrawled recipe, if you will, for concentrating the active compounds in Ayahuasca. No attempt had been made to hide it."

"Aya... what?"

Lost Hands

"Ayahuasca. Used by Amazon folk for their rituals. Make it into a kind of tea. Produces powerful hallucinations."

"Like John described to me and put down to the head injury."

"Police friend told me Wayne-so-called-Minto was in South America before he came here via Melbourne."

"Interesting! And those three bugs?"

"This is where it gets even more interesting. A certain Dean Tony Shaw keeps popping up. Partial anagram for Anthony James Wood. Lives in Wellington. So Wayne travels all that way to meet up with the guy in a waterfront bar called the Crab Shack. Got my dog to book a table for himself outside."

Anita laughed.

"Your dog?"

"New guy I took on couple of weeks back. Called Kauri. Pure Māori. Could sniff out a shifty puker the other side of the country. Has connections, too. So, thanks to my sweet little bugs, we get wind of the meet up between Dean, who definitely isn't, and Wayne, who probably isn't either. Dog decides to go there too. Same time. Only for the great mussels, he said."

"Never mind the mussels, Andy. Was it him? Tony James Wood?"

"No doubt whatsoever. Dog got a whole heap of photos of the bugger. Had shaved his head and grown a beard, dyed black, but nose and eyes the same. Facial contours too. Perfect Photoshop match."

"Oh my God! Anything on the wife, Sally?"

"Only that Sally *is* Sally. A nurse back in Scotland. Has

a sick mum. Early dementia, I reckon. Sally worries about her."

"But not about her husband languishing in jail for murdering a man who's still alive, huh? Andy, how can I ever repay you for what you're doing?"

"Anita, we're friends. You don't pay a friend to help dig out the truth."

Anita laughed.

"Dig out the truth with a dog, eh? When can I meet this Kauri fella?"

Andy glanced at his watch.

"Any minute now. With the photos."

Chapter 25

"Tell me what's happening, Sean," Sally asked Sean after he got back from Wellington. She refused to call him 'Wayne'. She'd had enough of strangers after learning how the man she had married, and had thought of as the best surgeon in the world, turned out to be the very person who had ruined Sean's life by killing his sister in a botched operation. Giving her lover a new name felt a bit like starting up all over again with a stranger. But whenever she tried to find out just why he had to take off for South America with that bumbling idiot, Cameron, without contacting her afterwards, plus change his name, he became angry. She was accused of 'not trusting him, not caring. Just like his aunt... and his stupid little sister, Felicity,' he texted on one occasion. Sean became a different person when angry, so she buried her doubts and went along with whatever the Sean, whom she had loved since nursing him nearly five years back, said and whatever he did.

Sally now hated John for destroying Sean's life, and she accepted, without question, her lover's version of the events that led to his father killing his mother. The poor woman's depression over the loss of her elder daughter was such that she simply could not go on, but nor could she do what she wished to do... end her own life. Sean believed that his father knew this and assisted her by fulfilling her wish. In Switzerland, this would have been called 'assisted dying', although in Scotland it was 'murder'. The pharmacist's Swiss interpretation of what happened was surely why Sean had always been told, since his teenage years, that his mother had 'topped herself'.

"True!" insisted Sean as was, not 'Wayne'. "My dad helped her. That's all there is to it."

Still it made no sense to Sally that Sean simply buggered off, but she was so happy to be back with him, and to be made love to by a true man and not a wimp of surgical drill. Plus, she felt no qualms, no guilt for her part in what happened after Sean contacted her by e-mail, out of the blue, whilst she was in bed with John shortly before their marriage.

John had been working really hard before the honeymoon, putting in extra hours, and she, having taken a week off for wedding preparations, had all the time in the world to listen to, and scheme with, Sean.

The two worked together, assisted by Mike, to formulate a plan that would do to John what his botched operation had done to Sean's father. Land him in prison on a charge of murder. Sally felt no remorse, for no one would actually get killed, according to Sean.

Mike had been to New Zealand and even worked there, for a while, clearing trails in the Milford Sound rainforest area. He once had a job in Queenstown, near the airport, and knew of a guy called Tony Wood. A pilot who took pleasure-seeking tourists on fun flights over the fiords in a little six-seater prop plane.

It was Tony who came up with the idea when Mike asked whether they could stage something spectacular to hit the headlines and turn Tony into the hero he wished to be for the woman who dumped him for one of the other pilots. A 'bludger' of a bastard, according to Tony who was only too pleased to help out when told that it would involve putting the man who had stolen and married Mike's best friend's girl, a fella called 'Wayne', where he belonged: in jail for killing Wayne's beloved elder sister.

*****

It was Sally who showed John the webpage she 'spotted' whilst browsing 'Tourist Flights over Milford Sound'.

"Just take a look at this, John," she said snuggling up to him on the sofa as he watched the BBC News on the television, only half-awake following a gruelling day in the operating theatre.

John grinned at her after seeing the advertisement about an hour-long flight over one of the last paradises left on Planet Earth in a six-seater prop plane that would '...*Blow his Mind!*'

"As long as it's only my mind it blows!" John said.

"Your jokes are rubbish," Sally said, pretending to laugh. His jokes were not the only rubbish things about the John whom she thought she knew before Sean got back in touch with her after nearly two years. "It'll really make our honeymoon, honest it will," Sally persuaded her fiancé. "Our first chance to be together in paradise, right!?"

"First of many, I hope," John answered, putting his arm around his soon-to-be-bride and kissing her on the cheek. Sally could now only stand her fiancé's kisses by closing her eyes and imagining those lips to be Sean's. Same when John made love to her. Faking sexual arousal and climaxes was difficult at first, but she soon discovered that she was quite a good actress. *'Playing the part'* was how Sean put it to her when she suggested to her ex-lover that she should just call off the marriage, forget about 'the

156

bugger', as Sean called John, and join him in New Zealand. She felt sure they would recognise her Edinburgh nursing qualifications and experience there.

'*No! The higher the height he falls from, the greater the pain,*' messaged Sean. '*My childhood with a sister like Verity was my paradise. Destroyed by that bugger who killed her. Only way he'll learn a lesson for what he did.*'

Sally felt uneasy about the idea of the pilot crash-landing '*somewhere in the wilderness*' on the pretext of killing himself and all his passengers to achieve newspaper headline status in order to make his ex-girlfriend feel guilty, and with Mike and Sean, alias 'Wayne', ensuring the staged air crash would be quite safe after Mike, an experienced pilot, and Sean had subdued the 'crazy' pilot Tony and taken control. Tony had agreed to take off into the undergrowth after the landing, and, with John all doolally after ingesting sweets filled with a South American psychedelic concoction, spring out on John and Sally, pretend to attempt to rape John's new bride and...

'*WALLOP!*' Sean texted to describe how the confused John would be stopped from really killing Tony and later told how the dead pilot's body had been disposed of in the fiord. '*My mate's friends in the Queenstown police will see to the rest,*' reassured Sean.

Sally's acting skills were pushed to the limit during the wedding ceremony, the reception and their first night as 'husband and wife', but she stuck with Sean's instructions like a limpet to a rock. Throughout the long flight, via Singapore where they spent the night in a hotel, she repeatedly rested her head on John's shoulder, took his hand on her lap, and smiled like a prostitute in the pay of some wealthy sex-hungry American. In Queenstown, she became more nervous because, booked into the same hotel as Sean and his Ozzie friend, Mike, she wondered how far her acting prowess would be tested on actually seeing Sean again after so long apart from him. She and her ex-lover had agreed to wait until they'd all boarded the plane before silently acknowledging each other. Anything might happen should they attempt to communicate in the hotel, although ignoring Sean — unchanged from when he took off one Monday morning in Edinburgh — and his companion, at breakfast, seriously tested the Scots nurse's self-control.

John, thankfully, took no notice of the two young men seated at a table the other end of the dining room, one of whom could not take his keen eyes off Sally. He was too absorbed in just staring at his new bride as though she were some kind of a goddess. Nor did he notice an older American couple, despite their voluminous size. Sally saw Sean talking to the pair who suddenly seemed delighted at what he told them for both turned to look at Sally and John, the husband with his back to the large Americans. John had his head down, the man nodded and Sally, almost imperceptibly, returned a timid nod.

*****

The same Americans showed up on the plane and sat in front of John and Sally. She and Sean had agreed not to text each other in New Zealand in case John should read the messages, so she had no idea whether or not the large couple were in on Sean's plan. They seemed friendly enough after sinking into the two seats in front of her and her new husband.

"Where you folks from?" asked the man, turning to

look back and smile at Sally and John.

"Scotland, actually. Edinburgh," said John as though the friendly round, red face was an intrusion into his private space.

"Jeeze, honey, these folks come all the way from Scotland," the man said to the woman beside him, presumably his wife. Sally could tell they were a true couple, as she should have been with her beloved Sean before the past actions of the so-called husband beside her took their toll on her one-time lover and forced him to vanish for nearly two years.

"Hey, what part of England's that in? It's where all the Scotch comes from, huh?"

"It's not!"

'Here we go,' thought Sally giving her husband a sharp elbow nudge. *'Grumpy bugger! They seem such a nice couple.'*

"Sure it is," insisted the American guy. "Best whisky comes all the way from Scotland."

"In England. Scotland's not in England," John told the man seated in front of Sally.

"Got me there. Could have sworn — "

"Britain. Not England," John rudely interrupted.

"Hey, well how about that, then!? Britain! Like Ireland too, huh?"

"Ireland's in Ireland," muttered John before receiving another nudge from Sally.

"Arnie! Arnie Manetti. And this here lovely lady is Joan, my wife."

Joan did have a warm, kind smile, and, together with Arnie, offered to shake hands with Sally and John.

Lost Hands

'So friendly! Typical American,' thought Sally.

"John and Sally McEuen," said her morose husband.

'If only it could be Sean and Sally Taylor,' thought Sally, smiling back at the Americans.

"Just married," she said, trying hard to appear natural. "On our honeymoon."

"Oh my, ain t that just cute!" responded Joan. Two honeymooner lovebirds on our little flight. And all the way from England."

"Scotland, Goddammit!" John whispered to Sally just before her attention was diverted by the arrival of Sean and Mike on board. She struggled to stop herself from getting up and hugging her true love for the first time after nearly two years apart. They sank into the two remaining seats behind Sally. John, her husband, with his hand on her lap, turned around and introduced himself and Sally to the 'newcomers'.

"Righto, mate!" said Sean with a weird Ozzie accent. "Wayne," he added. "This is Mike. You here for the tramping?"

"Nope. We're on honeymoon." The word stabbed at Sally's heart.

"Lucky you!" offered an unsmiling Mike.

'Lucky?' The very last word Sally would have thought of to describe her current situation.

"Kiwis?" asked John.

"Not bloody likely," responded the dour Mike. "Ozzies. From Melbourne."

"Great," replied John. "Not been there."

"Wouldn't want to, mate. Piss awful place."

"I'm sure it isn't," said John without conviction.

Lost Hands

"I'm sure it bloody is," insisted Mike.

"Candy?" offered Sean.

"Who?" questioned John.

"He's offering you a sweet to suck," explained Sally, caustically. "Helps the ears for take-off."

'What if he refuses?' she wondered. Thankfully, things went according to plan. Her husband took a sweet and began to suck on it just as Tony, the pilot, welcomed all on board. Sally feared the man might not be up to it, but it turned out he was a bit of a joker although his light-hearted reference to 'falling out of the sky' would not, she felt, sit well with a humourless Scot like John. She pulled her hand free from John's, laughing, when anxiety tightened his grip. She half wished to reassure him that their plan was for him to stay alive in order to commit a 'murder' that would demand a custodial sentence. Instead, she mouthed 'I'm okay' after Tony's humour, punctuated by chuckles, went a little over the top.

Arnie, lovely man, Sally thought, chipped in by asking John whether there was rainforest in Scotland. Her rudely sarcastic husband responded by saying there wasn't much of it left around Edinburgh. And when the American mentioned going to see the King at Buckingham Palace, John befuddled him by talking about Holyrood which Arnie confused with Hollywood. Sally gave her husband's hand a warning slap when John's blatant sarcasm crossed the limit, and before Arnie suggested that he and his wife, Joan, would love to one day visit Scotland.

Silence engulfed the plane's cabin as they climbed high above the mountain peaks and headed for the beauty of Milford Sound. After about twenty minutes, the plane banked steeply, throwing Sally sideways against her husband and making her wonder whether she had been stupid to go along with Sean's crazy plan.

"Jeeze, what was that about!?" yelled Arnie.

"He took my job as chief pilot and then my girl, guys," announced the pilot. That was too much, don t you think? I mean, you d have all done the same, wouldn t you? Eh? Is there anyone here who wouldn t?"

The plane looped about, throwing Sally and John the other way. She screamed.

"What the fuck s going on?" shouted Arnie.

The plane dropped like a boulder thrown by a god. The forested mountain rose up to meet it.

"Had to choose the right spot, see. A reasonable number of casualties to hit the headlines so as she d notice. Wouldn t want to be relegated to a small paragraph somewhere in the middle of the local rag. Small addendum tagged to the bottom of a news bulletin. Need a front-page headline. She should feel guilty, right? Couldn t kill *her*, could I, or she d never have known that guilt? Plus I was a better pilot than him, the bastard. Called himself my friend, the fucker! But you lucky lot, you re going straight to another paradise. No need for a silly brochure about that other place, eh? Get there, for free, from *this* paradise, guys! To the *ultimate* paradise."

It sounded almost too convincing for Sally. She trembled and looked at John, the man beside her, as though begging him, with her eyes, to 'do something'. The large American tourist in the seat in front of the them took the initiative.

"Out the way, you jerk!" he shrieked at Tony, the crazed, lovesick lunatic pilot. I flew in the Nam. I ll take over."

"Na! Better to go quickly," Tony replied without looking up. Wake up in paradise, ha-ha!"

'God, this is for real,' thought Sally. *'I'm gonna die!'*

Mike, Sean's Ozzie mate, pulled his way to the front of the plane to wrestle with the pilot, all staged, but, unexpectedly, the hefty American heaved himself forwards and took control. Sally recalled seeing Arnie and Joan talking with Sean and Mike at breakfast, in the hotel, but there had been no suggestion from her lover that the Americans would be involved in the 'plan'. Her understanding was that Mike would safely 'crash-land' the plane to allow Tony to vanish into the forest, unscathed, before leaping out and pretending to attempt to rape Sally.

"Out the way, you jerk. I flew in the Nam. I'll take over."

"Na! Better to go quickly," the pilot said, without looking up. Wake up in paradise, ha-ha!"

"Do something, John!" shrieked Sally. Not 'acting' now. "Help them, for God s sake! The maniac s gonna kill us!"

The American pulled Tony up and out of his seat like a father dealing with a naughty toddler, cast the man aside, then, attempting to get the plane to gain height, yelled,

"Fuck, we re almost out of fuel!" he screamed.

Lost Hands

Someone break the bastard s neck and get the hell back to your seats, guys."

Mike, in a pretend struggle with Tony, seemed to suddenly realise it was all for real. He slammed Tony's head down on the floor of the plane whilst Sally called her husband a 'fucking dummy' for not joining in the fray up front. The plane's undercarriage scraped the tree tops.

"Brace, everyone!" shouted Arnie.

John pushed Sally's head forwards before adopting the brace position himself. A loud bang, followed by metallic scrunching and an eerie hiss. The buckled plane, otherwise silent, and bereft of a cockpit and pilot, sat perched up in the trees.

"The door, for fuck's sake," shouted Sean from the floor behind the immobile pilot. He edged forwards on hands and knees. John, the nearest to the door, fumbled with it but nothing happened.

Useless sod! thought Sally hanging from her seat above her husband.

"Open the fucking door!" Sean repeated through the hiss of the dying engine whilst edging forward. She ll blow any minute!" He pushed John aside, kicked at the stubborn door till it swung open, pulled and pushed John out of the aircraft after screaming at the 'useless' Scottish surgeon to jump, then focussed on rescuing Sally and Jean, telling Mike he would "...Take the girl" and leave Mike to help the American woman. With the young Scot's bride's skirt risen up around her waist, Sean was only too happy to encircle her shapely thighs with a free arm whilst using his other to pull himself and his delightful burden from the wreckage and out onto a tangle of branches.

164

Lost Hands

"Help her down, for fuck's sake!" Sean yelled to John.

"Just grab my bloody legs, can t you?" shouted Sally.

John did so, clumsily lowering his pretty, young wife down to the ground with Sean still holding onto her hand from above. John seemed concerned that her white underwear was on view.

"Your skirt..." he said.

"Oh, for God's sake! Help Wayne and Mike, can't you?" Sally scolded.

"Stand clear!" warned Sean before clambering back up between the branches to assist Mike with the large American woman. John came to his senses when the wrecked plane belched out a black cloud of acrid smoke. He shouted out "Run, Sally!" and, as his wife ran towards a clearing away from the plane, he attempted to support the weight of the American woman from below. No way was he strong enough. She slid down, past John, banged her head on a branch and tumbled to the ground below. John, now a horrified, helpless doctor, peered down at her as her body jerked and twitched before going still.

"Oh, for Christ s sake!" yelled Sean.

Quite suddenly, with an enormous explosion, the plane burst into a brilliant ball of fire. For a split second, Mike, still in the doorway, was silhouetted before being engulfed in a fury of flames as John and Sean both fell from the tree.

When John came too, his wife was bent over the body of the macho 'Ozzie'. Choking in the haze of dark smoke, he staggered towards Sally.

"Help him, John," she said, looking up. His leg, it's badly injured. You're a bloody surgeon, for God's sake!"

165

Lost Hands

John stared at the other man's broken limb. Ripped jeans exposed torn flesh. There was a lot of blood. The jealous husband somehow transformed into an experienced surgeon. Kneeling down, he carefully removed jean material free from the wound.

"John, *please* don t hurt him!"

"I m doing my best!" snapped the woman's husband, anger evident in his tone. Anger with himself for being a wimp, with his wife for caring about another man, and with the other man for being a Hollywood macho hero and ruining their honeymoon.

"Aargh!" Sean yelled as John removed the fake-Ozzie's boot and sock. Sally sobbed for her lover whilst her husband used the other man's sock as a tourniquet to stem the loss of blood.

"We ve gotta get away from here. Quickly," John said. Sally nodded, coughing. The three survivors on the ground were all choking on lingering smoke drifting down from the burning aircraft jammed up in the trees. Together, Sally and John helped the groaning Sean away from the blaze to a clearing where they gently laid him down onto his back.

"The woman?" John said. Together, they returned to fetch Joan, halting to stare at her inert body.

"Dead!" Sally said, looking blankly at the large American. "Just a minute..." she added, stepping cautiously towards Joan, fearful of the heat from the blazing tree supporting the airplane. "Joan?" She knelt beside Joan, felt the woman's neck, and turned to face her husband. "She's got a pulse. Just."

Joan raised her hand, slightly, and opened her eyes.

Lost Hands

She tried to speak, but no sound emerged from her bruised face. She responded to John's questioning by tapping his hand; once for 'Yes' and twice for 'No'. John seemed reassured that she was able to feel and move all four limbs, concluding that she had merely been concussed, but at a loss to know how to reply when Joan asked, after John praised her husband for his bravery...

"Where's Arnie?"

"Bloody hero, he was," offered the injured Sean. Sally stooped down and hugged Joan.

"Was?" asked the American woman.

"Like Wayne said," Sally told her, almost in a whisper. "Because of your husband, we're still alive."

John turned his attention to the 'Ozzie', using a rolled-up jacket to support the other man's head whilst his wife gently stroked his face and cheeks; then he broke of a nearby branch to serve as a splint, using his belt to secure this to the injured leg. Sean yelled out an obscenity. Sally glowered at John.

"We ve gotta get help for him, John," she insisted, before glancing back at Joan. "Her too," she added.

"Where from? We re in the bloody wilderness. Remember? Fucking 'paradise'?"

Sally *reached* into a pocket and pulled out her mobile phone, offering it meaningfully to John whose own phone was somewhere amongst the airplane wreckage.

"Do something with that!" she instructed her husband, with annoyance. He discovered, unsurprisingly, that there was no phone reception.

"Sweetheart," Sally continued, much to John's delight, "something must be done. He can't walk. He mustn't suffer

167

any longer like this. He just can't! Have a heart, John."

John stood aside, watching impotently as his wife hugged Sean, stroking his hair.

"What is it you want me to do!?" he shouted. No response from Sally.

"Okay, okay!" John said. I ve got the message. I ll go and get help. No problem! Just a little jaunt down this steep, densely forested mountain, pick up a wandering lone ranger and all our troubles are over."

"John! No sarcasm, please. There s a time and place for that, and it s not here and now. We have to try is all I m asking."

"Other way around? I look after Tarzan?"

"Tarzan? He s just Wayne, John, and he needs help. We *all* need help. You don t seem to see it. What the hell is wrong with you?"

John shrugged his shoulders again.

"Sorry," he replied, at last, squirming with guilt. Sure, I ll go for help. Keep him warm, huh!?"

"Come here!" said Sally, her tone changed. "Let me kiss you!"

He stooped for his wife to plant a sexless kiss on his cheek.

"Another candy, mate?" suggested Sean in his mock-Ozzie accent. John gladly took another sweet from Sean. He had found the one he sucked on earlier strangely pleasing.

"Take care!" warned Sally as her spaced-out husband took off alone, through the undergrowth, down the steep mountainside, muttering nonsense to himself. Sean laughed, pulling Sally down to the ground beside him. She glanced at the American woman, lying on her back, eyes closed, then, giggling like a schoolgirl, straddled herself face down over her lover as he fumbled with the flies on his jeans, pulled her skirt up and her panties down for all-out sex.

Afterwards, when Sally thought all had gone to plan, and that Tony, the pilot whom John thought had died in the plane crash, had 'vanished', her husband re-emerged from the undergrowth.

Chapter 26

Justina felt as though she had been transported to a different and beautiful planet after Daniel, using Lina as her Lithuanian translator, contacted the girl's Art teacher, Ponia Ivanova, in Vilnius, to request that she stay on in Edinburgh for the whole summer term.

"We are doing a collaborative installation with our students on food from across the world, and Justina has such brilliant ideas," he told the Lithuanian woman. "She's got us all excited about Aleksandra Kasuba, but it seems your amazing student here might take things to a whole new level. She keeps telling me how you really helped her during a period when she was getting bullied at school."

"Och, those terrible girls!" Ponia scoffed, in English, after Lina explained what Daniel just said. Daniel was one of those people who always gets their own way simply by being nice to others. Ponia's reservations melted like butter pats in the sun after he praised her for teaching Justina 'so brilliantly', and she promised to discuss it with the school principal.

"She says they should be able to arrange one-to-one Zoom sessions with teachers back home for her," Lina translated for Daniel. "Like during COVID. She says the principal will be so very proud of the achievement of one of their star students."

"No problem!" added Ponia in English, grinning from an i-Pad screen at Justina who stood peering over Daniel's shoulder. A smiling Melanie suddenly appeared on Ponia's screen, before putting her arm around Justina.

Lost Hands

"Justina's new friend, Melanie," Lina explained in Lithuanian to Ponia. "Also a great artist. She's helping the police."

Ponia's face changed as though an unseen hand had flicked a switch. She looked fearfully at Mary who had now joined them and who, until that moment in time, had been so happy with the way things had gone after being taken to help a certain tearful Lithuanian girl in her church hall the previous Sunday. The girl's story had reminded the minister of her own escape from religious persecution in Nigeria, with Ade, in a past that was ever present inside her head. But the expression on the face of the woman on the screen?

*****

Melanie was born in the same year that Boko Haram unleashed unprovoked mass killings of Christians in Northern Nigeria. Mary's uncle, who had been a Catholic village pastor, was slaughtered in his church together with dozens of worshippers, during mass, when armed Islamist extremists swept into the village shooting those whom they deemed to be Christian. Mary and her husband, Ade, had been planning to return to their home in Lagos from Edinburgh where they met and fell in love as students. Mary studied theology, Ade law. Although brought up as a devout Catholic, with leanings towards joining a nunnery, her high academic achievements and her lovely nature resulted in one of her teachers back home suggesting to her, and to her parents, that she study for a Bachelor of Arts degree in Theology in Scotland where the same teacher's brother had graduated. It was Ade, a fellow Edinburgh student, a devout atheist with whom she fell in love on their

171

very first date, who later suggested she switch allegiance from the Catholic Church to the Church of Scotland and join the ministry.

Before Melanie came into the world, Mary had hoped that she and Ade might return to Nigeria; Ade to take up an academic position in UNILAG, one of the top universities in Africa, and herself to find work with the Presbyterian Church of Nigeria, or PCN, having been inspired by her nineteenth century Scottish missionary namesake, Mary Slessor. Like that other Mary, she so wanted to make a difference in a country she loved but wept to see being torn apart by violent religious fanatics. She even had Muslim friends who were ashamed to belong to the same religion as those rapists and murderers of men, women and children, and it took a lot of input from a level-headed Ade to dissuade her from returning to visit family back home in Northern Nigeria after she became pregnant. When her beloved, gentle uncle priest was added to the list of murdered Christians, she agreed that, at least for her little baby's sake, the Osondu family should remain in Scotland.

Mary was much loved in the Church, and, because Ade, now an accountant with an Edinburgh firm, was able to work from home for much of the time, she could throw herself into Christian ministry with a passion that soon reaped rewards in terms of numbers of friends and contacts.

When Melanie grew up to become a bright and enthusiastic teenager, Ade found time to pursue his own interests, particularly a passion for cooking. He met Daniel, one Saturday morning, browsing the cookbook bookshelf of Waterstones. It was Daniel who spotted a Black man obviously into cooking. A typical Glaswegian, he immediately entered into lively conversation with the African accountant.

Straightaway, he wanted to know what Ade's favourite dish was, whether there was a decent Nigerian Cuisine cookery book and whether he also preferred paella to risotto. After Daniel learned that Ade was an accountant, he almost kissed the Black man in the shop for he discovered that Ade knew, through his legal connections, David, Daniel's lawyer husband from New Zealand. Some twenty minutes later, they exchanged phone numbers, agreeing to meet up, which they did, with spouses and Melanie included.

Young Melanie and Daniel became great friends. She found him so funny and, later, when she was bullied for being Black at a girls' private school which, Mary had been informed, was particularly good for children gifted in the Arts, Daniel showed his true strength as a kind and understanding family friend. He was like a rock for the girl having himself weathered bullying, being gay, as a young lad in Glasgow. And like her father and Daniel, Melanie loved cooking. The threesome became quite competitive in the kitchen, too, each dying to know what score out of ten his or her particular dish might get from Mary and from David after a weekend culinary get together.

It was partly because of Daniel that Melanie became so interested in art. He immediately recognised her amazing draughtsmanship and encouraged her to use this at school where he met with her art teacher to see how he could help her develop her talents. Indeed, it was because of Melanie that he came up with the idea of creating an artistic installation at the college to explore the concept of food from across the world being brought together in a single harmonious mind blow.

The arrival of Justina on the scene seemed like a gift from the gods, particularly after he learned that the Lithuanian girl, too, had been bullied at school.

"Just because she's different from the cat pack," Mary quietly assured Daniel as Melanie and Justina sat down together at a work table before a large empty sheet of white paper, discussing how to fill it with 'food from across the whole world'. "Sorry, Daniel. That is not very Christian of me, but it's how it looks from the outside. A few other girls just ganged up together against my daughter. Justina, too, at her own school, from what Melanie tells me." She paused. "That Ponia lady in Vilnius. I really don't know what to make of her. The look on her face when Lina said Melanie was helping the police with the shady business to do with that pharmacist."

"Mr Taylor the pharmacist?" queried Daniel. "Not very 'Happy Family' sounding, ay? Should be Mr Pill or Mr Lotion."

Mary chuckled.

"Hmm! You know, you really do get to know people from their expressions in my job. Learn about the person behind the words."

"So being a minister is so much more than just a 'job', then, Mary. First thing I do when I get my 'Road to Damascus' experience will be to come and hear you preach."

"Your snores would be heard all over Edinburgh, Daniel. No, the look on that woman's face. After hearing

Lina's translation for the word 'police'."

"Like 'a naughty boy and the headmaster' kind of look?"

"Melanie had her own suspicions about Mr Should-be-Pill in the pharmacy, you know. Never came out till Justina told her what happened. Apparently the look he once gave my daughter when she went to collect a prescription said a lot, she reckons. She was in her school uniform. He remarked that her skirt was 'too short' and that 'he knew her headmistress'. Almost like he was threatening her. Or, looking back, and because of what he tried to do to Justina, it was as if he was…"

Mary paused again.

"Like he was offering to punish her himself for wearing a short skirt. Pff!" exclaimed Daniel.

"So the police visited Melanie's school. My dear friend, DI Calum Scott… he and Melanie, together, spoke to her headteacher. She was horrified but not too surprised to hear what Melanie told her and, well, the long and the short of it was Melanie wasn't the only girl to have experienced that sort of response from Mr Taylor in the pharmacy when there were no other customers present. Always the same remark about the girl's skirt being too short, and 'What would Mrs Wellersby, their headmistress, do?' if she saw her dressed like that?"

"Do you think Justina's art teacher back in Vilnius was in on it?" enquired Daniel. "And the fake notice about an art competition that appeared one morning in the girl's letterbox? Surely not!? Justina said her teacher was dead against her entering the so-called competition."

"That's the thing. Why? Perhaps because she reckoned

she could use this in her defence if it all came out."

"Did your DI's contact in Vilnius speak with her? That Ponia lady?"

"Like you said, she tried to dissuade Justina from entering. So, why would they?"

"So your policeman friend has been in touch with the police in Vilnius?"

"Yesterday. His counterpart in the Lithuanian Police is as sharp as a razor, he tells me. Vyresnysis Komisaras Budris. Can't get his lips around that lot, Calum said, so he calls the man 'Buddy'. Apparently, for quite a while now they've had reports of missing girls..."

"All with connections to that Sonia woman?"

"Hmm!" humphed Mary thoughtfully. "Calum hoped Sonia might open up more under pressure, but he says she's scared. Survived the system in Russia by becoming one of 'them', but he thinks she doesn't feel safe, even here, in prison, in Scotland, from their hit men if she were to betray the Bratva. The Russian Mafia."

"Well, just as long as those brat people allow Justina to stay here a little longer! And woe betide any Russian mobster who dare tackle Daniel. Being a woman of God, you'll know all about Daniel's triumph over the lions."

Mary laughed.

"I see you'll not have to come to my bible study class, Daniel. But religion aside, how long will it take for you and the girls to come up with an overall design for your installation, then?"

"How long is a piece of string, Mary?"

"The longer the better as far as I'm concerned. Something clicked between those two girls. Somehow I just knew it would when I met poor Justina for the first time in the Church Hall."

"What about the girl's parents?"

"Her father died. But her mother is just so proud of her daughter. As she should be. But..."

Mary went silent again. Daniel, as always, could read the minister's mind.

"Ponia, right? Something's wrong. Get your personal policeman friend to ask that Buddy guy in Lithuania to suss her out."

Mary nodded.

"I'll give him a call later, back at the manse."

Back home, relaxing in the sitting room whilst Ade, with Lina's help, prepared an evening meal for all five of them whilst the girls happily chatted away in Melanie's bedroom, Mary dozed off, only to be awoken by a shrill scream upstairs.

She scaled the stairs two at a time, rushed into her daughter's room fearing some awful calamity must have taken place, only to find Melanie seated on her bed beside Justina, her arm around the Lithuanian girl whose phone trembled in her hand. Both girls remained speechless when Mary asked what was wrong. Lina also appeared, alerted by the scream, and stood beside Mary. She repeated Mary's question in Lithuanian. Justina looked up, tears streaming. Melanie spoke...

"It's her art teacher in Vilnius. She was found dead. Someone killed her."

"Ponia?" queried Mary, mortified.

Justina nodded. Mary joined her daughter to sit beside Justina and cradled the sobbing girl in her arms whilst Lina returned to the kitchen downstairs to inform Ade about a murder almost two thousand miles away.

Chapter 27

Moments after Andy said that his dog, Kauri, would turn up any minute, the doorbell rang. He winked at Anita, left the room and returned with a young Māori man with long, flowing hair and a short beard. His bright eyes fixed on the lawyer, the 'dog' grinned and offered her his hand.

"So pleased to meet with the best defence lawyer in the Land of the Long White Cloud!" he said. "Plus I have some very interesting photos for you. All authenticated. Take a squizzy[8]."

Kauri sat beside Mary who needed little convincing after seeing the images of the still-alive-murdered pilot, taken by himself, in Wellington, plus earlier pictures of the man.

"Chur[9], Kauri. Whatever's going on, it's a whole different yarn[10] to the one that came out in that courtroom. You are an absolute ace. Problem is, what to do now?"

"Your bro, Anita," Andy offered. "That takatāpui[11] in Scotland."

"David? What about David?"

"Sally's Scottish, isn't she? Like your guy in jail. Her husband."

Anita nodded, slowly, as jumbled thoughts slowly rearranged themselves inside her brilliant brain.

"And whatever that Wayne fella is, he is not an Ozzie.

---

[8] look
[9] Thanks
[10] story
[11] gay person

179

You're so right, Andy. Like me with you guys, David has connections in Edinburgh. He could do some digging."

"Get him to dig hard enough and he could join us for a boil-up, eh?" Kauri suggested.

Anita laughed.

"Good on you! David and his artist husband are full-time foodies. Though Daniel's the chef. We might promise to teach him a thing or two about Kiwi cuisine if he could find out more about Sally and her non-Ozzie. I'll message my little bro. Been meaning to get in touch with David a while now. And maybe John himself knows more than he lets on. Could be he's protecting Sally? I really do not know that man apart from the fact that he isn't a killer."

*****

"Where is your mother now, Justina? It is her on your phone, right?"

"With the policeman in Vilnius. He comes to our home. Lina, you talk please. I cannot think."

Lina, who spoke over the phone with the police officer in Vilnius, explained to Mary, later, how Ponia must have been followed on her way to school the previous day, for her body was found by a dog-walker, hidden in the undergrowth in Vingis Park, in a pool of blood, her throat slit open.

"How awful!" exclaimed Mary. "Did they say any more? Like, who was responsible?"

"Russian Bratva," answered Lina. "No doubt. And perhaps Justina's art teacher back home wasn't the person Justina thought she was."

"Killed to keep her silent? Do you think she was in on that art competition scam all along? With Sonia?"

Lina nodded.

"I'm sure of it."

"What are you saying?" Justina asked Lina in Lithuanian. "Ponia and Sonia together?"

"Yes. And you, Justina, must stay here in Edinburgh. Mary… call your policeman friend. Mr Scott."

Mary did, and learned that DI Scott had already been contacted by Vyresnysis Komisaras Budris in Vilnius, advising that Justina should stay in Scotland until it might be safe for her to return home. He told Mary that he was just about to call her when his phone rang. Together, they agreed that Justina and Lina would remain with herself and Ade, plus police protection, and that Justina's mother would go into hiding in Vilnius. On hearing this, Justina asked if she, too, could come to Scotland, but 'Buddy' as Mary's police friend called his Lithuanian counterpart, said even the travel to Edinburgh would be too dangerous for her.

"Animals!" exclaimed Lina on hearing this.

"No," said Mary, quietly, "just evil humans. The Devil is at large in Russia, but even Russia, the largest country in the world, isn't big enough for him."

"We all fight him, huh? Together!" suggested Lina.

Mary smiled.

"Not fight. Just believe in God, Lina. In justice. And in our love for one another."

"How?"

*****

Lina had proved a Godsend to the police. Before coming to Scotland, back in Vilnius, a language university graduate, like Justina she had been duped into believing she was visiting the UK to take up a position... in her case as a translator for a multi-million-pound export business. It all appeared so genuine, with a very professional website, an online interview that left her feeling as though she was floating on top of the world, totally unaware that she was stepping onto a dark trail that would lead to inescapable prostitution. Again like Justina, she was met at Edinburgh airport by the well-dressed, affable Sonia. As a linguist, she was used to Russians, and was impressed by Sonia's fluency in both Lithuanian and English. In the taxi from the airport, she jokingly asked why Sonia herself wasn't applying for the seemingly lucrative position that Lina was about to fill. "Already been there," answered the Russian woman, without elaborating on the 'there'... prostitution.

The truth engulfed Lina like a dark cloud as soon as she entered her 'lodgings' in Muirhouse. Her passport and other personal belongings were immediately confiscated by a silent brute who stank of vodka, urine and sweat, and she was warned that any attempt to alter things by 'escaping', or pleading with wealthy clients, would be fatal for her family back in Lithuania. She would only be allowed to talk to her widowed mother in the presence of Sonia or one of the Russian woman's accomplices, and would be forced to stick to a given script, saying how wonderful her hosts in Scotland were, and that all was going well with her new job. Small amounts of money, a mere fraction of what the young woman earned 'on the street', were sent to the mother as proof that 'all was well'. Lina even contemplated suicide after being 'put out to work', but thinking about her mother back home kept her alive, for she had been warned that killing herself would be regarded as 'escape' by Sonia's immediate boss, exacting the same outcome for family back home.

That day, after Justina's arrival, when the police broke into the apartment, arrested Sonia and her thugs, and released herself and the other girls and women kept captive, was the most wonderful in her life to date. Curiously, the horrific experience of her six months in the clutches of the Bratva gave her a strength she never knew she had before. It was as if an inner, undefinable power, of which she had been totally unaware, had taken over her soul. Never again would she become putty in the hands of the Devil. She now went to church every week, said prayers several times a day, and stayed on, as instructed by the police, with the most wonderful people she had ever met...

The Osondus.

Lina applied for refugee status, and, in view of her knowledge about the goings on in that stinking Muirhouse apartment, and the links with the Russian Bratva through Sonia, clearly needed police protection for herself as well as for the Lithuanian girl staying at the manse. Mary, against the idea of deadly weapons being used by one human against another, on religious grounds, felt uneasy about the twenty-four-hour presence of an armed officer, but her good friend DI Scott insisted. The two teenage girls rather enjoyed chatting up the young male officers. Less so the female ones.

After learning that her beloved art teacher back in Vilnius was also 'one of them', Justina felt as though she was being swept along on a turbulent river of mixed emotions. Anger, despair, revenge, fear, acceptance and determination all mingled in a swirling mental maelstrom

Lost Hands

as, slowly, with help from Melanie, Lina, Mary and Daniel, her flow of thoughts became calmer. She and Melanie, sometimes with Lina's help as a translator, would sit and talk for hours. And at the art college, together with Daniel, they worked, alongside other students, on the installation whenever they had time off from school, for Justina now attended the same school as Melanie, wearing Felicity's old uniform, thanks to the paedo pharmacist, with additional online lessons from her teachers back in Vilnius. Thus the art competition scam became a reality, for Daniel saw to it that, the following term, Justina would become the first winner of the 'Daniel McMurray International Art Scholarship' allowing her to formally become a student of the ECA.

Life for the young Lithuanian artist slowly became not only normal, but super-normal. Thankfully, her English rapidly became as fluent as Lina's, for Lina met a young medical student called Patrick, at church, moved in with him and within a year they married. Her parents came across for the wedding before their daughter became Mrs Duncan; a wedding that filled Mary's church and hit the headlines of the local weekly press; a wedding that stung the one-time pharmacist, languishing in Saughton Prison for murdering his wife, like a wasp from hell.

James Taylor's appeal, on the grounds of merely carrying out the wish of his wife, Elsie, claiming that her depression, following her elder daughter's demise at the hands of a rogue surgeon, made her suicidal, had been denied thanks to DI Scott who was also at Lina's wedding. The ongoing investigation of the pharmacist's sex movies of underage girls, linked to the Russian Bratva, remained 'under cover', but Mr Taylor's lawyer, at the last minute, persuaded his client to back off from the appeal or it might 'all come out'. Worse than it first appeared, threads of intelligence information now linked the vile criminal web, in which the pharmacist had become trapped, with a certain Russian oligarch, calling himself Petr Velikiy[12], who lived in a spacious villa just outside Menton, on the glorious Côte D'Azur, and...

A personal friend of the newly elected President of the United States of America.

---

[12] Peter the Great

PART 4

Chapter 28

"It's a beautiful thing," the President of the United States of America said of his friendship with Peter Velokov, renamed Velikiy, or 'The Great', by those close to him. "A great guy," echoed the President. "Just like, thanks to me, America is again great."

Felicity, now happily married, felt trickling tears tickle her cheeks as she watched the BBC News broadcast on television. Her Aunt Maggie had recently revealed to her DI Calum Scott's concern that behind the sexploitation ring masterminded by the Russian Bratva was the untouchable billionaire oligarch residing in a villa in the South of France. She had promised to tell no one else, including her husband, Ranjit, but to think that the man, whose face had appeared on the television screen, was responsible for movies of herself, school skirt pulled up, beaten by her father, being sold, online, to paedos across the world, was now praised by the most powerful person in the world, was too awful to bear alone. She reached for her phone and called her aunt.

"I'm sorry," she sobbed, "I thought that was all in the past, with Dad doing time for killing Mum, but seeing the man behind it all on the telly brought it back to me."

"Shall I come over?"

Lost Hands

"Yes!"

"I was going to call you anyway because there's been a development. DI Scott was on the phone to me just yesterday."

"Oh yes?" There was uncertainty in the tone of Felicity's voice.

"Something that might help you to get closure. And that lovely Lithuanian girl, too."

"Justina?"

"Uh-huh! I hear she's doing really well at art college in Edinburgh."

Felicity was tempted to say, 'Bully for her!', but stayed silent. She had too much respect for her lovely aunt. Without that woman, there was no telling how things might have turned out.

Later, together, the two women shared the Edinburgh detective's news, quite possibly game-changing, and agreed to travel northwards together the following week. Now pregnant, and on maternity leave, Felicity had mixed feelings about returning to the beautiful city of her traumatic childhood, but Ranjit insisted she should go. Also, he had an old medical colleague friend, now working in Edinburgh, he wished to meet up with. It was his weekend off, so he offered to accompany them on the train.

"If it helps the truth to come out," he said, "perhaps those demons of yours will finally be put to rest.

*****

"Slut!" repeated John, over and over, as he staggered towards the copulating couple.

Sally disengaged herself from a wild embrace with her lover from the past, stood up and stepped back from her

187

swaying husband. She pleaded with him, explaining that things weren't as they seemed, that the injured man, lying on his back on the ground, needed endorphins to control the agonising pain from his injured leg...

"That's all," she insisted as John reached down to pick up a broken-off branch with the intention of walloping the injured 'Ozzie'.

Sally screamed,

"Stop it!"

Wayne-come-Sean dodged the blow, only for John to drop the branch, reach down and encircle his rival's sturdy neck with deft, surgical hands. Sally pulled and clawed at her crazed husband, shouting,

"Don't, John! Don't, don't! I had to do something. No painkillers. Only endorphins. You know that. You're a doctor. Sex releases endorphins in the brain. Helps to kill the pain. He was in agony. Please stop it, John. There's no need."

John, doped and dazed to the point of delirium, paused and released his hands from their grip around the throat of the bastard on the ground when the man went still. Moments later, Sally, having picked up the same branch, whacked her husband across the back of his head with it.

John fell stunned to the ground as Sean, gasping, came too. John also recovered consciousness and sat up, rubbing the back of his head.

"Slut!" he exclaimed again, followed by a sudden change in mood...

"Oh, my dear, sweet wife! I love you so much. All that tenderness. Those times we ve had. We re going to have such a life together, you and I."

Lost Hands

John rose to his feet. Sally screamed, turned, dropped the branch and took off into the undergrowth.

Lost Hands

Chapter 29

"**We** have to go together," Aunt Maggie said over the phone. "I can't explain why right now, but I just know you'll understand after we get there."

Felicity struggled, for a fortnight, with the horror of returning to Edinburgh, the location of her tormented childhood and early teen years, but Ranjit persuaded her not to back out. They joined her aunt at Kings Cross station, Ranjit trailing two suitcases, for a train journey to a city that, for reasons she could never comprehend, had once, in the past, been referred to as 'The Athens of the North'. More like 'Hell' as far as she was concerned, but she had grown into a sensible, strong-minded woman and was determined to help her aunt in any way she could to unearth yet more truths that might help to keep her hated father locked up for good.

On arrival at Waverley Station, and exiting onto Princes Street, Felicity realized, for the very first time in her life, that the city in which she had been born and brought up was not only magnificent, but also strangely beautiful. Her ancient castle, perched on a rocky outcrop like a crown on the head of Mother Earth herself, reminded Felicity of the love she felt for her own mother, the rock of her childhood. Had it not been for the woman's recurring bouts of depression, she might have had the strength to stand up to that bully now languishing in Saughton Prison for her murder. If only the man could also be brought to justice for the crimes he committed against herself, Felicity felt she might finally get closure. Was this what Aunt Maggie had in mind, she wondered? All she knew was that the dreaded trip to Edinburgh had something to do with a minister of the Church of Scotland. The minister at the church to which she, Verity, Sean and her mother were dragged along every Sunday for a morning service that just went on and on, and would, on occasions, be followed by Sean and her father taking her to the pharmacy for a painful, filmed beating 'before God' for 'her sins'. Aunt Maggie had promised Felicity that the present minister was a 'lovely woman' who knew all about her brother-in-law's perverted past, and who wished to finally meet her to help her come to terms with what happened to her as a child.

Maggie and Felicity booked into an Airbnb close to the church. They had been invited to dine that evening at the manse, and Felicity spent most of the afternoon lying on her bed, talking to, over WhatsApp, and getting strength from, Ranjit, who was staying, more cheaply, at the College of Physicians in Queen Street.

"We should go now," interrupted Aunt Maggie, looking at her watch.

"Remember, I'm with you all the time, my darling," Ranjit said from Felicity's i-Pad screen. "Love you more than you can ever imagine."

Felicity laughed, then the tears began to flow again.

"I wish you were *really* with me," she said. "Like right now! Here in this Airbnb."

"I am, I am," he repeated. "Can you hand me to your Aunt Maggie."

Aunt Maggie took the phone.

"Look after her... promise!" Ranjit demanded.

"Don't you worry. This Mary Osondu sounds simply

amazing. I know she'll look after my wonderful niece every inch of the way." She paused. "She's hoping Felicity might help her with her back pain, too," she added glancing and grinning at Felicity.

"Once a physio, always a physio!" groaned her niece, retrieving the phone.

"Remember what the psychiatrist said last week, darling," encouraged Ranjit. "This isn't about anger. It's about understanding. And understand this. I love you more than you can possibly imagine."

Felicity smiled through her tears.

"Love you, too," she whispered before closing the call.

Later, on their way to the church, Felicity halted at the street corner where a familiar church spire came into view. She recalled that very same spire, from her childhood and teenage years, which, instead of reaching up towards a God who had no intention of protecting her from her awful father, seemed to pierce her soul like the knife her father used to cut into the Christmas turkey. She remembered how every Christmas would end in a beating, or two, watched and filmed by Sean, in the pharmacy 'studio', with their mother hidden away in the parental bedroom, back home, in the grip of deep depression.

The tears returned.

"Remember, Ranjit is with you all the time," reassured Aunt Maggie. "Just think how lucky you are to have a husband like him. If only Elsie could have a life again with her own Ranjit!"

"If only!" echoed Felicity. "Come on. Let's do it."

Aunt Maggie knocked on the door of the manse, an austere, stone Victorian building that somehow reminded

Felicity of her father whenever he stood in the studio dressed in a ridiculous black headmaster's gown with a stupid square-topped mortarboard balanced on his balding head.

The door opened onto a pair of grinning girls standing together in the doorway, one Black with a refined Edinburgh Morningside accent when she spoke, the other white with an East European accent. Felicity immediately took to both of them.

"So you're Maggie and Felicity," the Black girl said. "Lovely to see you both. I'm Melanie, and this is Justina, the next ten times great Lithuanian artist."

Justina gave Melanie a playful punch in the side and both girls giggled.

"Please come in. Mum's in the living room with her detective friend and Daniel's Kiwi husband, David. David doesn't say much because Daniel does all the talking, but he's really lovely. Daniel too. He's our design prof at art college. Into cooking, like Dad, so they're both busy in the kitchen."

"Let them come in, Mel," urged a smiling Justina, pulling her friend back from blocking the doorway.

"Sorry! I'm just so excited. Mum says you're going to help get that horrible pharmacist put away for good. And —"

"That horrible pharmacist is my dad," interrupted Felicity as she followed her aunt into the large house.

Stepping back, Melanie clamped her hand to her mouth with embarrassment, but Felicity immediately put her at ease...

"But you're quite right. He's even more horrible than

193

you could ever imagine. Because of what he did before I ran away from home, I almost didn't come up to Edinburgh."

"Oh, I'm so glad you did. Please, come and meet Mum and Uncle Calum... that's what we like to call her detective friend... and David." She then added, quietly, "*He's* dead serious for a Kiwi, but a one in a million. A lawyer."

Felicity and Maggie followed the two girls into the living room where they were immediately greeted by Mary.

"Mary Osondu," the minister said, standing up and embracing first Maggie, then Felicity. "I'm so pleased you agreed to come up together to our wonderful city. And you, Felicity. You are so brave. I know how awful it must be for you to return to where you were brought up, but Calum — DI Scott — he truly believes this is the best way forward."

The two men stood and introduced themselves to Felicity and her aunt, before they were shown to a couple of empty chairs. Felicity thought it somewhat resembled a bizarre séance meeting as they sat, albeit comfortably, in a semi-circle.

"You're from New Zealand, I hear," Maggie said to David, breaking the silence.

"Uh-huh! A true Kiwi."

"Beautiful, I've heard. Particularly the South Island. A real paradise."

"Too right it is. It's where my sister lives."

"You've a sister?"

"Yeah. A lawyer like me. Two for the price of one, huh!?"

Melanie chuckled. "He's really very funny, like Daniel, though you wouldn't know it most of the time," she said, grinning at David.

"She has a family?" enquired Maggie. "Your sister?"

"Widowed," responded David. "No children. Only work, work, work!"

"And paradise?" added Maggie.

"I do wish we could go to New Zealand, Mum," said Melanie. "See a real kiwi. Do they really only come out at night, David?"

"Yeah. Like Edinburgh art students," said David.

Melanie and Justina looked at each other, then giggled.

"And you, Justina?" Maggie said, addressing the Lithuanian girl, hitherto silent. "I hear you came to Edinburgh on an art scholarship when you were only sixteen."

Justina looked at her mother's detective friend before responding with a shy head nod. He answered for the girl.

"That's part of the story we have to finish," he said. "Why we asked you up here. But we can talk about all that stuff later. After the meal. Melanie's dad and David's husband are preparing a feast you'll never forget, I promise."

Which proved to be true. An evening that was indelibly etched onto Felicity's brain, but, after returning to the Airbnb, her stomach full of the most delicious food she'd ever had, her head spinning with voices... new voices... friendly voices, the fear of seeing her father again, albeit safely locked up in Saughton jail, resurfaced, like stinking scum on a puddle in a rubbish tip, as she sat, silent, on the edge of her bed, staring at the floor.

Aunt Maggie sensed her niece's disquiet and came over to sit beside her. She hugged Felicity close and stroked her hair.

"It is best that you see him. So he can tell you himself."

"That he's sorry for destroying my childhood?"

"There's more to it than that. Whether or not my brother-in-law could ever feel any sort of remorse remains to be seen, but perhaps just knowing that you're not alone with what you went through in the past might help. Oh, if only Elsie had confided in me before..." Maggie paused, clearly uncertain as to how she should complete the sentence.

"Before what?"

"A letter addressed to me. Never sent, and obviously written just *after* the one I did get. Saying she was scared of him. Got handed in to the police by the new owners of the pharmacy. They found it hidden away, un-posted, when they were doing renovations in the storage area. DI Scott informed me about this just last week. Relevant to on-going police investigations, he said. My brother-in-law must've found it back then, hidden by your mother. The envelope was open, DI Scott said. He must've read it before he..." Maggie paused.

"Before the bastard killed Mum?"

Maggie nodded.

"Told the police it shamed him. On top of everything else. Elsie must've tried to hide the envelope, intending to send it to me, but never got the chance. Thankfully, it was still there. In the pharmacy. New owners had kept everything as it was till they decided to make changes."

"Even the... you know?"

"The studio? That's just a store room now."

"Thank God! Can I see it? That letter of Mum's?"

"After we've visited the prison. I honestly don't want

you to have to spend a second longer with the bugger than you need to. But I do agree with that police inspector. And the lovely Church of Scotland minister, Mary Osondu. That he must tell you himself."

"Tell me why he killed her and pretended it was suicide? There never was a suicide note, was there?"

"Not as such. Only word of mouth. That she 'couldn't go on any longer'."

"And that vile brother of mine?"

"Disappeared without a trace just before they arrested your father."

"And *he* denies knowing Sean's whereabouts?"

"Apart from the fact that he allegedly went off to South America with a climbing buddy."

"Can't they trace him through that so-called buddy? Passport checks, if they left the country together?"

"Apparently it's not that easy. Would be like looking for a needle in haystack."

"Sean used to pleasure himself when Dad beat me. Whilst recording everything with that awful camera on a tripod. The same one Dad used to take posh portraits and passport photos. I can't even look at one of those sorts of cameras without it all coming back to me. Thank heaven for i-Phones and smart phones!"

"Mary's coming with us. She insisted. Such a lovely woman."

"She had her own problems back home in Nigeria. Melanie told me whilst I helped her and the Lithuanian girl with the washing up. Her uncle, a Catholic pastor, was murdered by the Boko Haram. It's why they stayed on here in Edinburgh."

Lost Hands

"And Justina? Did she say anything to you about her own experience with your father?"

Felicity, frowning, turned to face her aunt.

"What? He did it to her as well?"

Aunt Maggie nodded.

"Tried to. There's a lot you don't know, Felicity. That I never told you because I just wanted to help you to forget the past."

"He beat other girls? With Sean behind that awful camera? Making movies?"

Aunt Maggie nodded again, and put a comforting arm around her niece's shoulders as they continued to sit in silence on the edge of Felicity's bed, each struggling with her own fear of the following morning.

Chapter 30

Sean watched with interest as a stuporous John staggered after his pretty bride when she took off into the undergrowth.

"All going to plan, thank God," he said to Joan, reverting to his native Scots accent.

"What's with the change in accent, Wayne?" the American woman asked. "Here... help me up."

Sean, after reaching for the branch that Sally had dropped, and using it to support the weight on his injured limb, helped Joan up from the ground.

"It's Sean, not Wayne. And that bugger who's gone after my girlfriend killed my big sister back in Edinburgh."

"Scotland? So you're Scottish? Like Sally?"

"Never told you the whole story back there in the hotel. When Mike and I learned you'd be taking this flight. And I'm so sorry about Arnie, though he did kind of mess things up. By getting in the way. Mike would've landed us safely. And Tony was going to make his escape. Then..."

"So this was all staged?"

"I feel really bad about your husband. I — "

"Bloody good riddance!" interrupted Joan.

"What?" questioned Sean, staring in disbelief at the large American woman.

"He's been a pain in the arse since the day we got married. His other women were the least of it."

Sean could scarcely believe a man the size and shape of beached walrus would ever have had much luck bedding 'other women', but Joan's apparent relief at losing her husband in the air crash gave him an idea. One that he could work out together with her and Sally after Tony had done his bit. He could see the pilot taking off after the honeymooners, unseen by John, through the undergrowth, and told Joan to follow him, reminding her he was still 'Wayne' till he told her otherwise.

*****

"Hi, little brother! How are you?"

Anita sat in her office, a mug of coffee in one hand, the other cupping the mouse beside her desktop computer screen.

"I'm fine, sis. And it all went well last night. The meal at the minister's place. Daniel and her hubby pulled out all the stops. Two lovely girls, she has there. Her daughter and a Lithuanian girl. Both art students. Plus there's something going on. With the daughter of a local pharmacist who's banged up in Saughton — that's the local male prison — for murdering his wife. And the Lithuanian girl... according to Daniel, she and the minister's daughter are both absolutely brilliant students. Best he's ever had. Organised a worldwide-food installation project together at ECA when they were only sixteen."

"Yes, you told me about that. I remember. Year before last."

"On the basis of that, the girl from Vilnius got a scholarship. Funded by Daniel's wealthy businessman dad."

"You never told me that."

"Well there's a lot more I never told you. Mary, the minister, was telling us, with her detective friend, whilst the girls were in the kitchen washing up, how Justina, the

Lithuanian girl, was trafficked to the UK by the Russian Bratva."

"Like the Mafia?"

"Precisely. The Russian Mafia. A woman called Sonia brought her from Lithuania to Edinburgh on the pretext she'd won a scholarship to study art at Daniel's college here."

"She was Russian, huh?"

"Yeah. Took the poor girl to a seedy apartment in Muirhouse — a rundown part of the city — where she was holed up with a bunch of women and underage girls from all over. Africa, Far East, Europe. Even another from Lithuania. Lina. Forced into prostitution. The Justina girl was taken to a pharmacy not far from Mary's church, forced to change into the school uniform that once belonged to the younger woman who came up from London — "

"Slow down, David. You're losing me. What younger woman?"

"The daughter of the guy banged up for killing his wife. He was into making movies of young girls, including his own daughter, being beaten with a cane for some sort of perverted online sex market."

"Run by the Russians?"

"Uh-huh!"

"No surprise there, then."

"But the Lithuanian girl sorted him!"

"What do you mean?"

"Instead of him beating her, *she* beat him. Felled him with a karate chop, grabbed his cane and struck him across the face with it. Scarred for life on his cheek, Mary says."

"Good. A permanent reminder of his crime."

Lost Hands

"The abused daughter who came up to Scotland, Felicity's her name, she said her elder brother was also in on it. He shot the movies. Same young guy was there when the Lithuanian girl whacked the pervy pharmacist dad, but cleared off when he realised he'd met his match with Justina. Guy called Sean. Apparently buggered off to South America when his dad got banged up. Scared they'd lock him up too."

"Which they should. Did they catch him."

"Na! *Had* a girlfriend, apparently. A nurse. Sally or something. She's — "

"Hang on, David. This girl called Sally. Did she recently get married?"

"Dunno. My dog says she was a bit pissed off about her lover buggering off to Patagonia one Monday morning, never to be seen again."

"Your dog?" laughed Anita. "My private detective friend has one of those too. Called Kauri. Look... the wife of a guy I defended and who got banged up for murdering an air pilot down by the Sound, she's also called Sally and sounds Scottish. Like her surgeon husband, my client."

"A doctor husband done for murder, ay? What is the world coming to?"

"Only I'm convinced he didn't do it. Got set up. The man he's supposed to have killed has turned up, alive and well according to Kauri, in Wellington. And another passenger on the air tour called Wayne, whose friend, Mike, really did die in the air-crash, shows up with the killer's wife, Sally. David, can you find out the maiden surname of this so-called girlfriend of your murderer's son? From the hospital where she works? Or will that detective fellow know it?"

"Whatever, consider it done, sis! What about at your end? Can't you find out that woman's family name from court proceedings? She'll have been a witness, right?"

"Sure was. For the prosecution."

"Hmm! Some wife! Lucky I stuck with a husband," said the brother.

"Yeah! We women are far more complicated, David."

"So... let me get this right. This newly-married Scots nurse of yours, Sally, she goes on honeymoon in our beloved New Zealand, the young couple — "

"Not so young," interrupted Anita. "My client, that is. Some twenty years or more older than her."

"Interesting! So they book in for one of those scenic air tours over the Sound, see the fiords. The mountains. The plane crashes. He thinks he's murdered the pilot — revenge or something — but he hasn't. Then the wife goes off with one of the other tourists on the plane. A guy called Wayne."

"That's the thing, David. I'm not sure he is. Called Wayne. And I'm certain he's no Ozzie as he claims to be. I thought it funny he wasn't called as a witness, too, alongside an American lady called Joan. At the trial. But what if he wasn't who he claimed to be? Feared his identity might be uncovered by the legal process. All I know is that he's supposed to have survived a severe leg injury and later claimed not to have actually seen anything, because I probed a bit to see whether we could use him for the defence. Just suppose, after all, he's really Sean. A Scot from Edinburgh, and the brother of the woman from London who's visiting your pharmacist in jail. About their mother's murder."

Lost Hands

"Cool, Anita! You always were the brighter of us two sibling lawyers. So, you've got your own dog, Kauri, digging down under and you want me to dig a bit deeper up here. Dig hard enough, and we could all meet up in the centre of the world."

"Journey to the Centre of the Earth. Jules Verne. Way ahead of its time. But you've reminded me. Someone said this Wayne guy fancies himself as a writer. Were he and Sally trying to turn some weird fantasy fiction book into reality by bringing the pilot back from the dead? Whatever, he'll not escape the nose of a Māori tracker, which is pretty much what Kauri is according to my private dick friend."

"Are you asking for the case to be re-opened?" asked David.

"Not just yet. Need hard evidence about the pilot fellow, but if Wayne turns out to be Sean, the wife's ex-lover, we've got him by the goolies."

"Isn't that what they call pebbles in Oz?" asked David, grinning.

"Yeah... well if we're talking the same Sally, she must have a heart of stone to do that to my doctor client. He really is a lovely man, David."

"Don't tell me too much, sis, or you'll make Daniel jealous!"

"Doubt it, somehow. You adore him. So d'you think they could be linked. My case here, back home, and your murdering father and his links to the Russians and child pornography?"

"Could be big, sis, but taking down the Russians would be like trying to blow up Mount Everest with a petrol bomb."

Lost Hands

"Well put, bro. I can't see us taking down the Russians any time soon, whatever that detective friend of your Church of Scotland minister thinks, but I will seek justice for my Scottish surgeon."

"Beware the wrath of my big sister, all you bad guys! So when are you coming to Scotland, Anita? Daniel can't wait to try out some of the Nigerian dishes he's learned from Ade, Mary's hubby, on you. He's our accountant."

"I might well do that, David. Depends on what further leads I can get down here. And whether or not Sally and her fake Ozzie lover head back to Edinburgh. Keep in touch, bro!"

"Sure thing! Love you, sis. Bye!"

"Bye!" Anita turned off her computer and sat for a while staring at the blank screen. Before speaking with her brother, the case of John McEuen had, itself, been like a blank screen. Now, two brilliant legal minds were about to come together to fill the screen with hard facts that would stand out like telegraph masts helping to broadcast the truth to a sick world.

Chapter 31

"That poor woman," said Justina as she and Melanie sat together in Melanie's bedroom, later that evening, both their stomachs close to bursting after a most amazing meal. Not Lithuanian, not Nigerian nor even Spanish, but delicious, albeit simple, Scottish.

"Felicity? The physiotherapist?"

"It was bad enough just seeing his eyes bore into me, visually undressing me after forcing me to put on his daughter's school uniform, but imagine living with the monster. Until the age of fourteen. Her poor mother, too."

"Murdered. Perhaps she *would* have killed herself if he'd not done the job himself."

"Suicide? A mortal sin for us Catholics," said Justina.

"My mum used to be Catholic. Like you. Never talked suicide with her, though," responded Melanie.

"Glad to hear it," said Justina.

"But surely it's even more of a sin to make someone *feel* suicidal, Justina. Anyway, let's not argue about religion. Just pray that it all goes well for the woman when she confronts that evil man in prison."

"I'm pleased your mum's going with them to visit him in jail. She's so strong. And understanding. My own mum loved meeting with her last year."

"Will she be coming again this summer? Instead of you returning to Vilnius. Don't think I could stand it again without having you here, Sister! Like last year."

Justina laughed and hugged Melanie.

"I'll try to persuade her. Safer here, anyway. Oh, those

horrid Russians!"

"I can't think of one Russian artist I admire."

"You don't have to! I've been thinking, Mel."

"Good. I like it when you think."

Justina chuckled again. "Another installation project," she said. "For the college show in the summer," she said.

"Tell me, Aleksandra Kasuba!"

"Don't make fun of me!"

"I'm not, I'm not! You really have the gift. Imagination. Spill the beans, as we say in English."

"Beans? No, not beans!" Justina looked at her friend, wide-eyed, before they both collapsed, together, into laughter.

*****

Sally, followed by her husband, followed the trail down towards a waterfall, her disorientated husband staggering after her, clutching at branches, muttering gibberish. She smiled to herself to think that Sean's sweets, injected with a powerful South American psychedelic, were doing their job, turning John into a zombie in free-fall. She refreshed herself at the stream, splashing her face and scooping handfuls of fast-flowing water into her mouth. John did the same. She felt tempted to tip him over the edge into the water, but refrained. She, after all, was no murderess. But she *had* promised Sean that she was with him every inch of the way to ensure the man who had escaped jail for killing his adored elder sister would finally end up in prison. So far, all had gone to plan apart from the tragic deaths of the large American and Sean's friend Mike. John's fault, too, as far as Sally was concerned.

As planned, Sally retraced her steps to the clearing

where Tony the pilot, prompted by Sean, emerged, quietly, from behind a tree before stunning John with a blow to the head. Sally and Tony, together, dragged the helpless John back to the clearing and laid him down on the ground. The pilot hid, again, as the other three stood and waited for John to regain consciousness.

"Thank God you're okay," Sally said after her husband came to.

"Gave us a hell of a fright, mate," added Sean.

"You okay?" John asked Sally.

"Better than you, by the look of that bruise on your head," she replied.

"What...?" John began.

"He's alive. Out there somewhere," Joan said.

"Who are you on about?" John asked, rubbing his head. He swayed like drunkard as he attempted to sit up.. "Who's alive?"

"The pilot."

"What?"

"Wayne spotted someone move between the trees after you left," Sally said. "Same coloured top as the pilot. He was following you."

"Thank God I found my feet again," Joan said. "He was gonna kill you, I know it. If only I could've run at him. You just didn't seem to be aware of him, like you were on another planet. Even talking to yourself. I screamed after he hit you, and he kinda vanished like a puff of smoke. Here..." She offered John her hand before helping him up onto his knees.

"God, you're strong," John remarked.

"Gonna have to be with Arnie gone," she replied.

Lost Hands

"But for your husband, we'd all be dead," John reminded her. "So that bastard clobbered me, then? Funny, I thought..." John looked at Sally, then Wayne.

"What?" queried Sally.

John remained silent.

"You thought *what*, John?"

"My mind playing tricks," he replied.

"It was a hell of whack you got, mate," Sean said. "Sure you're okay?"

John nodded. "What about your leg?" he asked.

"I'm good," Sean replied. "Thanks to you and Sally here."

Sally smiled. "Can you stand, John?" she asked.

"Think so," her husband replied. With Sally's help, he struggled, unsteadily, to his feet.

"We'll stick together best we can from now on," said Sean. "Down to the shoreline. Sure to catch the attention of a pleasure boat."

"Heard a helicopter," John said. "Surely they'll see us here in the clearing."

"Fire's too close," remarked Sean. "That tree's alight already. Must get going, unless you and your young wife here want to be kebabbed." He looked at Sally. Did he wink at her? John could not be sure. In fact, his mind felt so fuzzy, he wasn't certain about anything.

"What if that crazy pilot jumps out at me again?" John asked.

"All the more reason to get the hell outa here!" remarked Sean. He indicated John and Sally, standing side-by-side. "You two guys take the lead."

Together, they headed down the trail that John

thought he recalled having taken earlier, with Sally, but now wondered whether it had all been in his mind. When the muffled sound of a waterfall found his ears, he felt more certain that he and Sally had already walked the same trail; like before, it grew louder and clearer until, once more, he felt a fine spray stroking my cheeks.

"Sally, please tell me we *were* here together. Before you found me again. This is exactly as I remember it."

"John, you were badly concussed. We've never been here before. I promise you. It's all in your imagination."

'Including seeing you copulating with that Ozzie?' John asked himself. He remained silent as they approached the waterfall before stepping sideways down towards the rushing stream below.

John stopped and crouched to drink from the fall where Sally and he had, earlier, in his head, refreshed themselves. Sean (or Wayne as John knew him), now standing behind him, fumbled in his pouch and took out another sweet before offering this to Sally's husband after glancing at the only woman, apart from his sister Verity, that he had ever loved. John eagerly snatched it from him and popped it into his mouth, noisily grinding the sugary fragments between his teeth and quickly swallowing them.

Sean laughed.

"Another?" he suggested.

No way could John refuse. Those little sweets had a real hold over him. But they also gave him a damnable thirst which he slaked with handfuls of water from the stream.

"Could be a little tricky for Joan and me down there," remarked Sean, peering from a promontory at the Scottish couple below. "You and Sally go on ahead, John," he suggested.

With Sally in front of her husband, the honeymooners slowly inched their way down a scree slope to a more levelled off area of dense scrub.

"Stop, Sal!" John screamed when he saw man-shaped shadow flit between two trees ahead of Sally. "Over there. That pilot guy!" He gesticulated, like a madman, at the forest ahead. Sally looked and shrugged her shoulders.

"John, you're still suffering from concussion. Nobody's there."

Cautiously, her husband caught up with her. He picked up a rock and slowly approached the tree behind which the shadow had vanished. Nothing! He listened, intently, for any sound resembling that of someone moving around in the forest scrub, but the noise of the waterfall was deafening. He turned to look back and saw Joan help Sean down the scree towards him and Sally.

"Everything okay, John?" Sean called out in his fake Ozzie accent.

John shrugged his shoulders without replying, dropped the rock and followed Sally on down the mountainside towards the fiord below. There was now a well-worn trail that zig-zagged beside the fall.

Chapter 31

Felicity climbed into the taxi, followed by Mary and Maggie. All the time, during the short, silent ride to the Stenhouse district in the outskirts of Edinburgh, Maggie held her niece's hand. The taxi halted outside the austere gate of 'HMP Edinburgh', better known as 'Saughton', Mary paid up, offering a generous tip, before the three women emerged into the gloom of the grim prison precinct.

Felicity held back as the other two women approached the prison entrance. Maggie stopped and turned to face her niece.

"I can't do it," Felicity said. "I cannot face him. It'll all come back. The nightmares. The abuse. The shame. The pain. I just can't!"

Maggie went back to where Felicity stood alone and took hold of her, gently, by the shoulders.

"Felicity Prakash, you can, and you will. My sister was so proud of you, though perhaps she never told you so. She was too beaten down by him. You have an amazing strength. I've known that since you were a little child, and I always had my own suspicions about the man who called himself your father. Do this for Elsie's sake. For your mother. Do it for..." Maggie looked back at Mary. "Do it for God. Please. And we mustn't be late. Have to be there at least thirty minutes before the visit. And Mary and I will be with you all the time."

"You know something, don't you?" said Felicity. "Can't you just tell me yourself?"

Maggie shook her head.

Lost Hands

"Has to come from him. But know this. You are stronger than my evil brother-in-law. It's he who should be scared of you. And you don't have to look him in the eye. Just stare at the scar on his right cheek. The one that lovely Lithuanian girl gave him when he tried it out on her."

Maggie smiled at, then hugged Felicity who now allowed herself to be led to the entrance where the strict process of clearing the three female prison visitors began. Identification documents were carefully scrutinised, the three women were searched then passed through a metal detector before being shown to a waiting room where they were to remain until the specified time. To Maggie's great relief, the FCO (family contact officer), with whom she had spoken over the phone, showed up, as she had promised to do, and kindly reassured Felicity that no harm could come to her. Her father would be across a table, although far from reassuring Felicity the very mention of her father in connection with a 'table' rekindled the fear she always felt as a child when taken to the studio at the back of the pharmacy where she would be forced to lean across a table (he called it a 'desk') for the awful man to beat her with a cane. Far too young, back then, to know anything about sexual perversion, and totally unaware that her 'punishments' were being recorded on film not, as she was then told, as a reminder for her to behave but for dirty old men across the planet to pay for, and take evil pleasure in, thanks to the Russian Bratva.

The time finally came for the threesome to be taken to the visit room. Felicity's father, in stark prison uniform, was already seated at a table on the other side of which were three empty chairs. Without acknowledging her father,

Lost Hands

Felicity sat on the middle of the chairs with Mary and Maggie on either side of her. It was Mary who spoke first.

"I believe you have something to tell Felicity. Something that might help her understand why you did those things. To her and to her mother."

As advised by her aunt, Felicity looked up and, avoiding the eyes of the seated prisoner, stared fixedly on the linear scar striping her father's right cheek; a sign of his weakness when felled by a girl one third his age. The one-time pharmacist opened his mouth, looking down at his hands clasped together on the table in front of him. No sound emerged from his lips. It took a prompt from Aunt Maggie, plus a period of silence that, to Felicity, seemed like an eternity, before he finally spoke...

"I'm not your father," he said, looking up and directly at Felicity.

Stunned, Felicity remained silent. Like a fast-play rewind of a crazy horror movie, memories of her tormented childhood zipped through her mind as she stared at the scar on the face of the monster across the table. Her mother appeared, in her mind, worn down and helpless; her elder sister, too; always a mystery to the younger girl and the one who could never do any wrong; and her hated big brother going about the house with a permanent smirk on his cruel face. Had any of it actually happened, she kept asking herself? Was it all part of an unreal nightmare? One that she only awoke from that morning when, as a fourteen-year-old girl, using money that she had stolen from the pharmacy till and hidden in a drawer, ran away, taking a train from Waverley Station down to King's Cross in London and from there, by tube, to Hampstead where she

214

waited, seated with her back up against the front door, and only a small bag of essentials, till her Aunt Maggie arrived back home from work. She recalled sitting there for hours, hungry and thirsty and thinking that if her aunt refused to take her in she would somehow find her way to the River Thames and jump into the water when no one was looking.

Felicity turned to look at her aunt, her eyes questioning the older woman, almost asking whether she already knew.

"I only recently found out. From a letter your mum intended to send to me but got intercepted. By *him*!" The way Aunt Maggie said 'him' said a lot more than the word itself. It seemed to link all three women together and, although neither Felicity nor Maggie could call themselves religious, just the presence of Mary, and the strength of her faith as a Christian, seemed to bond them. Mary's religion was all about sharing a love for others rather than championing 'self' all the time like the man seated opposite and unrelated to the woman he had always called his daughter.

"That's how *he* found out the truth," Maggie said looking with disgust at the man who, until that moment, Felicity always thought of as her father. "It's why you did it, right? Killed my sister?"

"She cheated on me. But never said. All those years later, she finally admitted it. But not to me. Sean, he found the letter before she posted it. Recognised his mother's handwriting. So he opened it up. A confession, it was. Finally. I knew all the time, of course. Had even challenged her with it. About that weekend when I went to a conference down in Birmingham. That's when it started. An old flame of hers. I knew from the timing of *her* arrival." He looked at

Felicity. "She said it must be a big baby when she was obviously so much further on with the pregnancy than she should have been if I was the father. And you weren't. A big baby. She rarely let me... you know... Look, I'm sorry, Felicity, but— " he began.

'Trawling for sympathy?' thought Felicity. Rage took over.

"Sorry!?" Felicity stood up. "You don't even know the meaning of the word. But I swear to God I'll make you *really* sorry when it all comes out. Which it will! What you and Sean did to me all those years. And those dirty little movies! Do you know what they do to paedos in prison?"

With a violent backwards scrape of her chair that made the man who was no longer her father flinch, Felicity got up and hurried to the door, brushing past a prison officer and quickly followed by Mary and Maggie. She hurried along the corridor and, after briefly stopping to check out, left the building, finally coming to a halt just outside the entrance to the HMP Edinburgh. She stood, fists clenched, whilst Maggie and Mary, together, also got up. Both put their arms around the younger woman. She was clearly way beyond tears.

"He insisted on telling you himself," Maggie explained, breaking the silence, and clearly worried her niece was truly upset that she hadn't been warned prior to the prison visit. "Perhaps..." She paused, obviously trying to work out how best to express what she imagined was the motive behind the pharmacist's request. "Perhaps he was hoping for empathy because of your mother's infidelity."

"Empathy for killing her? Can you blame my mother? For seeking a brief escape from the bastard?"

"Not at all, dearest. But at least you know now it wasn't *you* that made him treat you differently from Verity and Sean. Maybe understand why he did what he did, however wrong and horrible it was."

Felicity remained silent for a few awful moments.

"We might have a problem," Mary said. The other women turned to face the minister. "Ade was speaking to David about it yesterday and— "

"So everyone except me knew!" Felicity interrupted, fuming with anger.

"It's not like that, Felicity," promised Mary. "No one wanted to hide anything from you."

"Listen to Mary, Felicity," urged Maggie. "Please! She's trying to help."

Mary continued,

"...David thinks it highly likely that his lawyer will try to re-open the case and lodge a plea for a reduction in sentence on the grounds of diminished responsibility, now with hard evidence of a confession of infidelity in that letter meant for you, Maggie, and that only recently turned up in the pharmacy. I'm not sure whether we should thank the new owners for handing it in to the police or not now."

"Oh my God! That would be awful. Surely that could never happen?" responded Maggie.

"As David often says, 'The law is an ass!' And that coming from a lawyer!"

"Can't we stop him? Oh, Felicity, I am so sorry. There must be something we can do."

"Brilliant, Mary! I'll ask David if I can sue him. Take out a civil action if your police officer friend, Calum, isn't interested," Felicity responded.

Lost Hands

"It isn't that he's not interested, Felicity," said Mary, in her friend's defence. "It's because what happened in the pharmacy is part of an ongoing investigation into something much, much bigger. And it goes to the very top. Police work is far more complicated than we civilians could ever imagine. Particularly when it involves trying to break up a criminal network like the one that man who isn't your father got himself mixed up in. But I'll talk to David. He owes me one for all the meals Ade and Melanie fed him over the years!"

"There's something else I must do, Aunty," Felicity said.

"Sweetheart?"

"Find my real father."

Lost Hands
PART 5

Chapter 32

Even in hell there are glimpses of light. For me, Anita's visits are like moments of brightness and warmth from a God I have never had any time for. Without any doubt whatsoever, the woman is an angel. Of this, I, albeit a total non-believer, am certain. Periods between her visits resemble dark grey clouds engulfing every waking moment after emerging from the black nothingness of sleep before slipping back into its oblivion within the confines of my prison cell.

Having said this, being a surgeon has earned me a certain respect from my fellow inmates. Often, at mealtimes, a prisoner will come up to me and seek my medical opinion on some inconsequential symptom, and even thank me for my advice and reassurance. The more perverse are curious about what I do... or did... with my hands during an operation; want to know what it feels like to run one's hands over a length of living bowel, or whether I've ever had arterial squirts of blood splatter my face. The more squeamish keep their distance if I talk, in surgical detail, about making that life-saving incision into a belly. When it comes to discussing nurses, and whether we doctors have the pick of the pool, so to speak, in bedding them, I merely grunt or go silent for I am painfully reminded of Sally. Whether or not I was drugged, as Anita seems certain was the case, the pilot's attempt to rape her in front of me remains etched on my hippocampus, that little hidden area deep within each and every brain where memories are permanently stored in extra-special cells; permanently, that is, until death or Alzheimer's takes over.

No, not all the inmates here are one hundred percent bad. Even the other two incarcerated murderers seem almost human. And so far, no one has beaten me up for pleasure. There have been a few threats of violence, but, because of my standing as a doctor, I have 'protectors'; hideous heavies who would thump the shit out of anyone should they dare to attack me. As for the prison warders, they, too, often bend my ear on what to do about a mole on a certain unmentionable part of their anatomy, or a streak of blood showing on the toilet paper after they wipe arses following a shit, and I, for one, must seem like the model prisoner. But the restraining walls, and the inability to simply do what I want, as and when I wish to, are hell-defining. Until I am with Anita again. When I'm with her, I can even forget about Sally.

I do so wish I knew more about the woman. She did, however, inform me that she has a younger brother, also a lawyer, practising in my home city of Edinburgh on the other side of the planet. Coincidence? We doctors don't believe in such things. Everything has a purpose. And a meaning.

My incarceration too?

*****

A shadow-turned-human sprang from the moss-carpeted undergrowth between John and Sally up ahead of the other two.

"Watch out, Sal!" shrieked John. But Sally could do nothing as the deranged pilot grabbed, and pulled her to the ground before fumbling with his trouser flies. John slipped and scrambled through the lush vegetation, dragged the man off his young wife and, with the pilot now pinned to the ground, on his back, John's weight pressing onto his belly, the surgeon encircled the pilot's thick neck with trembling surgical hands. Trembling with rage, or trembling because a surgeon's hands are created to save, not take, lives, John was unable to fathom. His mind was just a fluid fog.

"Stop, John, stop!" screamed Sally, now upright. She broke off a branch before bringing this down with a forceful whack on top of her crazed husband's head. John fell sideways, unconscious. The pilot picked himself up, and Sean and Joan, watching from a distance, joined them. Sally felt her husband's pulse.

"He'll be okay," she reassured. "He was barely conscious from that drug you gave him, anyway."

"Tony can carry him over his shoulder down to the water," Sean said in his native Scottish accent, clearly now wishing to take over. "Tony, you disappear like we planned. Just go into hiding for a while, then reappear with your new name when you've grown a beard. Catch up later, right?"

"Righty-o, mate!"

The pilot heaved the unconscious honeymooning surgeon onto his back, and, with surprising strength, continued on down the trail, alongside the fast-flowing stream,

All five remained silent till they reached the steep shore

of the fiord. John, still stunned and stuporous, made odd, grunting noises as they laid him out on the moss. Tony had already disappeared back into the forest when Sean waved his arms and shouted at a passing pleasure boat. He was noticed by the skipper who deftly turned his craft around, dropped anchor, and sent one of his crew, in a dingy lifeboat, to rescue the stranded trail finders huddled on a rock at the water's edge, one lying on his back.

"We had to knock him out before he killed us too," explained Sean in mock Ozzie after the dingy drifted into shore. "Tried to stop him, but he was like a wild animal. Got there too late to save that other guy. The one he strangled and weighted with rocks before tipping him in the fiord. If it wasn't for this injury of mine, I could have prevented it. I feel so bad!"

Sean showed the guy his injured leg.

"Plane crash. Up there. A tourist flight over the Sound. Went badly wrong. Two killed. Not the pilot's fault, but he survived, and this fellow here suddenly goes berserk and decides to kill the poor man. Can you contact the police from your boat? We're all three of us witnesses."

Somehow, Joan, Sean, Sally and a semi-conscious John were fitted into the dingy before being transported to the bobbing tourist boat where John, mumbling again, was perched on one of the benches. Sean high-fived with Sally and Joan grinned her approval as the boat pulled away.

John came too, peering in disbelief at the others.

"Sal? You okay?" he asked.

To his confused horror, she responded by asking her husband, "What have you done?"

"Did they get him?" John asked, ignoring her question.

"The mad pilot."

"Are you completely insane?" John could not understand the anger in her tone when he clearly remembered saving her from being raped by the pilot before blacking out. "He was helping me when I stumbled. And you bloody killed him!"

"Shh!" warned Sean. "There may be hidden ears on this boat." He leaned down and whispered in John's ear. "We... Joan and me... we were too late. So, whilst you were out for the count, thanks to Sally, though too late to save the guy, we filled him with rocks and tipped him into the fiord. Just hope it's deep enough to swallow him forever and that they believe our story. That he died in the crash. It's up to you, John. The police might be waiting for us at the quay. Better have your story worked out before we dock, huh?"

"But he *was* trying to rape you!" insisted John, addressing his wife who merely shook her head. He asked for water and Sean supported him whilst Sally went to fetch a glass of water from the bar.

"It's not true, is it?" John asked Joan whose expression displayed a damning disgust. Instead of denying what he had just been told, she nodded.

"But he killed your husband!" John rebuked. "*And* he attacked Sally."

"Not from where I was standing. And what do you mean, 'He killed my husband'? That was a dreadful accident. But to blame the poor pilot you strangled, how low can you get?"

John remained silent in shocked disbelief till the boat had docked, and after he had been escorted, at the quayside, to a waiting police vehicle. Before climbing in, he turned to look at his wife again, but all he saw was her contempt. It wasn't until he was incarcerated in a cell in Queenstown Police Station, on a charge of murder, that he felt able to formulate any meaningful words. They were addressed to the female lawyer assigned to him. A late middle-aged woman with a genuine smile and greying hair, Anita Mulholland.

Chapter 33

"Melanie, it's a brilliant idea!" exclaimed Daniel. "Why didn't I think of it myself? Shame on me! Naughty Daniel!" He slapped his wrist.

Grinning, Melanie glanced at Justina before both girls collapsed into giggles.

"But so little time before the Festival! You girls must get cracking right away. I'll be in touch with relevant agencies tout de suite!"

"You mean David?" asked Melanie.

"Best lawyer in town. Just happens to be my husband. Can get a tad grumpy, though, if you approach him in the wrong way."

"So that's why Mum told me to ask you first," responded Melanie. "But that poor woman up from London. She's absolutely devastated. Her whole childhood destroyed because of that bastard in jail who isn't even her proper dad."

"Dracula!" corrected Justina.

Melanie grabbed her friend by the arm.

"That's so cool!" she said.

The other girl shrugged her shoulders.

"Why?"

"An eye-catching poster for the exhibition. Dracula. With a scar on his right cheek. And two children looking up at him. Wide-eyed. Terrified."

Slowly, a smile began to light up the Lithuanian girl's face.

"And a hand. The hand of God. Protecting the

children," she suggested.

"Or two hands? Like in prayer?" questioned Melanie.

"You've got me lost, girls, all this talk of hands."

"Brilliant, Daniel! Lost Hands!"

"Oh, I really must stop being brilliant," said the girls' design prof, emphasising his statement with a foppish one-handed gesture.

"No. The Title. Of the exhibition. 'Lost Hands'. Hands that should protect children lost... to turn into hands that harm them."

"Hmm!" Daniel made the girls laugh again by pulling a funny face.

"How much do you think we could raise for Felicity?" Melanie asked. "For her legal costs."

"Well... my husband, with a little persuasion... in bed of course... will offer his services for free. So... talking legal costs... advertising..." Daniel raised his eyebrows and looked beseechingly up at the ceiling as if seeking help from a higher authority with whom Melanie's mum had a better connection.

"She will win, won't she?" asked Melanie.

"*David* will win. Of course he will. And Felicity *will* finally get justice. Even if that letter to her aunt they uncovered in the pharmacy *does* mean a retrial, and some stupid lawyer *does* manage to get his sentence reduced, Daniel will make damn sure he's locked up again the day he's released. Dracula will get put back where he belongs. In his coffin!"

*****

The evening after learning that the pathetic specimen of a man whom they had faced across that table in the visit room at Saughton prison was not her father, Felicity enjoyed, together with her aunt, a wonderful meal of true Nigerian cuisine thanks to the combined efforts of Melanie and her dad. David was busy working on a case of domestic abuse so was unable to join them, but Daniel, never one to miss out on his accountant friend's awesome cooking, was there, in full flight, having been inspired by Melanie's idea of an art exhibition about child abuse. He had already spoken with someone he knew in Children First[13], one of Scotland's leading agencies for troubled and abused children, who thought it a wonderful cause for a special exhibition and offered to help in any way she could.

"There's something else," Felicity said, sheepishly, when she spotted a pause for a breather in Daniel's verbal outpourings. She looked pointedly at Maggie.

"Yes?" her aunt asked.

"I have to find my real father."

Silence filled the room. All eyes fixed on Felicity. Everyone seated at the table, apart from her, suddenly felt overwhelmed by guilt for not even thinking about the other consequences of what Felicity had been blankly told by that prisoner the previous day. It was Mary who made the first move. She stood up, came round to where Felicity sat staring ahead at nothing in particular, and put both her arms around the younger woman.

"Of course you do. And *I* will help you."

"See! Angels do exist," announced Daniel. "We have one right here in this very room. Married to the best chef in Edinburgh. A toast to Mary and Ade, everyone!"

The ice broken, glasses were raised.

---

[13] https:www.childrenfirst.org.uk

Lost Hands

"To Mary and Ade!" all, including a still tearful Felicity, exclaimed.

Later, back in their Airbnb, Felicity, clutching to her bosom a photocopy of the letter from her mother to her aunt, questioned Maggie about the murdered woman's mysterious lover, awareness of whom took almost fifteen years to see daylight. Maggie, always game for a puzzle, welcomed the challenge after berating herself for not, earlier, thinking about tracking down Felicity's true father. She had been too concerned about the threat of her brother-in-law escaping justice by claiming diminished responsibility because of her sister's affair.

Maggie's mind trawled through memories of happy teenage years when she and her younger sister, Elsie, would share opinions about boys from a nearby school over cupcakes and cups of coffee in a place, just off Princes Street, most Saturday mornings. She recalled her wee sister blush every time a certain shy, red-haired lad called Robbie was mentioned.

Apart from attending the same church, Robbie was a pupil at the boy's school which shared certain sports facilities and sixth form classes with the sisters' school. And at the end of every summer term, the two schools came together with an annual end-of-year dance. Maggie clearly remembered a particularly deep blush colouring her sister's face when she suggested Elsie should ask Robbie to accompany her to the dance when she was just fifteen. She could tell that Elsie wanted for this to happen more than anything in the world, but, like Robbie himself, was far too shy.

"I've seen the way he looks at you in church," Maggie

recalled telling Elsie. Finally the parents intervened, and Felicity's grandmother proposed to Robbie's mother, on a Sunday morning, following a church service, that it would be 'so nice if Robbie could take Elsie to the school dance.'

It happened, and something truly 'clicked' between the two teenagers, as Maggie's mum put it. They went out together at least once a week, and Elsie even proudly admitted, in secret whispers to Maggie, to having been snogged and kissed by Robbie 'till she wanted more'. But the 'more' never happened. Not back then. More than being besotted with Elsie, the red-haired boy almost worshipped her, but he was also respectful and studious, unlike most other boys that the two girls came across, and never 'tried it on'… the girls' terminology for attempts to lure them into having sex.

Over the summer holiday the following year, the young lovers went in different directions to divergent holiday destinations with their parents. After her return, Elsie seemed to avoid Robbie. When questioned about this, the younger sister would snap at Maggie, claiming it was, 'None of her business' and 'Why didn't she have a serious boyfriend herself at nearly eighteen?' Felicity's granny reckoned that Robbie had had a 'holiday romance with a local girl in Spain and was too embarrassed to talk about it with Elsie'. Sadly, Elsie and Robbie, as teenagers, never got back together again, and avoided each other at church, but somehow Maggie knew this was not want Elsie truly wished for. She had always known that there was a real depth to the love her sister felt for the shy. studious, musical redhead. Even years later, Elsie would still blush whenever the topic of 'first love' was brought up.

229

Lost Hands

"I think I know," Maggie said to her niece in that Airbnb in Edinburgh over a full Scottish breakfast the following morning.

"Know what?" asked Felicity whilst also What'sApping her husband, Ranjit, who was breakfasting alone in another part of Edinburgh.

"What are you talking about, darling?" asked the Indian doctor's serious face on Felicity's i-Phone.

"Know who the real father is," Maggie informed Felicity and Ranjit. "Wait here. Left my phone in our room. Have to make a call."

"Are you sure about suing the bastard?" Ranjit asked his wife after Maggie had left to fetch her own phone. "Won't it make things worse? Bring it all back? All that loveless pain. And we can't change the past."

"I need closure, Ranjit. Plus they're all so lovely here. And the minister's friend, Daniel, he's a real hoot. Never remembered *any*one in Scotland actually being funny during my childhood in Edinburgh, but..." Felicity paused.

"Your childhood was stolen from you. That's the problem. And I do understand. That it's not *just* about revenge, is it?"

"No. Justice. Whatever that means. Not revenge. God, if he ever gets let out of prison, I'm scared I'll kill him myself."

"You wouldn't. *Couldn't*, darling."

"I know, I know! I s'pose I'm still frightened of the bastard. Sitting across that table from him in prison was bad enough."

"It seems that Church of Scotland minister woman — "

"Mary Osondu!" interrupted Felicity. "She *does* have a

name!"

"Sorry, darling! Mary. Looks like she has lots of connections. And her lawyer friend seems pretty positive about you successfully suing him for what he did to you, from what Aunt Maggie says. And now she thinks she knows who your real father is. That's got to be good news."

"Suppose he's another Dracula!?" Felicity said.

"Well, you'll have that woman of God to help you out, then. With a wooden cross."

"Ranjit!"

"Sorry. Look, no way can he be anything like the guy banged up in prison. Not if your mum actually sort comfort from him to bring you into this world, you wonderful woman. Makes you 'special'. Which, for me, you most certainly are. Perhaps the man you always thought was your father kind of knew this. Knew you were special. *And* someone else's daughter. So he took it out on you. I dunno! I'm not a psychiatrist."

Felicity laughed.

"Thank goodness!" she said. "I'd never have married you if you were one of those." Aunt Maggie reappeared in the breakfast room, talking into her mobile. She looked up at Felicity with a broad grin, turning the phone around for Felicity to see Mary's smiling face before sitting down. Felicity waved at Mary, then turned her own phone around for Ranjit to do the same before switching it off.

Whilst two unfinished, full Scottish breakfasts grew cold on the table of the breakfast room of that little Airbnb in the west end of Edinburgh, Mary, Aunt Maggie and Felicity pondered over how a shy, red-haired, musical teenager from a murdered woman's past could be traced and, hopefully, contacted about, quite possibly, a daughter he never knew he had.

Chapter 34

"At last!" said Sean, holding Sally up close as they watched her befuddled husband being driven off, away from the fiord quayside, in a police vehicle, and waited for an ambulance to take them, together with the American woman who sat large and motionless on a quayside bench, to the Lakes District Hospital in Frankton near Queenstown. "Justice for Verity! Finally!" he continued. "I so wish you had known her. It was like she was my true mother when I was a child. Mum was just too bloody depressed most of the time."

"Why *did* you leave me that awful Monday morning?" asked Sally, still staring at the receding police vehicle. "No warning. Just buggered off to South America with your climbing buddy and not a word for nearly two years!"

"Can't go into it just now."

"I know there was something else going on. With you and your father. Before he got put away."

"All right, all right! I was scared he might blame *me* for what happened."

"Killing you mother?"

"Well... that. And other things. Look, we're gonna have to hang around here a while. Get my leg fixed. Again! With that very same extra-special nurse looking after me, right?"

Sally turned to look at Sean and smiled.

"Of course!"

"And absolutely no contact with Tony whilst he sorts out a new identity. Agreed?"

"Of course!"

"Ah! There's the ambulance. You can play at being a nurse again."

"What do you mean, 'play'?"

"Remember. I'm Wayne. From Melbourne. Like the guy who got killed. Mike."

"You never told me how you got into all those funny accents."

"Part of being a writer. Living the experiences of my characters, I s'pose."

"What happened about that book you were writing? The time travel one about an Inca princess or something that you told me about after you caught me unawares in bed with that creep of a husband of mine? Before we planned all of this." Sally emphasized the 'this' with a sweep of her hand.

"Still there. In my head. Most of it. Unwritten."

"And Joan? Did she really want to get rid of that interfering husband of hers?"

Sean looked meaningfully at Joan and nodded.

"Didn't plan to," he replied, "but more than pleased after it happened.

*****

"Tell me more about your so-called 'dog'," I say to Anita. I have stopped thinking of her as a lawyer. More as a friend. But I cannot believe anything other than recycled shit could come out of re-trial.

I really do want to know more about Anita, wonderful woman that she is, but cannot summon the courage to ask. I know she's widowed, but does she have children? Even grandchildren? What does she do in her spare time, if she has any? Seems to me I'm now getting a prison visit from her just about every other day. Not normally allowed, she tells me, but with her being my lawyer different rules apply.

She laughs when I ask her about her 'dog'. First genuine laugh I've heard for what seems half a lifetime, albeit less than six months since the trial and my conviction.

"You mean Kauri?" Anita confirms with me. "The man's name refers to the Māori word for the resin of a particular native New Zealand pine. Huge trees. Bigger than redwoods, I've heard. And kind of mystical. Plus the name also means all sorts of other things in the Māori language. Strong... wise..."

"Is he?"

"Who?"

"Your dog. Strong and wise."

"More than that. He's a miracle. He'll seek out the truth, I know it. Look, John, you've been used. I'm sure of it. Cheated. Don't know why, but believe me I'm going to see justice done and get you out of this godforsaken place."

Much as try not to, I start to cry and the woman I feel strangely drawn too, gets up and comes round to my side of the table between us, after giving the watchful prison warden a meaningful nod and a wink (after all, I did reassure him that his tummy symptoms he pestered me about the other day did not warrant investigation), encircles me with her arms, and pats me on the back. Why, I ask myself, do I find this so comforting?

*****

"I love it, Melanie," Daniel said, peering, over the shoulder of the minister's daughter, at the A3 sheet bearing a huge, scary drawing of a facially scarred Dracula. "What if you made the scar red, but kept the rest of your Dracula black & white? Might draw the punter's eye straight to the crux of what this is all about. Abuse during childhood leaves a permanent scar. Never goes away. I've been talking to David about people he's represented and suspected were abused as children. Nearly always covered up. Like scars. Makes him cautious when talking to folk about their problems at home. Domestic abuse cases are his specialty."

"Covered up! You can say that again! I s'pose some people might misunderstand him if he tries to poke around into their past."

"Oh... they do, they really do, my dear girl! But it's the old cliché, 'still waters run deep', with David, ay? Anyway, the scars never go away, he says, but seeing justice done for what that man did to his daughter might help the woman come to terms with her past."

"What they call 'closure', right? Do you think David really could get that Dracula creature banged up for good because of what he did to that poor woman, Felicity? When she was a child. I mean, Justina here easily felled him two years ago, aged sixteen, but what if she had been just a little child? I can't bear to think about it!"

No response from the Lithuanian girl who appeared totally absorbed in working on a design for the installation.

"If anyone can do it, that person is David," reassured Daniel.

"Getting the poster right is one thing, Daniel, but filling a whole exhibition space about childhood abuse... kind of scary!" Justina said.

"Think laterally, dear girl. Justina...?" Daniel turned his attention to the other girl who had done nothing but amaze him since becoming his youngest student ever at the tender age of sixteen. "You're the ideas girl. Can you give Melanie some ideas before we get all those lazy ECA students fired up?"

"I'd like to talk to them first," replied Justina. "I was never abused myself, but some of them might have been. And I would like to meet up with David's contact in Children First."

"Excellent, my dear!" exclaimed Daniel. "If I wasn't so gay, I'd give you a hug!"

Melanie giggled.

"And if *you* weren't gay, I'd ask you to take me to the college dance. The boys in my year here are all so boring!"

"Discerning, you are, Melanie! A most applaudable attribute. Yes, yes! A dark red scar. Thanks to your dearest of friends here, Justina. That's perfect!" Daniel glanced at his watch. "Now just look at the time. Must leave you girls to it. Got a boring lecture to give. How many points d'you think I should get if I have them all snoring within five minutes?"

"Definitely ten out of ten!" remarked Melanie, giggling again.

"Melanie, what *would* I have done without you and your mum after I escaped from that pharmacy two years ago?" asked Justina after Daniel had left the room.

"Justina, you would've made a go of it whatever happened. By the way, have you seen the way that lanky, English, third-year guy, Kevin or something, looks at you?"

Justina grinned at Melanie, but said nothing.

Chapter 35

"Legal aid?" queried Felicity. "Didn't even occur to me, what with Ranjit being on an NHS doctor's salary, and me a full-time physio."

"Well..." began David, leaning back with his hands clasped behind his head. "Where child abuse is concerned, things can be very different. Rules become fuzzy round the edges. And I've a friend in government who can bend a few ears. In the Ministry."

"Not Mary's type of ministry?" questioned Felicity, looking at the Black female minister hanging on every word of the discussion between the other woman and her husband's lawyer friend.

"Which reminds me," said Mary as David shook his head. "I got in touch with the present minister of the church that your mum and your aunt both went to as teenagers. He's kept up with the previous guy who's still alive and kicking, praise the Lord, but — "

"Wish he could kick that man who abused me for the whole of the first half my life," interrupted Felicity.

"Christians don't kick people, Felicity, but we are taught to help one another. Good news is that the old fellow is still alive. Bad news is he's had a stroke and lost his speech, though according to Sam Donaldson, the present minister, he still has all his marbles."

"Sounds a bit of a long shot to me if we're trying to track down that red-haired Robbie boy," said Felicity. "No longer a boy," she added thoughtfully.

"Maybe not so long. Maggie texted me whilst shopping,

just before you arrived. She remembered red-haired Robbie was deeply into music. *Classical* music. Anyway, Sam promised to get back to me about meeting up with the old minister. D'you have any old photos of your mother, Felicity?"

"No. Took absolutely nothing with me when I escaped down to London back then. But I know Aunt Maggie has. Brought an old album with her up to Scotland. 'Just in case', she said. We looked at the photos together on the way up to Scotland in the train."

*****

Sally sat by herself in the waiting room area of the Lakes District Hospital whilst Joan and Sean were checking out. Joan, having suffered a head injury, was to be kept in overnight whilst Sean, the laceration on his leg stitched up with no hint of a fracture showing on the X-ray, was discharged. A divorced, close female friend of the still-alive-dead-pilot, who was in with them from the beginning, had promised to put them up in a spare room, for they knew they would have to 'stay around awhile', being key witnesses to the alleged murder. Joan, meanwhile, was to give a statement to the police before heading back to Wisconsin to begin a new life without the burden of a husband she had grown to hate.

Later, seated on the bed of their temporary accommodation in Queenstown, with her lover's arm around her, Sally called her line manager at the Royal Infirmary in Edinburgh to explain the situation.

"How awful!" exclaimed the voice in the phone. "No way! Mr McEuen arrested for murder? I simply cannot believe it. Is this some kind of a sick joke, Sally?"

Lost Hands

"Wish it was. He might get let off if they can prove it happened because of a head injury sustained during the crash. But the way it looks... he kind of lost it. Blaming the poor pilot. Engine failure, they reckon. An old prop plane. We tried to stop him, but couldn't get to the scene in time. Dense rainforest, you see. All that moss everywhere. So slippery. And the other two were too badly injured. Total nightmare. Tried to resuscitate the pilot after we pulled John off, but he was a goner."

Sean, his arm still encircling the imprisoned man's wife, raised his eyebrows and grinned.

"Thing is, we'll have to hang around here a while as material witnesses. Pretty certain it'll come to trial, the police say. But that could be months. Lawyers want us to stay on in New Zealand if at all possible. Such a serious case, they say."

"Oh my God!" announced the phone. "I'll let the Medical Director know about Mr McEuen. But Sally, will you be all right? Only just married to a man accused of murder? On the other side of the world!?"

"They're all being so very kind," answered Sally as Sean started to unbutton her blouse and fondle her breasts. She could hardly wait to get off the phone and let him make love to her again just as he used to back home in Edinburgh. It had been far too long, and no longer would she have to imagine that, with eyes tightly closed, John was Sean. "Look, I have to go now. Give the police a full statement. They say he's going to need a really good defence lawyer."

"Sally, don't you worry about things back here. We'll find locums. For both of you. Let's just hope he gets let off. Head injury, like you say. Probably had no idea what he was

240

doing. If John needs any sort of a character reference, let us know. I'm sure the Medical Director would agree to provide one. Oh dear, I still cannot believe it. Not John, of *all* people! Such a gifted surgeon."

Finally, the call over, Sally let go of her phone, which fell from the bed to the floor, as she and Sean, now both fully undressed, frantically made love again for the first time in nearly two years, limbs entangled, hands exploring every sweet corner of nakedness, before coming together in a passionate, noisy climax. Sally's crying out would have surely been audible all the way to Milford Sound. Meanwhile, John lay huddled, silent and alone in a prison cell, hands hidden between his legs, trying hard to remember, in detail, what actually happened on that mountain top above the paradise fiord of Milford Sound.

*****

Justina confessed that she had *more* than 'noticed' that lanky, English, third-year student.

"Not all boys are sex-mad pervs," said Melanie. "Talk to him. Better still, see if he can help us plan the installation. Say you've seen his work and like it. Think he could add something. Whatever, just come up with something. Being Lithuanian could be plus. Tell him all about Aleksandra Kasuba."

"I don't want to bore him."

"You, Justina Banis, could not bore anyone even if you tried."

"I'll get Daniel to do it," responded Justina with a smile. "Ask Kevin to get in touch with me."

"Daniel the matchmaker, ay? He'll love it. As long as he doesn't fancy Kevin for himself."

Lost Hands

"No way! He'd never be unfaithful to David. Anyway, Kevin's a straight as a Roman road. I can tell. And what about *you*, Melanie? You'll have to get over the disappointment you had after that holiday romance in Madeira last year one day. He was just a fun-loving, sex-mad bastard. Like all Americans. Forget him."

"I will." Melanie looked thoughtful. "I have!" she stressed. "Only I don't know who to trust, now."

"Well, you can trust me. And, most certainly, Daniel."

"Talk of the devil," said Melanie as Daniel re-entered the studio.

"The devil?" queried Daniel endowed with super-sharp hearing. "Am I really that famous!?"

Melanie laughed.

"We need you to fix Justina up with a date."

"Not easy for a hardened queer like me, my dears," Daniel said. "How are you both getting on?"

"That's just it," said Melanie. "Justina needs help from a third year boy called Kevin."

"Yes. I know who you're talking about. Good eye for colour, that one. Into photography, too."

"Can you, erm — ?" the Black girl began, looking at her friend who, smiling, pretended to be absorbed in making notes about the exhibition.

"Delighted to," interrupted Daniel. "Light the blue touch paper and see what happens, ay? It's about time we had a bit of romance in this institution. Brighten things up, it will."

Justina merely continued to smile without saying a word.

Chapter 36

Anita came off the phone after a long conversation with her private detective friend, Andy Rongo. The 'dog', as he insisted calling his full-blooded Māori 'assistant investigator', Kauri, had not only recorded evidence of the murdered pilot being alive and well in Wellington, but also many cozy meetings between him and the imprisoned surgeon's young Scottish nurse bride, always together with the fake Ozzie who was obviously her lover. The advantage of being Māori, Andy always said, being himself half Māori, was that he could melt, unobserved, into the background and collect all the information his senior partner might need to strengthen their case.

For the first time since the sudden death of her husband, Jimmy, just over a year back, Anita felt curiously uplifted as she headed in her car for Queenstown Police Station. There, she demanded an immediate meeting with Detective Inspector Tang, the senior police officer who had been involved with the arrest and detention of the Scottish surgeon accused of murdering the Wilderness Paradise Air Tours pilot following a plane crash on a mountain beside Milford Sound.

"I'm sorry. He's in a meeting right now. Please give me your— "

Anita had had enough of police incompetence. Already, her respected client had suffered months of unjust imprisonment for a crime that was never committed. Before the young woman manning the desk could complete her sentence, Anita came out with…

Lost Hands

"This *will* get out there. Into the national press. International even, my client being Scottish. But I just thought Kenneth would like to be told first. That he put away an innocent man for a murder that didn't happen. Tell him I'll remember to wave to him when he's back on traffic duty. I can— "

"Just a minute," interrupted the woman. "I'm sure he won't mind leaving the meeting for a short while."

"Not too short," advised Anita. "I'm a lawyer, by the way."

"Yes... I... erm... I recognize your face."

"Anita Mulholland. Defence lawyer. Be quick," stressed Anita. "I've an appointment with our Southland MP within the hour. He'll want to know all about this miscarriage of justice. At least I can be sure that *he* will listen to me."

"Please. Wait here. DI Tang will be with you very soon."

"Too right, he will!" responded Anita.

And he was. Anita had only just counted to ten inside her head before the detective inspector, the fabled three stars decorating his epaulettes, appeared and quickly ushered Anita into his office along a corridor. He had not been given the whole story by the woman at the desk, but enough to allow sheer terror to alter his face. The senior police officer, known for that almost-permanent mysterious oriental smile that invariably unnerved anyone being interrogated by him, now had a look of imminent death imprinted on his face.

"Please... take a seat," he said, nervously, to Anita. "The McEuen case, I believe. You have something to tell me."

Still standing, Anita let rip.

"Too bloody right, I have. For a start, the guy he's

244

supposed to have murdered, according to you lot, is alive and well, and living, of all places, in Wellington. Is that funny or is it funny?" she blurted, red with rage.

"Wait. *Please* sit down, Mrs Mulholland. I remember the case well. Three witnesses saw it happen. Saw him strangle the pilot before they could stop him. They dragged the body down to the water, but whilst they awaited the arrival of a boat, with the Ozzie fellow being badly injured and the American lady suffering from a head injury, the surgeon overpowered his wife and pushed the then stone-weighted body into the Sound. Over five hundred metres deep in places, the Sound. And there was a strong current that day, if I remember. Plus there was no forensic evidence of his remains at the plane crash site."

"And John-the-surgeon's wife never once visited him in prison. Is that odd or is it odd?"

"Wait... what are you trying to tell me?"

"Not just trying. I *am* telling you that Tony Wood, the pilot, is alive, and goes by the name of Dean Tony Shaw. Dean was his father's name, Shaw his mother's family name. But more importantly, the surgeon's wife and the other man at the scene, one of your so-called 'witnesses', who says he's Ozzie but isn't, they're lovers. And shacked up in Wellington."

"I remember her. A pretty woman. A nurse, I believe, from the same hospital as your, erm—"

"As my imprisoned, innocent client. Yes!"

"Look, Mrs Mulholland, I'm sure there is no need for you to, erm... tell the, erm..." The DI paused, clearly fearful of even mentioning the word... 'press.'

"Oh yes there is! How else are we going to get justice

for my client."

"We could apply to reopen the case. Get the police in Wellington to look into this claim of yours. I know the— "

Before he could say the word 'superintendent', Anita butted in.

"*I* know the truth," she barked. "It *will* come out. But it might go down better with the public, who perhaps have a better respect for truth than our local police force here in Southland, if you were to get my client released immediately."

"Please... do sit down, Mrs Mulholland."

"*You* can sit if you feel a bit faint... understandably," Anita said, "but I wish to remain standing."

Which she did as the detective inspector sank, like a discarded dummy, into his chair behind the desk. Anita glanced at her watch. "I'll take my leave now, unless you have any further questions for me. Mustn't keep our MP waiting. I'll give you forty-eight hours. If my client isn't released without bail pending your so-called further investigations, you can read all about it. Splashed across the front pages of the New Zealand Chronicle, the New Zealand Herald, Daily Southern Cross, The Post, of course, in Wellington... oh, and I promised Mr McEuen to get in touch with The Scotsman newspaper in Edinburgh. Plus, of course, the BBC. Get worldwide coverage in the English-speaking world, they do."

She took a memory stick from her bag and held it up in front of the dazed detective inspector.

"I will leave this with the girl at the desk. Has all the necessary video recordings on it. Get your forensic boys and girls to check it's not AI if you must, but they'll need to get their skates on." She turned to leave the office, opened the door, then halted. Without looking back at the DI, she said so loudly that people seated in the waiting are at the end of the corridor could hear every word.

"Please remember that as a higher income tax payer a fair amount of my earnings goes towards paying your salary, Detective Inspector Tang. The press will want to be able to reassure readers that this is money well spent!"

Open-mouthed, those seated whilst awaiting police attention for whatever personal reason, watched the imperious-looking lawyer, her head held high, leave the police station. She drove, just within the ever-changing speed limits, to reach the MP's office in the nick of time. Her prepared verbal delivery could not have been more different to the angry outburst aimed at the detective inspector. In it, she praised the performance of the MP's political party, and humbly beseeched him to forgive her for taking up his 'precious time', but she told him that she would have felt guilty if she had not informed the man of a 'matter of the utmost importance for voters in his *rohe pōti'*, deliberately using the Māori word for 'electorate' knowing that the guy was a keen supporter of Māori rights.

*****

The day after Anita said she was going to the police about Kauri's revelation, mid-afternoon, one of the wardens beckons to me, whilst I'm walking round and around, in the exercise yard, together with other prisoners, before taking me to the prison governor's office. Being in a foreign country, albeit English-speaking, I fear the worst. Solitary confinement? Has the New Zealand government suddenly re-introduced the death penalty for murder?

247

Lost Hands

"Sit down, Mr McEuen," he says.

Mister? Is he playing games with me?

A chair, opposite the governor and pulled away from the man's desk, and ready for me, is indicated by a generous sweep of his hand. Not quite knowing what to do with my own hands, I sit down and look at him.

Why is he smiling like that? A crocodile smile before sending me to my death, perhaps?

"You're free to go. I believe your lawyer is already waiting outside the prison. In her car. It's a white Toyota Yaris."

I look at my hands. They're still there, unchanged with unclipped nails, so I cannot have suddenly died and woken up in another dimension, I tell myself.

"Your belongings are in that bag over there. You're phone as well. All charged."

I turn and stare at a large hold-all that he indicates with another wave of the hand.

"What...?" I begin.

"A call from the Minister of Corrections. Just after lunch. All charges against you are dropped, and he offers sincere apologies on behalf of his government for any inconvenience you might have suffered whilst remaining in detention in our facility here."

"Facility?" I ask. "Is that what you call it?"

I want to tell him that the food in his so-called 'facility' is crap, and the bed like a bloody tombstone slab, but do not wish to try my luck. In fact, I suddenly have a desire to get up, grab the bag and run from the building, still in prison uniform. Instead, in the toilet, I change into the clothes I wore when driven away in a police car from the

248

Lost Hands

Milford Sound quayside all those months ago, pick up the phone and, whilst seated on the toilet, dial Sally's number...

'The number you dialled is unavailable' says a soft, female Kiwi voice lurking inside my phone.

Phone in hand, I leave the bag behind, in the toilet, because some other poor sod might find a use for it, 'sign myself out', so to speak, and emerge from hell to enter the sunlit paradise of South Island, New Zealand. Sally's choice for our honeymoon. And now I know why.

I spot a white Toyota Yaris. The driver's door opens. Anita gets out and just stands there, arms wide. I walk into those arms, tears streaming. She, too, is crying. How odd... a woman recently widowed and me cuckolded on my honeymoon and having wrongfully done time in jail for a crime that never happened... here we are like a pair of long-lost lovers.

She wipes her tears, ushers me into the front passenger seat, even buckles my seat belt for me, gets in beside me and starts the engine, and so far not a word has been exchanged between us. I guess that sometimes words are unnecessary. Whatever, it's not until we've been driving a good few miles, it occurs to me that I should thank my lawyer.

"Thank you," I say.

"It's the dog you need to thank," insists Anita, glancing sideways with a grin that seems to kick those months of incarceration into a past that can never happen again.

"Look forward to meeting him," I say before we drive on to a spacious house on the outskirts of Queenstown where a recently widowed defence lawyer and her recently released prisoner client, who happens to be a surgeon, might become something very different. Friends, perhaps? More than... even?

Anita shows me to a spare room where, already, she has laid out my clothes, and other personal items released by the police, on the bed. For a while, I sit there alone and think about what I once thought were the best nine months of my life to date... courting Sally, her saying 'Yes' when asked if she would marry me, the shot-gun wedding ceremony and reception and the flight to New Zealand for a honeymoon in paradise. Was it all a sham? The apparent pleasure of our lovemaking faked?

Later, I join Anita in the sitting room where she's watching the news on television. Were those thoughts flashing through my mind, a few minutes earlier, telepathic, for on the television screen was coverage of the arrest of Sally and that non-Ozzie, Wayne, plus the 'dead' pilot, Tony Wood? I stand there in horror as I see myself appear, full screen, my name, 'John McEuen', underneath a passport head and shoulders image of me, the broadcaster talking about my arrest and my imprisonment following a wrongful conviction for murdering the Wilderness Paradise Air Tours pilot, Tony Wood, after a plane crash in the rainforest.

"Ahem!" I exclaim.

Anita turns to acknowledge me with a smile and pats the empty space, beside her, on the sofa. I fill it, staring at my hands rather than the television. The broadcaster referred to me as a 'Scottish surgeon'. For almost an entire year, those hands have been useless to humanity. Not made a single incision, explored an open abdomen for some life-threatening mischief, carefully repaired any damage they inflicted in the process before carefully cleaning and stitching up the iatrogenic[14] wound.

Another hand comes into view. A mature, confident female hand, placed on top of my own 'lost' hands.

---

[14] Created by a doctor for a medical purpose

Chapter 37

Sally was awoken by a series of loud bangs on the front door. Sean, still semi-comatose after downing almost half a bottle of whisky the evening before, rolled over and mumbled something incomprehensible. Sally, still naked after a 'nightful' of lovemaking, got out of bed, slipped on a dressing gown and headed for the door.

"All right, all right," she muttered. "Keep your bloody hair on!"

She opened the door only to be rudely pushed aside by an armed officer who, with his semi-automatic sticking out like a phallus from hell, hurried into the room from which emanated swearing of Sean's annoyance. Another of the three police officers, in black and female, grabbed her arm, swivelled her around and, with Sally's hands behind her back, snapped on a pair of cuffs.

"Sally McEuen, I am arresting you for falsely claiming you witnessed your husband, Dr John McEuen, murder the Wilderness Paradise Air Tours pilot, Tony James Wood on the eighteenth of August, twenty twenty-four. You do not have to say anything, but anything you do say may be written down and used in evidence..."

"I feel sick," interrupted Sally, before promptly vomiting up the previous night's fish-topped pizza over the officer's feet.

She was escorted to the bedroom where Sean, also now only wearing a dressing gown, had already been handcuffed by the third officer. The guy with the semi-automatic brushed past Sally to search the rest of the apartment whilst

Lost Hands

Sally and Sean, in the presence of police officers, were briefly uncuffed and told to get dressed before being escorted, re-cuffed, to a waiting police vehicle outside their apartment block. Bemused faces appeared at several windows, their owners clearly having wondered what all the noise was about so early in the morning.

"We already have Tony Wood in custody," Sally and Sean were both informed, separately. "He's made a full confession. As has Joan Mannetti in Wisconsin in the United States of America. You have the right to call your lawyer."

Seated on either side of the female police officer, the cuffed lovers were driven to Wellington Central Police Station, formally charged and locked up in separate cells to await the arrival of a lawyer. The same one who had known all along that Tony Wood was alive and well after Sally's husband had been found guilty of his murder.

*****

After lunch, Melanie and Justina were back in the studio, sharing ideas for the forthcoming installation project, when the door opened and an anxious voice called out...

"Justina Banis?"

The two girls turned to look at the third-year student standing in the doorway.

"Kevin?" the Lithuanian girl said, softly.

Kevin nodded. Melanie hid a smile and continued to draw on the A3 sheet spread out on the bench whilst her friend was more than keen to enlist the help of the third-year student with their project. Soon, it seemed as though Justina and Kevin had been really close for years, and Melanie could not stop smiling at the fortune of her best friend.

It turned out, later, that Kevin, who suffered from a slight-though-noticeable stammer, had also been bullied at school, and, like Justina and Melanie, took refuge in exploring life, and the world in general, through art. Daniel proved to be right about the young man for, with Kevin's help, the project really took off.

Daniel identified several first-year students who were able to contribute meaningfully. Sooner than expected by the professor, designs for an installation, which would both inspire and shock the world, were ready to be put into action. A representative from Children First applauded their efforts and promised to help with the publicity.

*****

"I had a phone call from my dear friend, Calum. Detective Inspector Scott to others," said Mary.

She was seated opposite Maggie and Felicity in a coffee bar in St James' Centre where they had agreed to meet up whilst the two women from London used a free morning as an excuse to go shopping.

"And?" asked Maggie, reading from the look in the minister's bright, friendly eyes that she had something of major importance to tell them.

"Got the go ahead. At last."

"Go ahead?" queried Maggie.

"To sue the pharmacist for what he did to you, Felicity," Mary replied, looking intently at the younger woman.

Felicity appeared uncertain as to how she should respond. Following the revelation in Saughton Prison, initial anger had been displaced by so many conflicting emotions it seemed her mind had been turned into a whirlpool of jumbled thoughts.

"This has to be good news, Felicity," the woman's aunt insisted, placing a comforting hand on her niece's arm.

"There's more," said Mary. "A *lot* more."

"Tell us," urged Maggie, smiling whilst Felicity remained still and silent and staring at an un-drunk cup of coffee.

"I always knew that Calum, my detective friend, was up to something big. Could tell from the way he closed the hatches, so to speak, whenever I tried to get him to open up. Somehow, I knew that the pharmacist in prison was only a tiny part of the whole story."

"Not tiny for me," interjected Felicity without looking up. "Ruined my whole childhood and killed my poor mother."

"I'm sorry, Felicity. I wasn't trying to downplay what he did to you. That was one of the most awful things I've encountered during all my years of ministry to date. No, the point is why didn't the police take action for what he did to you and all those other women and girls after they broke into that flat in Muirhouse and arrested the Russian woman and her accomplices? I just knew there was more to it. Calum had to maintain confidentiality... secrecy... whilst dealing with an OCG — "

"OCG?" interrupted Felicity.

"Organised criminal gang. In this case, not just nationwide, but international. He's been working closely with the Met down in London, together with other forces across the UK and in Europe. Particularly a senior officer in Vilnius. Vyresnysis Komisaras Budris." Mary chuckles. "Calum says he can't get his lips around the name, so calls him 'Buddy'. Ever since Justina's art teacher in Lithuania was murdered, they've been tirelessly working together to break into the OCG responsible. Now they have insider intelligence in several countries. It's vast. A multibillion-dollar enterprise. So you can see what I mean, Felicity, when I say that awful man who beat you for his and others' pleasure was just a tiny part of it."

Felicity nodded her understanding of what she had been told, albeit without much conviction.

"I understand, now, why Calum's kept the whole affair so close to his chest. This OCG goes to the very top," the minister said.

"Top?" queried Felicity, looking up at Mary.

*****

Sean sat sullenly across the desk from a steel-jawed DI and his sexless sergeant who might just have passed for a woman, in the Scot's eyes, if dressed in a skirt and top.

"So you're clearly not Australian as you claimed before Dr McEuen's trial, and you're not Wayne Minto either. Tell me, clearly, who the hell you are."

"Sean Taylor," came the reluctant reply.

"Son of James Taylor currently serving life in Edinburgh Prison, Scotland, for the murder of your mother. Am I right?"

Sean nodded.

"For the sake of the recording, please answer my question. Are you Sean Taylor?"

"Yes. I am."

"And did you conspire with Anthony Wood, also known as Dean Shaw, to deceive the South Island police into believing you had witnessed him being strangled to death by the husband of Sally McEuen, and disposed of in Milford Sound, before you could stop him, because of injuries you sustained during a plane crash that was planned by yourself, Mr Wood and Mrs Sally McEuen?"

Sean glanced at the useless defence lawyer seated beside him. 'Useless' because everyone present knew that there *was* no defence, nor any mitigating circumstance that might reduce his sentence at the trial.

"No comment," answered Sean, acutely aware that his father doing time on the other side of the world would not go down well with the jury.

Later, the same fierce DI and featureless female DS confronted Sally with the same question, with the name 'Sally McEuen' replacing that of 'Sean Taylor'. The same defence lawyer advised her, in a sideways whisper, to say, "No comment" when, sobbing uncontrollably, she had failed to reply after a period of several minutes. She had wanted to say, instead, how her bastard of a husband had killed her lover's elder sister, Verity, when Sean was still a child, and how this had affected him in every walk of life since then, and that all they had wanted was justice for Verity since the judicial system in Scotland had failed Sean and his father. So far, no mention had been made of the latter being in prison in Edinburgh for murdering his wife, and Sally was thankful for this for she still remained convinced, in her own mind, that the pharmacist was merely carrying out the woman's own wish... to end a life destroyed by Verity's death as painlessly as possible by using pills from his pharmacy.

'Pills prescribed by God?'

Sally, of course, was not at all religious. Nor was she

privy to the other side of the story. One that involved Sean's mother making contact again, nine months before his little sister Felicity was born, with the only true love of her miserable life: a man who was once a shy, red-haired boy passionately keen on classical music.

Chapter 38

Mary's Church of Scotland minister friend, Sam Guthrie, picked up her, Maggie and Felicity, from the manse, after Sunday morning service, and drove them to a suburban house in the south of the city to meet the old minister, Miles Macauley, of the very same church that Maggie and Elsie had attended as children and teenagers. A friendly, Black nurse carer opened the door. From her accent, Mary knew at once that she wasn't Nigerian, soon learning that she was from Zimbabwe, having fled to the UK with her doctor husband to escape persecution by Robert Mugabe.

"Marisa, his fulltime carer, has been a godsend for poor Miles since his stroke," Sam explained as they were led to the sitting room where the old minister was ensconced in an armchair by the window.

"Thank you," responded the nurse. "Coffee?"

The three other women shook heads in unison.

"No thanks," Sam replied for them. "But we will need your help talking to Miles."

The old minister raised his eyebrows and lifted his left hand by way of agreement with the man who took over his ministry. Chairs were placed, by the nurse, in a semi-circle around Miles before all sat down, Marisa beside the old man, intently watching his distorted face as he listened to Sam's explanation for their visit: to find out what happened to a musical, red-haired boy from the past who, quite possibly, might be the father of the younger woman he had brought along with him.

Lost Hands

"These ladies are the sister and the daughter of a girl in your parish who went out with this boy for a while," explained the nurse for the old minister's benefit.

"An Elsie Taylor," added Sam.

The half-smile that appeared on the old minister's watchful face indicated that he immediately knew of whom Marisa was speaking. With a half-grin on his wrinkled face, he raised his left hand and moved the arm about in a rhythmic sideways sawing motion.

"What's he doing?" asked Felicity with a puzzled frown.

"A violin," explained Marisa. "He's making as if playing a violin."

The half-smile returned on the hemiplegic man's face, together with a left-handed thumbs-up.

"A violinist! The boy was a violinist," confirmed Maggie. "I *remember* now! Elsie told me. *And* his full name. It was Robbie Lombardi. Half-Italian."

This time, the old minister added a series of head nods to his lopsided-grinned affirmation.

"He's really as bright as button," Marisa said. "Are you sure you won't have a coffee? He would love to know more about you three ladies. Plus the reason for wanting to know about the red-haired boy with the violin."

Mary agreed to coffee for all of them. Sam included. Not only so that Maggie and Felicity might learn more about the subject of a murdered woman's teenage love, but for Mary to share her past life in Nigeria with a fellow African woman. Soon, over coffee, periodically with help from Marisa, the three ministers shared church experiences, past and present, together with Maggie, whilst the two African women talked about their love and sadness for home countries in a continent that seemed to be changing faster than anywhere else in the world. Meanwhile, Felicity shut herself off from the discussions going on and carried out a Google search for her presumed father on her i-Phone…

'Robert Lombardi… professional violinist… trained under… bla-bla-bla… at the Glasgow Conservatoire… won such and such an award at… and at… and at…'

Felicity sat wide-eyed as she learned about a world-famous classical violinist she had never even heard of until her aunt blurted out his name following the old minister's attempt to mimic violin playing with his one free hand. Could this amazing man truly be her father?

She read on. Updates about the violinist. Surely not!? He was to give a concert in the Usher Hall, Edinburgh, the following week. The 'Bach solo violin sonatas and partitas' followed by the 'Bruch violin concerto in G Minor'. Felicity had just about heard of Bach, and she felt so stupid to be ignorant about classical music should this man turn out to be her true father. She interrupted her aunt's discussion with the three ministers by showing her a recent image of the world-famous violinist, his hair still showing a tinge of red flecked, mostly, with white.

"Is this the red-haired boy Mum fell in love with?" she asked. Maggie nodded, then hugged her niece when the younger woman burst into tears. "At long last you'll get to know your true father."

Conversation between the ministers stopped. All, including Marisa, looked with sympathy at Felicity being comforted by her aunt.

"It might not even be him," sobbed Felicity.

Lost Hands

"Oh, it will be," Maggie reassured. "I'm certain of it. I knew your mother well enough to read her mind. Plus the violin thing reminded me. Something she said over the phone the week before... you know."

"Him?" questioned Felicity. "That horrid man!? Before he killed her."

"If only she had learned to 'fiddle', your mum said. I thought she meant the other sort of fiddle. To swindle my brother-in-law about something. Money to escape from him, perhaps. And she was in such a state, I seriously wondered whether she knew what she was even saying. But I think she was referring to Robbie, her teenage boyfriend, and his passion for the violin. What if the thing between him and that girl in Spain was just about music, nothing more? Perhaps your mother got it all wrong back then when they were teenagers, and it came out if ... or when ... they met up again."

"I'm going to book tickets for his concert on-line," said Felicity. "Here and now. For you and me, Aunty. Somehow I must get to see him backstage. I'll demand to see him," she insisted.

"I wish I could bring Miles, too," said Marisa, "but not in a wheel chair. We both love classical music. Have the radio tuned into the BBC Third Programme most of the day!"

Felicity booked tickets online for a concert the thought of which filled every waking moment of her time in Edinburgh. They proved very understanding, in the hospital where she worked, after Ranjit, one of their most popular doctors and now back down in London, had, in person, explained the situation to her superior.

Lost Hands
***

"Will they let me see Sally?" I ask Anita.

"I think not," she replies. "Could be seen as interfering with the legal process. You, John, are now a witness for *her* prosecution for misleading the police. Giving false evidence under oath. I'm afraid this is going to be huge. Never known a case like it."

I want to say that I've never known another woman like Sally, but as I sit and see, on the television screen, the story of my last nine months played out, including footage of the jail where I was incarcerated because of what Sally and her accomplices did, I realise I've never even known my wife. Her pretty face displayed for all to see, on the screen, is now that of a total stranger, not the beautiful scrub nurse I fell for as she handed me surgical instruments over the anaesthetized bodies of countless patients in desperate need of my experienced surgeon's hands.

Chapter 39

Kevin's input with the 'troubled children art project' proved invaluable. His real passion being photography, he used his skills to create images that even astounded Daniel.

"That young man will go far," the prof whispered to Justina when Kevin was out of earshot, having gone to fetch yet another portfolio of photos, some of which, he thought, might be of use for the installation. "Make sure he takes you with him, Justina."

"We've only just met," replied the Lithuanian girl, trying hard not to smile too broadly.

"I believe I said the same thing about David first time we got together. Same sort of smile as you have, I had. Look, do not let your past come between you. You could help him. You're a strong girl. That boy is brilliant, but has no confidence at all. With you, he might open up. Blossom, so to speak."

"I know," Justina said, glancing up at Kevin as he returned to join them.

"I agree," said Melissa, also looking at the young photographer.

"Agree what?" asked Kevin before placing his portfolio on the table in front of Justina.

"You and Justina. Made for each other," announced Daniel.

Kevin said nothing but turned rather red as he showed the girls a collection of images of children he had put together after hearing about their project. The images themselves confirmed for Justina what Melanie had just

Lost Hands

declared. That she and Kevin were made for each other. Before the week was out, they had slept together. Plus the project now seemed to have a momentum of its own. Like Kevin in the presence of Justina, it blossomed. Kevin's hauntingly harassing yet beautifully powerful images were perfect for publicity material, and were to be used as a 'lead-in' for the installation. Justina's proud mother, flown in from Vilnius, for the summer, immediately took to the young man when he accompanied her daughter to pick her up from Edinburgh Airport.

*****

Sally was released on bail, but had to remain in the country. Her demented mother in Edinburgh was now in a care home and appeared to have no idea who she was when Sally, tearfully, spoke to her on WhatsApp. Sally had never before felt so alone, so desperate, and simply yearned to be with Sean again. For reasons she could not understand, *he* was not let out on bail. Something to do with his father and a court case against him coming up back in Scotland. Why, she wanted to know, should this have anything to do with her lover? The lawyer acting for her, about the only person she now spoke to in that paradise-turned-hell, made no sense of it. Nor could *he* understand Sean's repeated claim that John, her husband, had killed his elder sister.

"That is *not* what happened from information I received," the lawyer, a certain Mr Blake, told her. "The girl was in septic shock from a ruptured appendix. Far too late, though your husband, John McEuen, a much-respected general surgeon, apparently did everything he possibly could to save her life. And I understand something else has come to light. The prosecution are claiming that the girl's

265

father was, in some way, responsible."

'Sean's father? That as well? How could <u>he</u> possibly be responsible for her appendicitis? They've all gone mad!'

Sally only knew when it was too late that it was John who had been the young surgeon operating on Sean's sister and who had been taken to court by Sean's pharmacist father for medical negligence that, according to him, was responsible for her death. The man's claim that Felicity, too, was complicit by causing the appendicitis because of her 'bad behaviour', requiring frequent 'correction' by her father, did, to Sally, seem rather far-fetched, but she just went along with everything Sean said. Because she loved him. As much as she, then, hated her husband-to-be. To destroy him in paradise had seemed the perfect way for her to reclaim her true love... Sean Taylor.

*****

Felicity spent most of the time every day, before the concert in the Usher Hall, reading review after review about the world-famous violinist, Robert Lombardi, and she also bought a set of headphones so that her aunt would not be forced to listen to numerous YouTube recordings. Sometimes, with tears in her eyes, she would remove the headphones and hand these to her sleepy aunt.

"Have you ever heard anything so beautiful before?" she asked Maggie, referring to the slow movement of the Beethoven Violin Concerto in D major. "Listen. And just look at the expressions on his face. I just wish Ranjit could come up to Scotland to join us for the concert."

"Why can't he? Isn't he off again next weekend?"

Knowing Ranjit had another weekend off, Felicity's face lit up. After watching her aunt's face respond to the magic of Beethoven brought back to life by a man who was quite possibly the father she had never known, and who probably knew nothing about her, she agreed. First, she booked another ticket online for the Bach and Bruch concert, one of the few remaining unsold seats, before messaging Ranjit. Being in the middle of a clinic, his immediate and simple reply of a 'thumbs-up' emoji did not surprise Aunt Maggie. She had always known, since that memorable moment when, after returning from work, she found her tearful fourteen-year-old niece sitting on her doorstep with nothing but a handbag and a mobile phone, that Felicity had a strength and determination unlike that of anyone else in the family. Seeing, with her niece, that world-famous violinist on YouTube, she now knew where the girl got it from. Certainly not from her sister.

In the days leading up to the concert, Felicity and her aunt ate at the manse every evening. Daniel and David always joined them, and with Melanie too busy with the installation project to help her father in the kitchen, Ade had to pull out all the stops to produce meal after delicious meal reflecting cuisine from across the world as expressed in the installation that won Justina a place at Edinburgh Art College after she came under the protection of his beloved wife, Mary. Ranjit also showed up again on the Saturday afternoon, well before the concert, so, unsurprisingly, Ade felt encouraged, that day, to point his culinary skills in the direction of India.

After an early pre-concert dinner, Felicity's husband could not stop complimenting his host on, quite probably, the best curry he had had in years. Mary gave Felicity a long and warm hug before Ade drove her, her husband and her aunt into the centre of town to drop them off near the Usher Hall well in time for the concert. Felicity wanted to see the celebrated violinist straightaway, before the concert, but both Ranjit and Maggie dissuaded her. How, Maggie asked her niece, might this affect the poor man's performance during the concert? No! On her insistence, instead, a hand-written note was produced and kept hidden in Maggie's bag with a request for it to be handed to the soloist during the interval. Felicity kept her fingers crossed that the great man, once a shy, young, red-haired boyfriend of her mother, might, with his violin, not only connect her with the God whom Mary preached about in her Sunday morning sermons, but also agree to see her.

*****

"I telephoned the Royal Infirmary in Edinburgh, John. They put me through to your Medical Director. He wants to speak with you."

Anita, phone in hand, stands in the doorway of the spare room where I spent a restless night wondering what on Earth will become of me if Sally is to be tried and convicted for what she and a man, who wasn't who he said he was, did to me after that little prop-plane ended up in flames on a remote rainforest mountain. Somehow, my release from prison has fanned, in my confused brain, fears for my future. What the heck will I do? Stay on in New Zealand and find a new life, new profession, or look for my lost hands by returning to Scotland, and use these to save lives all over again?

I sit up, take the phone from Anita who makes as if to leave, but I beckon for her to remain in the room as I speak with my Medical Director back home.

Lost Hands

"John, it is so good to actually talk to you at last. We knew something was wrong when we heard about what happened. And about the trial. We held off getting a replacement for you when I was contacted by your lawyer after the trial."

I look at Anita.

"She's an amazing woman," he says.

"Yes, she is," I confirm.

"So your job's still here. Waiting for you. I should add, your agency locum leaves a lot to be desired. Lots of requests for second opinions, if you get my meaning. Like one of your colleagues said the other day, you're irreplaceable, John."

"There's to be another trial here. Sally's."

"I know, I know," responds the Medical Director. "And yes, *she* has been replaced. Look, I realise you were only just released from prison yesterday, and I know how awful the whole ghastly business must have been for you. Absolutely no pressure, but we really look forward to having you back. And maybe you don't actually have to be there for the trial. Could be done remotely. For you. Back here. With us. In the Royal Infirmary."

After having had a restless, sleepless night, with my mind in a muddle, I'm not sure what to say. I look to Anita for help.

"He says my job's still there, and they really do want me back."

"And you, John? What do *you* want?"

I know what I really want. To be with her, this most remarkable of women. What do I say? What *can* I say? Anita's raised eyebrows give me the answer. And hope.

269

Lost Hands

"I'll call you back later, Simon," I say to the Medical Director in Scotland before handing the phone back to Anita in New Zealand.

Chapter 40

Felicity, after taking her seat in the Usher Hall beside Aunt Maggie, immediately stood up again and searched the stalls for Ranjit. She saw him and waved. He waved back at her, which curiously gave her much-needed courage.

"How silly of me!" announced Maggie. "You two should be sitting together."

"No," insisted Felicity. "This, tonight, is about you and me and my mum, your sister, and *his* girlfriend." She tapped the image of the violin-playing man with a tinge of red in his wild hair on the programme cover. "Ranjit understands. Like always."

Maggie smiled at the 'like always'. Two words that said it all. Spoke of the strength in the teenage girl who arrived, unannounced, on her doorstep, desperate for help, all those years ago. As the women sat together, waiting for the concert to start, with Felicity repeatedly turning to look at, and wave to, Ranjit, Maggie reflected on those happy days in an almost-forgotten past when she and her little teenage sister sat together and talked about boyfriends which, in Elsie's case, was only ever 'Robbie' as the great musician was referred to back then. Why she went into a huff when Robbie owned up about learning flamenco guitar with a Spanish girl whilst staying at a hotel on the Costa del Sol that fateful summer, Maggie could never understand. Nor why her sister broke it off with Robbie. The girl even refused to go to church with them on Sundays, and Maggie recalled Robbie looking forlornly at her and her parents seated without Elsie. She even remembered Robbie politely asking Felicity's granny whether Elsie was 'All right?' and appearing truly upset when told she was 'Fine!'

'My stupid little sister got it all wrong!' thought Maggie as the great violinist came onto the stage, alone and without an orchestra, to an ear-splitting applause from his ecstatic audience, to perform, on stage, the Bach solo sonatas and partitas. From memory! She and Felicity sat, mesmerized, together with hundreds of classical music lovers, listening to Bach being resurrected after nearly three hundred years. Later, she and Felicity learned how the great composer might have been lost forever but for another towering figure in the world of classical music, Felix Mendelssohn.

The solo performance was followed by a Haydn symphony which the orchestra got on with whilst Felicity could think only about her mother and what that awful man in Saughton prison had done to her.

During the interval, Maggie's 'urgent' note was handed in, with a promise from the usher, who took it, that this would be handed to Robert Lombardi as soon as the whole performance was over. They were to wait inside the main entrance for his response. In truth, Felicity had difficulty focusing on the music during the Bruch concerto, particularly having already watched the man who could be her father play the same piece, many times, on YouTube, over the previous few days; the man, who, with his bow and violin, had drawn Felicity into a world of sound that seemed to portray every possible human feeling and emotion, one that the woman never knew existed before learning that the monstrosity she had always thought of as her father turned out not to be.

Lost Hands

Finally, in the foyer, after the performance was over, the world-famous violinist, her true father, appeared. Staring at him, Felicity froze. Maggie broke the ice.

"Thank you so much for seeing us like this," she said.

With a shy smile that Felicity's aunt remembered so well, Robert Lombardi stepped forward and offered his hand. Maggie shook it as though reconnecting with a young red-haired Robbie, the love of her little sister, then stepped sideways to put her arm around Felicity.

"She is even more beautiful than Elsie made out," said the violinist, looking kindly down at Felicity.

"You knew?" Maggie asked.

Robbie, as Maggie insisted on calling him from then on, nodded.

"I am ashamed to say that I did. When she got in touch with me after she lost your elder sister, Felicity." He looked around checking there were no other ears to hear what he said. "Because of what that man did to the poor girl," he added.

"You mean Felicity," corrected Maggie. "What he did to your daughter here."

"No. The elder one. Verity, I believe, was her name." He turned to face Felicity. "Oh Felicity... come here, my darling daughter! Let me hug you!"

He opened his arms wide. Arms that had created the heaven of Bach with an instrument fashioned from maple, spruce and ebony, nylon strings wrapped in precious metal windings, and a bow using hair from a Mongolian horse that once ran wild and free like the notes in the Bruch Concerto. Felicity wept as she had never wept before. Her biological father comforted her whilst a stream of satisfied music lovers, filing out of the auditorium, passed by, many pausing to puzzle over a scene that brought tears of joy to some.

"My darling daughter!" the great violinist repeatedly exclaimed for the benefit of all.

When the foyer was finally empty apart the father, the daughter and those who came with her, in addition to Mary and Ade who were to give them a lift, Robert Lombardi was introduced to Ranjit, his son-in-Law, who had been respectfully standing apart. He hugged Maggie again, telling her she did not look a day older than when he first saw her with her beautiful sister, in church, all those years back. He laughed when she replied, "Not a day but a hundred years," then suggested they meet up the following day before his scheduled journey back down to London where he was professor of violin at the Royal College of Music in South Kensington.

"Ranjit and I work in London," Felicity said, excitedly.

"Wonderful!" exclaimed Robert. "But what about tomorrow? I'm staying with my mother up here. Father passed five years back. She, *your* grandmother, Felicity, lives alone, but is rather frail and wouldn't be able to cater for a crowd. A truly wonderful crowd, mind you."

"Come to the manse with our lovely friends, the Osondus. Please," begged Maggie. "Mary Osondu here, the minister, her husband loves to cook. Their daughter too. It's in the genes, I suppose."

"Genes, ay?" responded Robert looking at, then taking hold, again, of Felicity's hands. "I am so very sorry, but please allow me to give my side of the story tomorrow, Felicity. And thank you, Mary."

Lost Hands

"We know it's complicated, Mr Lombardi," said Mary. "Maybe more so than any of us here could possibly imagine."

"May I bring Felicity's grandmother along?" asked the violinist.

"The more the..." Maggie paused. 'Merrier' did not seem an appropriate word. "The better," she added. "The Osondus also have a Lithuanian girl staying with them. An art student. She, too, is part of the story."

"I can hardly wait. I'll give you my phone number. Please text the time and place and I and Felicity's grandmother will see you all tomorrow. I must go now. Mother will be worrying. I'm afraid that's pretty much all she does now. I was an only son, you see."

"I remember," said Maggie. "And how I used to think, if only you had an elder brother!"

Robert laughed, then looked serious.

"I never married, you know."

"Because of Elsie?" questioned Maggie. Looking down at her, Robert nodded.

"Tomorrow then!" announced Maggie before Robert politely took his leave and Felicity, tearfully happy, followed Mary and Ade, together with her husband and her aunt, to the Osondu's parked car. Ranjit hugged and kissed his wife before heading back to the college in Queen Street whilst Felicity and Maggie were driven, again, to their Airbnb.

Chapter 41

Anita's eyes take in every word as she looks at me whilst my past life with Sally escapes from my mouth in what seem to be almost meaningless sentences. My mind travels back to those times before Sally, for my life seems to be divided into three periods... before, with and after Sally.

"A workaholic?" suggests Anita on hearing about my barren sex life during the 'before'.

"Guess so." I look down at my hands resting on my lap. "And now they just don't seem to know what to do with themselves," I add. "They're lost. Those hands."

"No," responded Anita, "They are not lost. Resting. That's all. You're a surgeon. And a true doctor. I can see that. Let them lead you back to that hospital. Take up your scalpel again. Save lives."

"If only it were that easy."

"Life is never easy. I thought mine had come to an end when my husband, Jimmy, died, but I live on. Try to do some good."

"I'm sorry!" I apologise. "And you've saved my own life, that's for sure. Don't know what I'd have done without you."

"People often make fun of us lawyers. 'The law is an ass' and all that kind of stuff. But we're really a bit like you doctors. Trying to put things right."

"Will Sally go to prison?" I ask.

"A lot depends on *her* lawyer," Anita replies. "They'll have a difficult task on their hands. From what you told me, she truly thought her lover had disappeared forever after he left for South America that Monday morning. That was shortly after that you two got together, if I'm right."

"You are. And I don't think she was lying back then. About us."

"Well, I'm just glad *I'm* not her lawyer! That's all I can say."

"Wish you were!" I respond.

She frowns. A frown that makes me uneasy.

"What would you do, John, if she does get let off? By claiming he manipulated her in some way or other... perhaps. Would you want to get back together with her after what she did?"

In a flash, I realise there was more to Anita suggesting she put me up in her place than just simply 'helping me out'. At the same time, I know that my own feelings for the woman are changing. In prison, she was like a lifeline for me. Here, in her home, as a free man again, she seems a lot more than that. Because of her own facial expression, deep down I know the answer to her question. I just don't have the courage to spurt it out. Not yet. So I merely shrug my shoulders by way of a reply.

"Whatever," Anita says, "I *will* look into the possibility of you going back home and acting remotely as a witness in both their trials. I can't envision anyone objecting. Almost anything can be done online nowadays."

"Except imprisonment!" I add. "Yes, I think I do want to go back home. See if I can do something with these hands again. You told me your brother is also a lawyer, working in Edinburgh."

"David! A one in a million. Married to an artist. A professor in the Edinburgh Art College. Quite possibly the funniest man on Planet Earth. Just what David needs. I could almost count on the fingers of one hand the number of times I saw *him* laugh as a child!"

"Surely not!?" I exclaim. "When did you last see your brother?" I ask.

"When he got married. Ten years ago. Me and Jimmy took time off to go to the wedding. It was amazing. And I thought David was so lucky to be living in such a wonderful city. He couldn't make Jimmy's funeral, but sent me a bottle of whisky. Daniel's idea, bless him."

"You liked it? Edinburgh, not the whisky?"

"Liked? Loved, more like!"

Loved? I look sideways at the woman seated in the armchair beside mine and wonder.

*****

Melanie insisted that Justina ask Kevin to join them for the meal with the world-famous violinist and his mother.

"I'll be busy in the kitchen with Dad, and you'll need someone to talk to."

Justina laughed.

"Just talk?" she said, sheepishly. "He might want to see my room."

Melanie's turn to laugh.

"That's a 'yes' then. Text him. Now!"

Justina, still grinning, did so and received an immediate response. A thumbs-up emoji, together with a red heart.

"He likes cooking himself, but I *do* think he'd prefer to see my room," she told her bosom friend.

"Well, as long as you two can get dressed again in time for lunch!" said Melanie.

Lost Hands

"Melanie!" scolded Justina, grinning.

The following morning, Melanie and her dad were up early to prepare a meal for twelve people since Daniel also got wind of the feast from Melanie and insisted that he and David should *not* be left out. Justina told Kevin to come way before lunch time, so that, before enjoying the meal, they could 'enjoy each other's company' in her bedroom... just short of having full-on sex. Kevin said that much as he wished to, having sex in someone else's house would be disrespectful. Instead, shortly before lunch, he went to assist Ade and Melanie in the kitchen, the latter repeatedly giving the poor young student meaningful 'did they or didn't they?' looks.

Robert Lombardi and his mother arrived early... the violinist's excuse being that his mother could wait no longer to see her only grandchild for the very first time. More tears were, understandably, shed when this happened, and old Mrs Lombardi could not stop looking at Felicity throughout the meal which turned out to be more amazing than anything her much-travelled musician son had experienced anywhere in the world. Ade proudly stood and took a bow in response to the loud applause he received after the main course, including tuneless whistles from Daniel who had become funnier and funnier with every glass of wine.

"Robert, can you play us an Argentinian tango with your violin?" he said out of the blue. "I'd so like to have a go at it with my darling David here. He really does need loosening up." David scowled at his husband. Unlike Daniel, he became increasingly silent with each sip of wine of which a single glass was sufficient.

"I'm sorry, Daniel, but I do not have my instrument

with me. A Guarneri violin. It's been valued at eight million dollars, so I don't think my insurance company would be pleased if they knew I was carrying it around Edinburgh with me."

Ade's jaw dropped from the shock of hearing the value of the violin.

"That's even more than my wedding ring's worth," announced Daniel. "A lot less than the value of David, mark you."

"And it would be far from setting a record price for either a Guarneri or a Stradivarius," continued Robert. "But you know what? The music they make, some of these instruments, it's priceless." He glanced at a silent David whose face, either because of his husband, or because of the wine, had turned deep cardinal red.

"I so wish my mum had introduced me to *real* music," said Felicity to distract attention away from the embarrassed lawyer. "Like what we heard played last night."

"I, your father, must put that right, then," Robert responded. "But before I do so, you, your aunt and I need to talk. With your grandmother." He glanced at Ade. "In private?"

"Whilst Melanie and I prepare the desert, you could use my office," suggested Ade. "Daniel can play tango music on YouTube and the rest of you guys could teach him how to dance."

"Only with David," stressed Daniel, barely able to stand, let alone dance.

"I'll dance with Kevin," offered Justina.

And so, with Mary and Ade deeply engaged in spouse-talk, Justina tangoing with Kevin and Daniel being sharply reprimanded by his husband for "Drinking far too much," Felicity followed her father and grandmother into the accountant's small office just off the landing at the foot of the stairs. Robert closed the door, quietly, behind his daughter and her aunt and beckoned to the two women and his mother to sit down before finding a seat for himself.

"I have some explaining to do before asking for your forgiveness, Felicity," he said.

Chapter 42

Sean, in custody, was making it increasingly difficult for his lawyer to know just how to help him. All he did was to go on and on about how the death of his sister, Verity, caused, he insisted, by the incompetence of a surgeon who should have taken her to theatre straightaway even if he was in the middle of another operation at the time; the same surgeon who, later, stole then married his girlfriend.

"All one big cover-up!" he claimed, referring to his elder sister's death. His lawyer kept saying how this was all very interesting but legally of no relevance when it came to defending Sean in a New Zealand court of law for the crimes he and Sally McEuen had committed. He even suggested Sean undergo a medical assessment, at which Sean flew into a rage.

"You think I'm mad!?" he screamed. This, alone, made the lawyer wonder whether his client was, indeed, 'mad', but to be banged up with the criminally insane would, in his opinion, be a fate worse than death.

"You must give me time to think this one over. If your sister's death had been more recent, it might've been easier. Do you believe that Sally was somehow coerced into marrying him? That might have allowed your anger to get the better of you if we can prove it."

"Anger? What anger?"

"Understandable, from a juror's point of view, if perhaps Sally was given the wrong information by the surgeon. Maybe you tried to get in touch with her, and he got wind of this. Intercepted the correspondence?

Lost Hands

Prevented her from knowing how you wished to get back together with her before it was too late?"

"What are you on about? Have *you* gone mad?"

No, Sean did himself no favours, and his lawyer was at his wit's end when a date for the trial was set. Thankfully for Sean, Sally *was* allowed to visit him, although only in the presence of a prison officer who, to Sean's increasing annoyance, kept looking at the young Scots nurse as though he fancied her for himself. It took all the inner strength of will that Sean could muster to stop himself from thumping the bastard.

Meanwhile, Sally kept thinking back over that extended period when she truly believed she would never again see the love of her life, having had no response to her repeated attempts to get him to contact her by whatever means, and when she both admired and, in need of sex, bedded the surgeon whose face, for her, had, initially, been reduced to a kind and bright pair of eyes peering over a surgical mask across an opened-up abdomen.

Sean's other claim, alongside that of his father's, that the younger sister, Felicity, had been responsible for causing the appendicitis that killed Verity because of 'bad behaviour', made no sense to her as a trained nurse. And during her time with John, none of his patients had come to any harm. All the surgical staff at the Edinburgh Royal Infirmary praised his skill and his judgment. What if, through no fault of his own, she would sometimes ask herself, Sean was wrong?

*****

"Please understand that everything I did was coloured by the love I felt for your mother," Robert said to Felicity.

283

Lost Hands

"Just tell us what happened that summer when Elsie broke it off between you two," asked Maggie. "You were inseparable before you both went on holiday. All she said after you came back, whenever I asked her about it, was that you'd found someone else. She wouldn't listen to me when I tried to tell her she'd got it wrong. And no way would she let me talk to you about it. What happened?"

Robert drew in a deep breath before replying, as if, in doing so, he might find the answer to Maggie's question hidden deep down in his soul.

"I never married. Because of Elsie. It would have felt like a betrayal even though it was she who broke it off. And even after I heard she got engaged to that pharmacist... a student back then... I never found anyone else I wanted to be with. Just threw myself into the cauldron of music, if you will. You could say I married my Guarneri."

The violinist went silent.

"So?" persisted Maggie. "What really happened that summer."

"A Spanish girl. In a hotel in Nerja. Daughter of the proprietor. Outside our window. I heard her playing flamenco on the guitar. Early the first morning after we arrived. Awesome. Profoundly atmospheric. No way like Bach, but I just wanted to hear more. So I got dressed, went out and sat there beside her on a bench in a sort of Spanish garden. No one else around. Just a few orange trees. When she stopped playing, I spoke to her in pigeon French, not knowing any Spanish myself. She laughed, and spoke back in near-perfect English. Apparently her parents insisted she learn English because of those Brits on holiday crawling all over the place."

Lost Hands

"That's why I'd never go near the Costa del Sol," Maggie interrupted. "Cheaper to share a beach with drunken Brits in Southend."

"Shush, Aunty!" admonished Felicity. "Let him tell us what happened!"

"Anyway, she taught me the basics of guitar playing," continued Robbie. "And asked if I could teach her to play the violin. I had a cheap one to practise with whilst on holiday. Not that I did, in the end. Whatever, she got the wrong end of the stick, so to speak, after we met up a few times early each morning. In that garden of orange trees. All was fine until she kissed me. Thought I was onto her. Went into a Spanish huff when I told her I had a girlfriend back home and only wished to learn more about Flamenco from her. So she went and told her father I had tried it on with her. He blew a fuse, even though nothing had happened between us, and I still loved Elsie to bits."

Robert paused, and Felicity could tell from his expression that it pained the man to have to tell her. She reached forward and placed her hand over his as fingers that had brought Bach and Bruch back from the dead appeared to be searching for strings to play on his knee.

"Thank you," she said. "I understand."

"We had to leave the hotel," her father continued. "Couldn't find another one. All booked up. So we came home early. I never did find out exactly what my father said to your grandfather, Felicity, but Elsie got wind of the story which was already circulating around the whole district, even before we were back at school. She was beside herself and would not listen to me when I, in all honesty, said there was nothing to it. I tried so hard to make her see reason,

285

and so regretted having been bewitched by that guitar. Not the girl. I am a musician, you see, and the music was hauntingly beautiful. The girl played so well."

"Mum had no self-confidence whatsoever, you know," Felicity informed her father.

"So right!" emphasized her aunt.

"Oh, I know that now. But back then I guess I felt hurt. That she wouldn't believe my side of the story. Whatever, she refused to see me again. Even stopped coming to church."

"I remember," said Maggie. "Told our mother she no longer believed in God. Because of what you did."

"And I did nothing other than listen to Flamenco!" responded Robert.

"So... all *that* is ancient history. How do you explain Felicity here?" asked Maggie. "How did you two get together again after all those years? What made it happen?"

Robert smiled to himself.

"How? What? Indeed! To tell you the truth, I believe it had already started when Verity was still a baby."

"It? What?" asked Maggie, totally unaware of what the man was talking about.

"You don't know?" He looked from the elder to the younger woman, then back again. "She never told you?"

The women glanced at each other, then shrugged shoulders in unison.

"About the man who killed her? The pharmacist?"

Felicity and Maggie still appeared none the wiser. Robert glanced at Maggie again, then at his mother, neither of whom said a word. Suddenly, Maggie got the message and offered to take the old lady back to the living room towards the sounds of Tango, voices and laughter.

"Thank you," said Robert before continuing to enlighten Felicity on her own.

Chapter 43

Anita smiles at me after I hand her back her i-Phone.

"I can tell you just can't wait to get into an operating theatre again and use those hands of your to save lives," she says.

"Bloody true," I answer. "And you're right. About Sally. I never even knew her. Just that I..."

I pause.

"Needed *some*one?" suggests Anita. I nod my head. "I was speaking to my lawyer brother, Daniel, last night. He was a bit grumpy about having to go to some big get-together in the manse of his husband's foody Nigerian friend and the friend's minister wife. Something to do with an important Edinburgh Festival project for the Art College. About historical child abuse. Their daughter's a student at the college"

"Historical child abuse?" I ask, wondering what this all has to do with anything involving me.

"Complained that he'll be bored out of his tiny mind and only going for the food," Anita continues. "But he hopes he'll be able to get to speak with a woman coming to the party, up from London to meet with a father she never knew she had."

"Hmm!" is all I can offer, unable to see where this is leading. But I do know, from Anita's eyes, that something big is about to erupt and that she's breaking me in gently. Preparing me.

"Thing is..." Anita pauses. I lean forward, believing, perhaps, that this will help her find the right words to say what she must, but finds it difficult to do so. "Thing is, he's been asked to help this woman. Legally."

"Yes," I say, puzzled as to why this should be of interest to a recently released prisoner in New Zealand. "You told me he's a lawyer. Like you. Is he any good? Must run in your genes."

"He's absolutely brilliant. This woman he's been asked to represent... she was most horribly abused as a child by a man imprisoned for killing his wife. Her mother."

"The child abuse project and the case you told me about? The pharmacist?"

"Also the father of Sean Taylor who pretended to be an Ozzie called Wayne Minto."

My heart does a somersault as my mind erupts like mental volcano. Disbelief, anger, hate, revenge battle in my brain as my mouth struggles to respond to her revelation.

"Sally knew?" I finally ask.

"Sally knew all right."

"So... Sally's lover who got me put in prison is the son of a murderer and a paedophile?" I ask.

Anita nods.

"But there's more. A *lot* more. Something that's only just coming out. Thanks, in part, to those Nigerian friends of David's husband. As I told you, the wife is a Church of Scotland minister. Mary Osondu."

'Scotland, New Zealand and now Nigeria? All on the same planet, I suppose,' I ponder as I await Anita's punchline...

"Sean was apparently involved. In the abuse of his younger sister. When she was a child. Together with his father."

289

"Oh my God!"

Suddenly, this compatriot of mine, whom I hate to the ends of the Earth, is far worse than I ever imagined. Pure bloody evil.

"His sister is wanting to take legal action against her father for what he did to her as a child, and Sean's involvement will all come out. It'll have implications for the trial, here, against Sean, for what he and Sally did to you."

Slowly, I get Anita's drift.

"I haven't seen my brother for over ten years," she continues. "Not since their wedding in Edinburgh. The only gay wedding I've ever been to, but it was amazing. And I felt so happy for David. He and Daniel are truly made for each other."

"So you want to go to Scotland to discuss the case going on here with this brother of yours... David. Right?"

"Right!" she replies looking me straight in the eye. I know, immediately, the other reason behind her wish to return to Edinburgh. I see it in her eyes. I, too, feel it.

"So we can go there together? Scotland?"

Anita nods.

"And there's more to it," she says. "The minister, Mary, is friendly with a high-up police officer in Edinburgh. Someone called DI Calum Scott. He's been very involved with the case. Over the years."

"Years!? Bloody hell, what is it with you lawyers? A twisted gut, and I'm in there, within hours, trying to put things right, whilst for you lawyers, it takes you half a flipping lifetime to get to the truth."

"Not that simple. Not in this case. According to David, it's big. Huge. Involves an OCG."

Lost Hands

"OCG? Explain!"

"Organised Criminal Gang. In this case, international. With links to the very top."

"The very top?" I ask. Earlier mention of a church minister makes me wonder whether God is somehow involved. Not one for religion, myself, but I never imagined He could somehow get Himself involved with organised crime.

"A Russian oligarch living in a luxury villa in Menton on the Côte d'Azur. And a personal friend of the President of the United States of America."

"Oh my God!" I exclaim.

"Yeah! The man who seems to believe he has that job as well! When questioned about this friendship, the 'great' man himself merely said, 'It's a beautiful thing.'"

I do like Anita's deliciously dry sense of humour. In fact, I like everything about her. And the thought of returning to Scotland, not with my new wife whom I hardly know, but with my lawyer about whom I wish to know more—*so* much more—the very thought of this is wonderful!

*****

David never quarrelled with his husband when the other man got as pissed as a newt. Which was quite often. He would merely sink back into a soothing space of silence, switch on those very special cells in his brain, the ones that helped others get on with their lives because of his legal brilliance, and let Daniel do his own thing with others. He was as unsociable as Daniel was sociable and at the very centre of whatever was happening around him. They could not have been more different, but Anita knew, as soon as she first met David, that the Scot was the perfect partner for her little brother.

When David saw Maggie escort the elderly mother of the violinist back to the living room, amidst the background clatter and blabber, he got up and beckoned for her to join him.

"We need to talk," he said. "About Felicity. Together with Mary." Maggie agreed and called out for the minister to join them.

"I hardly know the woman," said Mary about Felicity before taking a seat beside David at the table.

"Always better that way," suggested David. "Legally speaking, knowing someone personally can get in the way of justice."

"So, this is about Felicity taking civil action against the man who abused for her all her childhood and some of her teenage years?"

"And there's more."

"What?" enquired Mary. "Oh, the poor woman! Tell me."

"She has a brother," said David.

"So I've heard. Vanished over a year ago when their father, the man Felicity visited in prison, got put away for murder. I know it's terribly un-Christian of me to say it, but I always thought he was really..." Mary paused.

"Really what?" asked David.

"Creepy. Though I had little to do with James Taylor before. When he was a pharmacist."

"And not a prisoner!" interjected David.

"Quite. He *was* one of our parishioners. And he did sometimes come to church. But I never got to know his children. They would've been before my time as minister."

"As I was saying, Mary, Felicity has a brother. And I had a call from my sister in New Zealand."

"The lawyer who lost her husband last year. How's she doing? I cannot imagine being without Ade."

"Nor me without Daniel. But she's coping well. No, this is about a case she was involved with. An Edinburgh Scots surgeon accused of murdering the pilot of a small plane that crashed in the rainforest wilderness in the mountains of South Island. Milford Sound."

"Yes, I remember that. On the BBC news. He was newly married. On honeymoon."

"Spot on, Mary! Well, Anita tells me the whole affair has been turned upside down, so to speak. The surgeon, who worked at the RIE, has been freed and his wife and her accomplice, an ex-lover, will soon be on trial for the most extraordinary contempt of court conspiracy case either of us has ever encountered. The murdered victim has been found alive and well in Wellington."

"No pun intended, I presume, David, as you're not Daniel!" joked Mary.

"Sometimes I wish I were, Mary. Drawing people rather than trying so desperately to understand them."

"Guess we share that problem. Understanding. So, no murder was committed."

"They never found the body. Until it turned up. Still alive. In the murder trial, they had relied on three, supposedly reliable, witnesses. Including the doctor's wife. A nurse, also at the RIE. And what pretty much amounted to a confession, although Anita was always convinced the surgeon had been drugged by the wife's lover. Spiked sweets. But it gets even stranger."

"I'm all ears," said Mary.

"That lover, who claimed to be Australian, a 'mountaineer-come-explorer' and writer called Wayne Minto whom no one had ever heard of— "

"Not heard of him either."

"Nor had anyone else, it seems. But guess who he has turned out to be."

Mary studied the serious face of her New Zealand-born lawyer friend. Something in the man's expression was a giveaway. A glint in his eyes, perhaps.

"I don't believe it! Surely not? The missing brother?"

David nodded. Maggie looked at him, aghast.

"The missing brother," he repeated. "Sean Taylor, also the son of the man you visited in Saughton with Maggie here, and Felicity."

"Does Felicity know?" asked Mary.

"Not had the chance to speak with her alone yet. But I want you both to be there. With me. When I do tell her. You're so much more people friendly than I'll ever be. And we have to get this right. You can see now how it might affect the trial against her father. Felicity's always claimed the boy was involved in the abuse, recording on film what the man did to his sister. But the movies he took ending up on porn sites, online, all over the world!"

"None of us can ever know how awful that must be for the poor woman. Thank the Lord, she has a wonderful husband."

"The Indian doctor. Yes, he must be very understanding. I really do not know how I'd feel if I knew there were porn movies of a younger Daniel floating about

294

out there in cyberspace. Anyway, I promised Anita I would break the news to Felicity. And we believe this could impact on both trials. In Sean Taylor's case, perhaps positively if his defence council can beef up the troubled childhood scenario... claim he was coerced into collaborating with his father at his sister's expense. But with Mr Taylor senior we have another potential witness for the prosecution if the son plays ball and admits to filming his sister being beaten by their dad for a porn industry controlled by an OCG with links to a Russian oligarch."

"Yes, I've already had an earful from Calum about the extent of that gang. Child pornography seems to be just a tiny fraction of his global empire. And he's even matey with You-know-who," said Mary.

"Could you two ladies have a word with Felicity? On the quiet. Better she knows before they go back down to London."

"Later this evening," affirmed Maggie. "Overnight train. Oh... there they are. Father and daughter. Felicity's looking really upset."

"She might feel happier to know the man she thought was her father now has a better chance of going down again for what he did to her after serving time for murder. Where crimes against children are concerned, we can be pretty certain the sentence given by the judge will mean consecutive, not concurrent, incarceration. And to learn her brother will finally feel the full weight of the law for the part he played in the abuse she suffered as a child will surely be a relief to her. Knowing he was always out there, somewhere, must've been hard for her all those years."

"As always, you're right, David." Mary patted his hand

before getting up to speak with Felicity. "What a lucky man Daniel is," she added, turning round to watch Daniel happily gyrating away, now to pop music, with Kevin and Justina, whilst Ade and Melanie busily tidied up the dinner table.

Chapter 44

Anita makes all the arrangements. I'm feeling rather like a child again, reborn, being told what to do... accepting. I wonder if my apartment in Edinburgh, where I used to make love to Sally, in that other life, will still be there. With my father refusing to have anything to do with me or my affairs, and forbidding my poor mother to contact me, a cousin in Aberdeen, my only other close relative, had promised he would look after it and pay the council tax, or whatever else needed doing, but we really aren't that close, and for all I know he might even have sold it off. Anita, as always, takes over, contacts him, reassures the man I have been exonerated and freed and will soon be returning home to Edinburgh.

Oh, I can hardly wait to escape from paradise-turned-hell and get back home... with a true angel!

*****

Mary, together with Maggie, went over to Felicity and took her to one side, watched by David. Because of the background noise, thanks to his husband, he could not hear a word of what was said, but when Felicity looked back at him, her eyes widened by horror, he knew she had been told.

Mary beckoned for him to join herself, Maggie and Felicity. Back in the bedroom together, Felicity was shocked to know that her dreaded brother had turned up in New Zealand, but pleased to learn that he, too, was to face trial and almost certain imprisonment. Whether or not he would agree to testify against his father in Edinburgh was up to him, but Felicity could relish in the fact that failure to do so might result in legal action being taken out against him as well, in Scotland, for his own involvement in her childhood abuse. She wanted Ranjit to be involved in every step of decision making, so, via WhatsApp, whilst her husband was eating out again with a previous medical colleague, he, too, could speak with David and with Maggie. Together, they all finally agreed to use David's legal services to take action against both father *and* son should the latter fail to agree to act, remotely, as a witness for the prosecution in a trial that was sure to make headlines, not only in Edinburgh, but across the world, for its ramifications were vast. Ranjit reassured Felicity that he would be with her every inch of the way. He told her that he had spent most of the evening informing his dear friend, with whom he was dining, all about what happened, and the ongoing consequences, and that, as an independent opinion, the friend agreed with Ranjit that this was the right thing to do. The friend waved to Felicity from her i-Phone screen and gave her a thumbs-up. Far from being upset that Ranjit had shared her shamed past with someone she had never even met, she felt relieved. It was as if this stranger represented the world, and his approval meant the world was behind her and against the man who had almost destroyed her plus killed her beloved mother.

No more cover-up!

*****

"What are you talking about?" Sally asked Sean in the presence of a prison officer who, although as straight and upright as a New Zealand tree-fern, was clearly listening to every word spoken between the young lovers. "Why on Earth would you want to be involved in your father's prosecution when you told me he acted out of kindness for your mother whose depression had made her life unbearable? They should never have put him in jail, anyway. It was so cruel."

"Nothing to do with my mother. Another trial."

"*Another* murder?"

"No. My younger sister, Felicity— "

"The one he claimed was responsible for Verity's appendicitis? That did sound far-fetched to me, Sean. Speaking as a nurse."

"She's taking legal action against him because of how he used to punish her for bad behaviour as a child. Had to do it, of course. Her behaviour was affecting our poor mother badly. *Really* badly."

Sean paused and stared at the bare prison table separating them. Sally had begun to realise, since her arrest, that there were things that happened in her lover's past that she had no knowledge of. Now she knew it had something to do with both Sean's father and his little sister, and finally Sean came out with it...

"He used to beat her. With a cane. Like they used to do in schools in the old days. And I had to watch and, erm..."

Sean went silent again.

"Watch and what?" she asked with a mix of curiosity, anger and unease, for somehow she knew what was coming.

"Film it. With a movie camera. My dad was into photography, you see. In a studio in the back of the pharmacy. Passport photos. Parents and children. People with their pets."

"He used to beat his own daughter whilst you filmed it? That is..." Sean looked away when he saw the disgust written across Sally's face as she struggled to find a word to describe how she felt about her lover's revelation. Clearly, she couldn't. "And you let him do it? To your own little sister?"

Sean opened his mouth, but no words came out.

"Tell me this isn't why you disappeared off to South America that Monday morning. No bloody warning at all!"

Sean's continued silence gave her the answer she needed for her to do what she did... stand up, abruptly, with a loud backwards scrape of the chair on the hard prison floor, thump the table, to the alarm of the watchful warden, and shout,

"Sean Taylor, I never want to see you again! Never, ever! When you said it was about something that might help you get early release, I was so excited! But this? You should bloody be locked up again and again and again!"

She left, too angered for tears, and Sean wondered what she might have done had he told her the full story. That those movies he shot all those years back had, because of the Russian Mafia, or 'Bratva', found their way onto the dark web and various porn sites involving underage children. The world would most probably have forgiven her if she had killed him.

*****

Later, back in their Airbnb, Felicity and her aunt sat together on one of the beds and talked on till the early hours about a day that had changed everything for good. And about her true father's revelation...

*****

"Pure chance," Robert said. "That we met up again after all those years. In Jenner's café. I was up here in Edinburgh.

Lost Hands

For a performance of the Beethoven Violin Concerto. Father had only recently passed, and I decided to take a break from practising the last movement that morning. It was driving my poor mother mad. So I took her shopping. We were having coffee in the café when she appeared. Just like that. Your mother. It was my mother who first recognized her.

"'Isn't that the girl from church you used to go out with?' she asked. When I saw your mother I just did not know what to do. The guilt for what happened that summer all those years back had never left me. It was mother who called out to her. She joined us. I barely said a word. What could I say? I saw the wedding ring on her finger. It pained me to see it there. Proof that that the only girl I've ever loved was now another man's possession. I knew she'd got married, but nothing more. I asked her about her husband. At first, she remained silent, but when our eyes met, I knew. Knew that she was saddled with a monster. All I wanted to do was to help her in any way I could.

"Mother invited her back to our place. She always said that everyone had got it wrong about that Spanish girl in Nerja, and she truly felt for me after Elsie broke it off. Elsie had lunch with us, and whilst mother was in the kitchen preparing something, it all came out."

Robert went silent.

"About the man who called himself my dad?" asked Felicity.

Robert nodded.

"Elsie thought he was interfering with little Verity. She had no proof, but the way the little girl looked at him, and always tried to avoid him, made her wonder. Plus she was

301

aware that he would often stare at young girls in the street. But you know what your mother was like. She had no self-confidence. It's why she got the wrong end of the stick about my interest in flamenco that summer. I told her to talk to him about it. About her concern. Maybe get help from their doctor. But she said she was terrified of man. Just like little Verity was. Anyway, as I tried to comfort her, it was like we were back together again. Teenagers in love. We couldn't hold back. Mother understood when I told her I needed to show Elsie something in my room. My old bedroom that my parents had kept unchanged for whenever I was back in Edinburgh. And... well that's how *you* happened. Nine months later. Her husband knew you weren't his daughter. With Verity in the same house, he had lost interest in having sex with your mother."

Robert smiled to himself.

"My performance, that evening, of the greatest violin concerto ever written, got a glowing review in the Weekend Scotsman. 'Outstanding', they said. Only Elsie and I knew why.

"So... whenever I was back in Edinburgh, if possible, Elsie and I would meet up. Mother knew there was more to it than two old friends getting together to reminisce. She even suggested I broach the subject of persuading your mother to leave the bastard, but she feared he would claim *she* was the guilty party... which, in a way, she was... and have Verity all for himself. And life with a concert violinist? I couldn't force that on Elsie."

"Oh my God!" exclaimed Felicity. "I had no idea. I was so jealous of my big sister. I'd hide her toys. Even cut up her favourite dress, one day. I could hardly sit down for a whole week after the beating I got from father that time. Rather, the man I *thought* was my father. Poor, poor Verity!"

"We'll never know how far he went with your sister, but the week before your mother died she called me. I was on tour in America. She said she had it on her conscience. That he was blaming Verity's death on you and that surgeon. You for causing her appendicitis because of 'bad behaviour' and the surgeon for botching the operation. The truth, she told me, was that Verity was terrified of telling her parents about a pain in the tummy that came on that evening. Terrified because the girl was afraid he would want to 'examine' her. Use being a pharmacist as an excuse. This all came out when Elsie found Verity, rigid with pain, in bed, after she failed to appear for breakfast before going to school. Apparently they did everything they could at the hospital, and the delay in getting her to theatre was mostly to improve her condition in ITU to allow surgery to take place. They told her parents, before the operation, that it was touch and go as to whether she would survive. If they'd got her earlier, it would have been a very simple procedure, but she died from multi-organ failure due to sepsis."

Robert paused when he saw a tear trail on Felicity's cheek.

"I feel so awful," Felicity said. "For hating Verity so. It was always 'Verity this' and 'Verity that'. I didn't see it. And Mum's depression meant that 'Father', as I called him, was at the centre of everything back home. And I was angry with Verity for never supporting me. Now I know why. She was frightened of him. Like me. Only, from what you're telling me, she had even *more* reason to be scared. Look, Dad — you don't mind me calling you that, do you? — should we get a DNA test done?"

"Could do, if you wish."

Felicity nodded.

"I do. Anyway, would you be prepared to act as a witness if David thinks it would help? If what you just told me were to come out in court, it might help my case."

"Anything that helps, Felicity. I can always make a statement under oath in the presence of lawyers if I can't make the trial. There are ways of getting the truth out into the open. Look, why don't we join the others? My mother would just love to hug her granddaughter again, I know it. She may have lost her marbles for recent events, but her memory for the past is still pretty sharp. As for your aunt, Mother told me she remembers Maggie well. The 'serious one' she called her."

"Yeah... that's Aunt Maggie all right!"

Chapter 45

I'm happy for Anita to do everything. Even pack my suitcase for me. So strange for a surgeon, used to busying his hands inside bellies, whilst saving lives, to sit and watch someone else take control. But somehow the woman who has helped to erase my wife from my thoughts is no longer just a lawyer but has become my main meaning for staying alive. In prison I had contemplated suicide, but now, with Anita, that's all in the past. And I do not need to tell her how I feel. I know that she knows.

As I sit beside Anita who is fast asleep, on the plane, after an exhausting few days, I feel the lure of Scotland. I imagine my country to be giant magnet working its magic on this magnificent speeding metal body in which I find myself, high up in the sky… pulling me home.

Back in Edinburgh, I see how close the New Zealand brother and sister lawyers are. I feel real envy for their sibling companionship. Being an only son, I reckon I have a hole in my life that can never be filled.

David and Daniel insist we stay with them, so our hotel bookings are cancelled. Through the gay couple, I meet Mary, the lovely Nigerian Church of Scotland minister, and her foodaholic accountant husband, Ade. We're introduced to their bright, young design-focused daughter, Melanie, and to the girl's Lithuanian bosom-friend, Justina; both are frantically organizing other art students with their installation about historical child abuse, aimed to shock, not please, and Justina introduces me to her thoughtfully shy, stuttering Scottish photographer boyfriend, Kevin.

Lost Hands

And to Justina's mother recently arrived from Vilnius. She is sharing a room with her daughter, at the manse, and joins us for a meal the evening of our arrival. Felicity, the younger sister of the fake-Ozzie fiend who called himself 'Wayne', her doctor husband, Ranjit, and her Aunt Maggie, are all back in London, but we see and speak with them over WhatsApp.

During a magnificent, multicultural meal, in Edinburgh, it seems to me that everything has finally come together in a headlong rush, helped along by Italian wine; Ade's idea to celebrate Felicity's connection with a half-Italian father she had never met before. And Ranjit shows him a bottle of sparkling Franciacorta being enjoyed in London, to liven up a pizza delivery, whilst the great violinist makes a brief appearance from New York, on i-Phone screens, before preparing for a concert in the Carnegie Hall. Two looming trials, at opposite ends of the planet, are forgotten until, during a dessert featuring Melanie's favourites, panna cotta and Nigerian coconut balls, Anita gets a ping on her i-Phone. It's her 'dog' in Queenstown...

"Hi, Kauri. What's up?" She glances at her watch. "Nine in the morning with you? Must be important."

"Is John there?"

Anita hands me her phone.

"I think you should go somewhere a bit more private, John," says the guy in New Zealand. I get up from my chair.

"First right on the landing, John," Ade calls out, thinking I need the loo. I nod, and leave the feast to sit on the stairs, not the toilet. The Māori face on the screen introduces himself.

"I'm Kauri," he says.

"Yes," I reply. "Anita's told me all about you."

"Not all, I hope. Look, John, Anita's detective friend, Andy Rongo, asked me to call you guys. He's kind of tied up right now, but he saw something on the news this morning. About your wife, Sally. Are you sitting down?"

When he asks me that, I know immediately. It's what we're told to do as medical students. Make sure, when breaking bad news, that a patient's loved relative is seated.

"What about Sally?"

"They found her last night. Took her own life, John. I'm so sorry. Guess she just couldn't handle it any longer. Don't know the details yet, but she left a handwritten note. For you. Andy contacted the police and asked them to text the note to Anita. Told them you're in Scotland with her. To do with a trial back in the old country."

I sit, stunned, not knowing what to say. Kauri suggests I 'talk things over' with Anita. I take the phone back to the dining room. Anita looks up at me and I beckon to her to join me. She excuses herself and joins me on the stairs. She finds Sally's texted note and hands her phone back to me…

'I know you'll never forgive me, John. I have to do this because I can't forgive myself either. I honestly did love you when I said, "Yes". Sally XXX'

I hand the phone back to Anita who puts her arm around me, holding me close as I cry. Knowing that Sally did not hate me somehow makes it worse. As for Sean, I can only feel sorry for him. He, too, has lost the love of his life. He, too, was a victim if unaware of the truth about his father and his elder sister. And I am now more determined than ever to help Anita and her brother, the sibling lawyers, see justice is finally achieved by ensuring that the pharmacist rots in jail for the rest of his life.

Myself? My old life as a doctor who has re-found his lost, surgical hands, back in Edinburgh, will surely merge with a new life together with Anita. Five years older than me, she has already intimated that she's planning early retirement. Plus, she 'adores' Edinburgh.

Later, Daniel tells me to propose to her after hearing about Sally. I do. And she says...

The Author

To find out more about Oliver Eade, retired hospital physician, photographer and award-winning playwright and author of fiction for children, young adults and adults, please visit:
https://www.olivereadebooks.org/about-us

For other Silver Quill Publishing books visit:
https://www.silverquillpublishing.com/

www.ingramcontent.com/pod-product-compliance
Lightning Source LLC
Chambersburg PA
CBHW060402260626
47160CB00006B/2408